HAWKE'S POINT

HAWKE'S POINT

MARK WILLEN

Pen-L Publishing
Fayetteville, AR
Pen-L.com

First Edition
Printed and bound in USA
ISBN: 978-1-940222-44-8

Cover design by Kelsey Rice
Formatting by Kelsey Rice

For Janet

CHAPTER 1

The cold rain suited Jonas Hawke's mood. He didn't like large gatherings, and he especially hated funerals.

"Everyone hates funerals," Emma reminded him. "Have you ever heard anyone say they liked going to a funeral?"

"Undertakers, maybe."

"You're giving the eulogy, for heaven's sake."

"Only because I couldn't say no."

"Stop it. He was your partner for twenty-five years."

Jonas frowned as he buttoned his white shirt and tied a full Windsor in his gray speckled tie, both remnants of his four decades as a lawyer. The tie was a little too wide to be fashionable, but no one in Beacon Junction was likely to know that. Folks might notice, though, that the shirt collar was too big, exposing the loose skin on his neck.

Jonas wasn't vain, but he couldn't help being aware of how time had treated him. In his prime, he cut an imposing figure, with huge hands and clear blue eyes that could be either charming or intimidating, depending on his mood. When he was thirty, Jonas stood six feet, two inches tall and weighed close to two hundred pounds, a hard man to miss and even harder to ignore. He was well liked, despite a natural shyness at odds with his professional demeanor.

He was also well respected—both for what he'd accomplished and for all he would have accomplished if it hadn't been for the accident, which had set him to drinking more and doing less. For a while, people believed he would get over it and go back to being who he was. Eventually, he did recover somewhat, gradually emerging from the fortress he'd built around himself. But never completely, and now, at seventy-three, his appearance matched his retreat from life. His curved spine and shabby posture meant the top of his almost bald head was little more than six feet from the ground, and his one hundred seventy pounds hung loosely from his bones. One of those blue eyes was glazed over with a milky cataract, and his once-powerful hands were marked with arthritic lumps.

Emma helped him with his jacket, and he realized she was ready, just waiting on him. It had always been the other way around when they were younger.

"You look great," he told her, and she did, neatly dressed in a dark blue Chanel suit that she hadn't worn in five years, not since Jonas had argued that case before the Vermont Supreme Court. "Dynamite," he added, rediscovering a word he had once used regularly to describe her.

"A little tight in the hips," she said.

"No, really. Dynamite."

She smiled. "You look good, too. We'd best be going. You got your speech?"

He patted his pocket as he followed her out the door.

It was still raining, though not hard, when Emma and Jonas entered the white clapboard church and took a program from an usher in the vestibule. The chapel was filling from the back, as it always did on unhappy occasions, but Jonas and Emma had been assigned seats in the second pew, behind the immediate family. As they walked up to it, Jonas caught sight of their son, Nathan, and they nodded to each other. Emma was staring straight ahead and didn't see him.

The crowd murmured in whispers, as the relatives, friends, and business associates of Franklin C. Hargrave waited for the minister to begin. A couple hundred people were there, not bad considering Beacon Junction's population of 5,871. The firm of Hawke and Hargrave was a prestigious one; Jonas and Frank had known most of the town and many people in the neighboring communities.

The minister, a dour thirty-year-old, welcomed the mourners with the expected words from Ecclesiastes and then asked them to join in singing "Amazing Grace." Reverend Simms had only been in town two years and hadn't really known Frank except to say hello. That had prompted the request for Jonas to give the eulogy. As Jonas waited for his turn to speak, he began remembering all the good times he'd had with Frank, from the arguments over baseball to the deep discussions about law and morality and life.

Jonas felt the urge for a little whiskey and waited a few seconds for it to pass. He knew it would. He had quit drinking after his heart attack at sixty-eight. The doctor told him he'd have to if he wanted to see sixty-nine. Jonas had thought about it a good while before deciding that drinking wasn't all it was cracked up to be anyway. It sure hadn't helped him accept what had happened, and by that time, it wasn't even helping him forget. So he quit. It wasn't easy, but like most decisions Jonas made, once he had his mind set, he simply went ahead and did it.

Remembering his heart attack made Jonas think that Frank, who was ten years younger, had died out of turn. Frank had always been healthy, a jogger who could explain the difference between saturated fats and trans fats—and did so frequently whether you wanted him to or not. His heart trouble hadn't come until six months ago, long after Jonas's, and then, after Frank had open heart surgery, the doctors told him he'd be fine if he took care of himself. He did, but complications ensued anyway, and after a second round of surgery to insert stents, an infection developed, ending in his death a week ago. There'd been a hint of less than stellar work by the doctors, but nothing had come of it.

Jonas looked up at Reverend Simms, who was droning on about the mysterious ways of our Lord and assuring the family that Frank was destined for Heaven. Jonas hoped his own remarks wouldn't be so boring. He'd written them all out, a big change from his courtroom days when he would deliver inspired summaries from brief notes, ad-libbing and adapting, based on the message he got from reading the jurors' faces. With that on his mind, he made his way to the pulpit after the minister finally took his seat.

"Frank Hargrave," Jonas began, "was the best lawyer in the state of Vermont. I was proud to be his partner. He could have been anything he wanted to be, and some of you may know that there was a time when he considered going into politics. He was actually courted by both political parties."

Jonas glanced up at the audience, trying to find a pair of eyes he could meet. Ed Riley, the chairman of the Board of Selectmen, was staring out a window. Angela Dixon, a clerk at the dry cleaner's on Hunt Street, was studying her nails. Even Nathan seemed to have other things on his mind.

Jonas made a decision. He folded the text of his speech, stuck it in his breast pocket, and looked directly at Frank's family.

"Frank Hargrave was my partner for almost a quarter of a century, but I won't remember him as a partner," he began anew, his voice taking on a muscular timbre that demanded attention. "I'll remember him as a friend. As a kind, honest, caring man who had a positive impact on everyone he encountered."

Jonas paused and shook his head from side to side in a gesture of familiarity that he knew would strike home with his audience.

"You know, life is fleeting, and it's so easy to get caught up in day-to-day struggles and lose sight of what really matters. We identify people too much by their profession, their accomplishments, their financial status. I could certainly give a eulogy that highlighted Frank's résumé, but that would miss the point. I'd rather talk about his humanity, how much he cared about others and acted on those feelings, his integrity, his moral fiber, his ability to reach out and help those around him. What I'll remember most is how he cared for people and how he was able to touch so many lives in so many meaningful ways. I always envied that ability to connect with others."

As Jonas continued, his eyes swept the pews, instinctively reading the expressions and body language of the congregants. Now he saw Riley smile in agreement. Sarah Moore, the firm's longtime secretary, wiped away a tear. Harry Piles, who owned the grocery on Main, gave him a look of encouragement. Jonas caught Emma's eye and got a slight, almost imperceptible nod from her.

"Frank was able to combine the strength of iron with the softness of velvet. You never felt like he would judge you harshly if you made a mistake and let him down. I know that from personal experience.

"But you didn't have to be a friend or even an acquaintance to benefit from Frank's kindness," he said, his inflection getting softer but his voice still reaching the back pews. "Few of you knew it—he wasn't the kind of person to talk about it—but every Thursday Frank drove to Brattleboro to volunteer at the Social Service Family Court, representing young children who had no one else, kids who were abused or abandoned and needed someone to speak up for them."

Jonas took a sip of water. It was a habit he had acquired in court, using the pause for effect, but today he did it because his mouth really was dry. He could feel the eyes of the congregation staring at him as he swallowed. He looked again at Frank's family in the front row. Nancy, Frank's wife, hung on every word. One of her hands held a tissue and the other held the hand of her son, Michael. Nancy's daughter, Molly, leaned her head on the shoulder of her husband.

"Frank represented these frightened and forsaken kids and helped guide them through the maze of our social services system, even keeping tabs on some of them long after they were out of the system. It was anything but easy and it took a huge toll, but he never once considered giving it up."

Jonas told a few more stories about Frank, the words coming from his heart, his voice rising and falling, his hold on the mourners increasing with every sentence. If he'd been speaking to a jury, they'd have decided in his client's favor without leaving the jury box. At one point, he glanced at Emma and recognized a look of awe on her face. He knew he was showing her something she hadn't seen from him in quite a while.

"I remember one night in particular," Jonas said, surprising even himself that he was going to tell this story but not pausing to consider whether it was a good idea. "It was more than twenty years ago, a time of great personal difficulty for me, a time when I was being stubborn and ignoring Frank's counsel about a case I was working on, one I should have let him handle because it hit a little too close to home."

Jonas paused briefly to catch Emma's eye again, noting her concern and smiling ever so slightly to reassure her.

"Frank did what he could to get me to do the right thing, but when he realized I wasn't going to listen to him, he didn't walk away. No, he did everything he could to support me, and he tried to prevent my mistake from hurting me or anyone else. Later, when it was all over, I tried to thank him. He shook it off as though it were nothing, but I knew better. I was a lucky man to have known Frank Hargrave. I know you feel the same way. His memory will always be a blessing."

As Jonas walked down from the pulpit, there was a quiet murmuring. He went over to Nancy and kissed her on the cheek, and she squeezed his hand tightly, too emotional to say anything. Molly and Michael stood up to shake hands. Molly added a hug.

Reverend Simms let the mourners have a moment to digest Jonas's words before asking if anyone else wanted to speak. There was silence for a few seconds, but then Betty Brown, a ninety-three-year-old neighbor, rose with the help of a walker and told how every morning Frank would pick up her newspaper from the end of her driveway and deliver it to her front door. "Just knowing he'd done it made me feel so much better. Like I hadn't been forgotten."

Sanford Tyler, a carpenter, told about the time he'd been out of work and Frank had hired him to put in a room full of custom-built bookshelves. Two months later, when he came round to tell Frank he'd gotten a job, Frank tried to make light of the fact that the bookshelves were still half empty. "I knew better," Tyler said. "He didn't need the shelves, but he knew I needed the work."

Kathleen Belton came next, describing how Frank took time out of his busy practice to represent her at a foreclosure hearing, then sent her a bill demanding payment in the form of two apple pies. "He told me no one could make them like I could."

Ed Riley told how Frank had often been a voice of reason and compromise at town meetings. And Mark Stratton, Frank's nephew, remembered how once when he was a teenager and had been in the kitchen watching his Aunt Nancy cook, he'd looked at the olive oil and asked what "extra virgin" was. Without missing a beat, Frank had said, "It's when she brings her sister."

So many people lined up to share their memories that the service went close to two hours before Reverend Simms returned to the lectern to lead the closing prayers.

Jonas and Emma's exit from the church was slow as dozens of mourners stopped to shake Jonas's hand, each complimenting him on the eulogy, most saying how moved they were or how well he had captured how important Frank was to everyone. Nathan gave his mother a kiss and his father a warm handshake.

It was no longer raining when they stepped outside. "You were wonderful," Emma told him as soon as they were alone. He smiled tightly, fighting to control himself. He could see that she was, too. She kissed his cheek and said she'd see him later. Jonas was going on to the cemetery for the burial, but Emma had volunteered to help set up for the reception at Molly's house, and she had to hitch a ride with one of the other volunteers.

Jonas's Explorer was already in line behind the hearse, and one of the funeral parlor attendants held the door open as Jonas climbed in. He was pleased that Emma was going over to the reception. It would give him some time alone to collect himself.

Jonas was enough of a performer, however rusty, to know the eulogy had played well with the crowd, but he gave most of the credit to Frank. He had been an unusual person who would be fondly remembered and sorely missed by a lot of people. Jonas might be pleased with himself for having found the words to capture what was special about Frank, but he could take no credit for what made Frank special.

He was glad that so many others had also spoken. They made it clear how many lives had been touched by Frank, how much good he had done for others. But it also made Jonas wonder about his own funeral. What would they say about him? There had been a time when he, too, had been more outgoing, more willing to get involved. Not like Frank, though. Frank was something else, with an uncanny ability to touch so many people.

The drive to the cemetery took less than fifteen minutes. Jonas parked, walked to the hearse, and joined the other pallbearers. The coffin was already on a cart with wheels, making his job mostly ceremonial. He helped guide it to where the fresh grave had been dug. The wet ground was covered with a tarpaulin for the mourners.

The minister recited the final prayers and words of solace, while Nancy, Michael, and Molly stood stoically. Finally, Molly put a single white rose on the coffin, and the family walked slowly to the limousine.

Jonas lingered by the grave after the others had gone. He finally noticed the gravediggers standing off to the side, waiting for him to leave so they could finish their work. He got annoyed at their seeming impatience and then realized they just had a job to do.

He walked slowly to the Explorer and climbed in. He sat for a while before starting the engine and then took the long way over to Molly's house.

———•———

The house was crowded, and it had that mix of solemnity and awkwardness that always defines such occasions. People were there to pay their respects and to console the loved ones, but inevitably the side conversations drifted into the irrelevant and even irreverent, as people exchanged greetings and news with those they hadn't seen in a while.

Jonas entered determined to be sociable, and he got an opportunity when he saw Michael standing by himself off to one side. Michael had grown up in Beacon Junction, but Jonas knew he had never felt very comfortable in the small town environment. After graduating from the DePaul University a year ago, he'd found a job and stayed in Chicago.

Jonas walked over and greeted him. Michael started to thank him for his eulogy, but his voice cracked, and he turned away. Jonas turned slightly to give the boy some privacy, then realized that was the wrong thing to do. He walked Michael into another room and put a hand on his shoulder. "Your father was the best of the best," he said. "He was always very proud of you."

Michael turned, started to put his arms around Jonas and then hesitated. Jonas forced himself to reach out and they hugged. Michael made a noise that sounded like the start of a sob but tried to hold it back.

"It's okay," Jonas told him. "It's okay."

But Michael wiped his eyes, refusing to let himself go. Jonas gave him a few seconds to gain control of himself and turned the conversation to safer ground.

"How's the job going?"

"Busy. Busy but good. I really like Chicago. And at least I was able to make it back in time to see him."

Jonas put his hand on Michael's shoulder and squeezed. "He was always very proud of you," Jonas repeated, wishing he could think of something else to say.

Michael nodded. "I wish I could stay here longer to be with Mom."

"You go back if you need to. Your mother's got Molly here and lots of friends. We'll keep a close eye on her."

They each took a deep breath before going back out to face the crowd. Jonas wondered which of them dreaded it more.

"There you are," Emma said as soon as Jonas emerged. "You've been hiding."

Emma had a plate in her hand, and Jonas helped himself to a cracker and cheese, but before he swallowed, Emma moved along to talk to one of her friends. Jonas wandered over to the table with the drinks and got himself a club soda. He was glad there was only wine and beer; they were easier to resist than hard liquor. Whiskey, bourbon, scotch, vodka, rye, whatever—a few years earlier he was drinking it all, and all to excess. Emma and some of his friends, Frank included, told him how impressed they were that he could quit so abruptly, but they didn't know what he went through, what he was still going through. It was at times like this, when the stress and the emotion built up inside, that he missed it most.

With his club soda, he made his way to the food table and carefully assembled a miniature turkey sandwich, wondering, as he always did, why anyone thought these tiny pieces of bread made sense. It only meant you had to work twice as hard to make yourself a real sandwich.

He had resolved to be sociable, and the other guests made that easy. One after another, they came up to talk, as if sensing that Jonas's usual shield had been lowered. The message was always the same: Remarkable eulogy. You really captured Frank. I could tell how much you loved him.

Jonas thanked them all, and after the expected comments about Frank dying too young and how well Nancy seemed to be holding up, he asked each person what they'd been up to. The fact that he needed to ask showed how he'd lost touch with so many. And the fact that he had trouble keeping the conversation going after that first question showed he still had a long way to go.

He was surprised to see many of his old colleagues from around the state—not only defense lawyers but judges and prosecutors as well. They had all respected Frank.

David McConnell, the head of the Vermont Bar Association, greeted Jonas warmly. Jonas wondered if he'd recognized the case Jonas had referred to in the eulogy, and if so, what he thought of his admission. Maybe he'd said more than he should have, but the words had just come out on their own. It had seemed a natural way to illustrate Frank's ability to figure out what people needed and how he could help them.

Sam Martin, one of the three family doctors in town, took Jonas aside to say how surprised he was at Frank's death. "Not what I would have expected from such a routine procedure." Jonas raised an eyebrow, inviting Sam to continue, but he didn't.

Finally, Jonas worked his way over to Nancy, who excused herself from the group around her, took Jonas's arm, eased him into a corner, and gave him a big hug.

"You were always his best friend," she said.

"Maybe second best," Jonas said with a wry smile. "He always told me you were at the top of the list."

Nancy had been in control until then, but the tears came now and she squeezed Jonas harder. He embraced her, but it felt awkward.

⎯⎯•⎯⎯

On the drive home, Emma and Jonas were too emotionally drained to say much. They rode in silence, Jonas's eyes straight ahead and Emma's looking out the side window. After a while she turned to him.

"Did it feel the way it looked?" she asked.

"How do you mean?"

"I don't know how to describe it exactly. You were so much in control up there. Like when you would argue a big case. Like you knew how well it was going and were enjoying it. Well, as much as anyone can enjoy giving a eulogy."

He thought about what she said, and also about what it said about their marriage. She still knows me at least as well as I know myself, he thought.

But he didn't tell her that. Instead, he talked about what

the other speakers had said, and how it made him realize that Frank touched a great number of people in a way that was important. In the end, how you dealt with other people, how you helped them, was what really mattered in life. Jonas had once known that and had made it a priority, but he'd lost sight of it after the accident.

"I've wasted the last twenty-four years," he said.

"You're being too hard on yourself," she told him. And then, after a pause, "Besides, it's not too late."

———— • ————

It was mid-afternoon and the sun was peeking through the clouds when they got back to the Sunrise. They went up to their room and changed, Jonas donning his standard black polo shirt and khakis, Emma opting for a pair of light blue slacks and a white top.

The Sunrise was a ninety-four-year-old Victorian building that had known life as a hotel, as the home of Beacon Junction's richest resident, and now as a four-rooms-for-rent bed and breakfast that Emma and Jonas owned but their daughter, Sally, ran. Emma and Jonas got to live in it for free, of course, and served as unofficial host and hostess as needed, though Jonas could be downright unsociable when the mood hit him. When the Vermont weather allowed it, he'd sit in the rocker outside and read the classics. He had a list of one hundred that he was working his way through. He'd just finished *A Bend in the River* and was now on *To Kill a Mockingbird*.

He picked up his book and headed down the stairs and on to the front porch, a big old-fashioned gray-skirted structure with a white railing. The rain had long ended, and he started toward his favorite spot, the last seat in the row of tan wicker rocking chairs, the one farthest from the stairs and front door and most out of the way to visitors. But then he stopped and took the chair closest to the front. He smiled to himself. It's a step, he thought.

After a few minutes, Emma came out, saw him, and hesitated, then sat down next to him. "You going for a change of scenery?" she asked.

It annoyed him that she had noticed, more so that she mentioned it, but if he was going to turn over a new leaf, it meant being more friendly to his wife as well as everyone else, so he forced a smile. "Just 'cause I'm old don't mean I'm set in my ways."

"You won't find me calling you old. Hits too close to home."

He thought a second. "Does that mean you now admit we're the same age?"

"Don't push your luck."

Jonas nodded again and went back to his book. Emma seemed to take that as a cue and opened the new issue of *Time* she was holding on her lap, but before she could start on it, they both heard a car approach. It slowed, moving more tentatively as it got closer and then turned into their driveway.

It was a silver Chevy Impala or Ford Focus or one of those other American cars that all look pretty much alike. Everyone in town would know instantly what it was, a rental.

Jonas looked up from his book when he heard the car door open and watched the man retrieve his bag from the car's trunk. He was in his late twenties, average height and weight and looks. Even his luggage was nondescript—the kind of black carry-on suitcase that just about everybody used these days. He wore an Oxford blue button-down shirt and tan slacks, with a double-breasted navy blazer that looked out of place in Beacon Junction. There was nothing else to distinguish him in any way except for his youth and the fact that he was alone. Most of the tourists who stayed at the Sunrise were older, and most were couples.

As he approached the steps, Jonas offered a friendly hello before Emma could, and she seemed to suppress a smile. The stranger nodded in return. He hesitated a second before opening the screen door and entering the house. Emma got up and followed him in.

———•———

Emma caught up with the stranger at the desk in the alcove. He was standing there looking around, like he expected to find a little bell to ring and not seeing one, was wondering what he should do.

"Can I help you?" Emma asked.

"I have a reservation. Name's Delacourt. Steven Delacourt. Staying three nights, maybe four."

She invited him to have a seat and offered a cup of coffee, both of which he refused, while she went to look for Sally. When Emma returned a few minutes later, she found Delacourt wandering around the kitchen, which meant he had already been through the parlor and dining room. Emma hadn't found Sally, so she took Delacourt upstairs herself and got him settled in the Juniper Room, which he agreed was very nice. He asked if there was a map of Beacon Junction, and she showed him the one they kept in each room for the convenience of the guests, but when she asked if she could help him find anything in particular, he said no.

"I'm here on business," he said, though she hadn't asked. "Got some meetings with some people over at Harrison tomorrow. Thought I might want to walk around a bit this afternoon."

"Harrison's on the northern edge," Emma said, referring to the medical device company that was the only big business headquartered in Beacon Junction. She started to open the map to show him, but then sensed he was impatient for her to leave.

"Well, if you need anything, let us know. There's a copy of the *Clarion*, our newspaper, downstairs. It tells what's showing at the movie theater in Bellows Falls and other events that might be of interest. Saturday is the Memorial Day fair, but I guess you'll be leaving before then."

Delacourt stayed in the room only a few minutes before heading down the front stairs and out the front door past Emma and Jonas. Jonas looked up briefly and then returned to his book, but Emma kept her eyes on him as he marched out to the silver whatever-it-was he was driving. There was something about the man that piqued her interest, something vaguely familiar.

———•———

Jonas was still on the porch an hour later when Mary Louise, who did the cooking at the Sunrise, came out.

"Mind if I join you?" she said as she sat down next to him.

"You sat before you gave me a chance to answer."

"Teach you to be faster next time."

"In that case, glad to have the company." He liked Mary Louise. Everyone did.

"Besides, you're in the wrong chair," she told him.

"That seems to be the consensus. I had no idea my sittin' habits were so widely observed."

Mary Louise gave him her sexy smile but didn't respond directly. She was wearing blue shorts and a flowery blouse. Her thick and long red hair was tied in a ponytail that made her look younger than her almost forty years.

"Emma said you were wonderful at the funeral this morning," she said.

Jonas didn't respond. He opened his tobacco pouch and started filling his pipe. Mary Louise waited. When he finished, he put the pipe in his mouth but didn't light it. He limited himself to one bowl a day, usually after dinner. The doctor had wanted him to quit altogether, but Jonas figured switching from cigarettes to a pipe and rarely inhaling was good enough. He'd already given up drinking. He couldn't stop living.

"Actually, I feel pretty good about it," he said, as though no time had passed since Mary Louise had spoken. "Frank was the best and he always brought out the best in me. So it was fitting."

"I wish I'd been there to hear you."

"You never really knew him."

"No, but I would have liked to have heard you."

He smiled in appreciation. "I have to admit there was something about standing up in front of a crowd that got my juices going again. I wasn't sure I could do it. It feels good to know I still can."

"I'm glad."

They stared out at the street for a few seconds, and then Jonas turned back to his book, but Mary Louise didn't let that silence her. "What'd you make of the new guest this afternoon?" she asked. Jonas shrugged, figuring he was about to get a full report.

"Emma says he's meeting with the folks at Harrison," Mary Louise continued. "He's from Maryland, down near Washington. Maybe he's with the government."

Jonas put the bowl of the pipe to his nose to smell the unlit tobacco, a new Kentucky blend he was trying for the first time, and then put the stem back in his mouth. He knew she wasn't finished.

"Emma thinks he looks familiar. You seen him before?"

"Not that I recall," Jonas said.

"Well, don't be surprised if she asks you. She's in there wracking her brain about it."

Jonas didn't say anything to that, and for a few moments they sat in silence.

Finally, Mary Louise looked at him. "You okay?"

Jonas nodded. "Why does everyone always ask me that? I'd be a rich man if I had a dollar for every time someone asked me that."

"You are a rich man," she reminded him.

"You didn't answer my question."

"You can be quiet sometimes. It makes some people think you're unfriendly or that something's wrong."

Jonas rocked for a moment. "Be a better world if more people were quiet a little more often."

"If that's a hint, I'm ignoring it," she said.

"I didn't mean you, and you know it."

She looked at him for a moment and then smiled. He thought she might be about to say something, but she closed her eyes and let the sun work on her face. Jonas went back to his book.

The Sunrise had seven bedrooms in all: four for rent, one for Jonas and Emma, one for Sally and her husband, Jake, who did estimates for one of the two roofers in town, and one for Mary Louise, who ran the kitchen. Her breakfasts were out of this world. Everyone said so, and many of the townsfolk came by each morning to eat because the meals were better than anything they could get at home or in one of the local eateries, which were known more for the quantities they piled on a plate than for the quality of what they put there. Shortly after Sally found Mary Louise, or really after Mary Louise found Sally, word of Mary Louise's talent on the griddle iron, the skillet, or just about anything else that found its way into the kitchen spread through Beacon Junction, and people started showing up around breakfast time to say hi. Of course, Sally or Emma would be polite and invite the person to have a little something to eat. Soon it got out of hand, and Jonas suggested they open breakfast to anyone who was willing to pay for it. He thought that would discourage them from coming, but it didn't. Now Sally made a tidy sum from it.

No one knew exactly why Mary Louise left Boston or how she landed on their doorstep, but gradually they realized the arrangement worked out pretty well for Mary Louise, too, because it allowed her to pursue her other career, which involved catering to men in more ways than just filling their bellies.

Mary Louise's room was in the back of the house, divided from the other bedrooms by a big storage closet, a laundry area, and a stairway to the attic, all of which created a kind of privacy barrier. The back of the house also had a separate entrance, and if anyone were to watch it closely—not that anyone did, mind you—he might see the occasional gentleman caller. At first, Emma and Sally just thought Mary Louise had more than one suitor, but eventually they realized there was more to it.

Mary Louise met most of her clients in nearby motel rooms, but once she got to know and trust someone, she'd save the motel bill and let him come to her room at the Sunrise. Her clients were the cream of the crop, the most respected men in town and from places much farther away. They had good jobs—they'd have to, considering Mary Louise charged $250 an hour—and most had families they were devoted to, at least when they weren't devoting themselves to Mary Louise. Emma and Sally used to gossip about it in the beginning, but only to each other. They got used to it after a while, and they didn't object for fear of losing Mary Louise.

Emma found it hard to believe at first. She liked Mary Louise and couldn't match her up with any of the stereotypes that popped into her mind along with the word "prostitution." Sally shrugged it off as one of those things. At thirty-five, she saw herself as much more modern than her parents, though in truth she was more conservative than they were in many ways, especially when it came to politics. Running a business will do that to you. She was much more likely to rail about licenses and liquor laws and taxes than Jonas and Emma, who, like most of Vermont, were liberal to the core. There were lots of laws limiting what businesses might do but far fewer when it came to reining in what people were allowed to do.

Jonas figured that was one reason why no one made a big deal of Mary Louise's sideline, even though at least some must have known what was going on. Or maybe they just didn't want to risk losing those breakfasts. Jonas, being an attorney and all, generally believed in enforcing the law, but he was never bothered by Mary Louise. He knew prostitution often came with some bad side effects, but he felt the higher-end work that Mary Louise engaged in probably did more good than harm, if you could tote up different sides of a ledger that way. He certainly had the feeling that Mary Louise did it by choice— that she had other options, just none that paid as well. She didn't seem a victim, and certainly her clients were free to spend their money as they wished. If anything, he felt sorry for the guys who didn't have the money to spare for an hour's pleasure. But that was the way life was. Those with money were better off. That'd been the case for thousands of years as far as he could tell.

Though Sally and Mary Louise counted each other as friends, they didn't openly discuss Mary Louise's other job, but they came fairly close. Sometimes Mary Louise would start yawning as soon as breakfast was over and wink at Sally. "I better go get some beauty rest. I got to work double tonight." Sally knew that meant she had two clients coming, but she was too embarrassed to ask the question that popped into her mind: Did it mean two at a time or one after the other?

On the other hand, the closest Emma and Mary Louise

had come to the subject was when the box from www.
condomcountry.com had arrived. She handed it to Mary
Louise, pretending she hadn't noticed the return address.

"Damn," said Mary Louise. "They promised me it'd be in
a plain brown wrapper. Last time I ever order anything from
them." Emma had burst out laughing.

Neither Emma nor Sally knew it, but Mary Louise actually
talked about her second job a lot with Jonas. He had shown
her how to use some of the state's legal databases to screen her
clients for potential problems. And once, when he'd noticed
someone he knew hanging round the back stairs, he'd asked
Mary Louise if she realized he was married.

"I prefer the married ones," she told him. "They're not
looking for anything I'm not selling. It's the single ones you got
to worry about. First thing you know, they think they're in love
and they want you all to themselves."

Jonas liked being in Mary Louise's confidences. He rather
enjoyed the fact that she trusted him, though at moments it
made him feel old, as if she thought he was out of the game
completely. On occasion, he wondered what Mary Louise
would say if he hinted he'd like to sneak up the back stairs.
He knew she had a client or two almost as old as he was, and
he knew his equipment still worked, with the right patience
and care. But he wouldn't dare do anything but wonder.
Sometimes he longed to ask her a lot more about her work.
He'd never been to a "professional" and had a million questions
on how it worked and what it was like from her point of
view, and of course, he wanted to know why she did it, but
he was too self-conscious to ask any of that. At least so far.

CHAPTER 2

That night Jonas ate dinner early and alone, it being Emma's night to work for Meals on Wheels. Afterwards he decided to take a walk into town, resolving that if he ran into people he knew—and how could he not in Beacon Junction— he'd make a greater effort to strike up a conversation.

The sky was clear and it didn't take long to find other people out and about, but getting beyond the first step was harder than he expected. He saw Amos and Betty Coyle, near contemporaries, walking in the opposite direction on the other side of the street. Jonas waved and then crossed over to say good evening and ask how they were.

"Getting by," Amos said. "You?"

"Fine."

They looked at each other and then awkwardly moved on, Jonas realizing he didn't have a clue how to engage them in conversation. He saw Henry Jackson's son, Hank Jr., but he didn't really know him except to nod. And Beatrice Abbott seemed lost in thought as she sat on her front porch when he passed. Jonas decided he'd just enjoy the exercise and tried to pick up his pace, but he found his inability to connect with anyone disappointing and frustrating, and his thoughts turned back to the funeral, to Frank and the rich life he had led, and then to Jonas's own life and the mistakes he had made.

By the time he got closer to town, a melancholy had settled on him and he was tempted to turn back, but he wouldn't allow himself to. He soldiered up the final two blocks to Main Street, then north for about six blocks until he came to the village green, surprised to find it relatively empty. It was a little after six. The stores and offices were all closed, and most of the town was probably home having dinner.

He sat down on a bench and tried to enjoy the quiet but soon felt restless and resumed his walk. He passed a few people entering the Ventura Inn and hollered hello to George Moss, who was locking the door of his bookshop next door. Moss was both the bookseller and town guide. His store doubled as the information center for visitors.

Jonas went by Stan's Tobacco Emporium next to Moss's Bookstore and the Whippoorwill Gift Shop, which used to specialize in decorative birds but now just had a few, Moody's Natural Foods, which was a vegetarian co-op, the Masonic Lodge hall, and the Do-It-Right Hardware Store, where the cranky seventy-nine-year-old proprietor insisted on knowing what a customer planned to do with the supplies he was buying so he could offer lots of unsolicited instruction on how to do the job correctly.

Jonas turned down Ellicott, past the First Congregational Church, which was bigger than the First Baptist, a simple white building with a simple white steeple, but not as big as the Church of Christ, where Frank's funeral had been, and not nearly as ornate as the Catholic church on the other side of town, which was adorned with stained glass windows and elaborate carvings.

Along Ellicott, Jonas passed the municipal building, which looked like a church but was actually home to the town clerk and registrar, the police department, the library, and the office of an irritable but competent accountant who leased space, giving the town a little added income. The fire station was across the street, next to the Chittenden Bank.

He decided he'd gone far enough and circled back up to Main, planning to head home from there, but that's when he ran into Ellen LeFevre, about the last person he wanted to see. Oh, he liked Ellen, liked her a lot, but she was a living reminder of all that might have been but never would be.

Ellen and Lucas, Jonas's eldest child, had been sweethearts all through high school, the perfect couple that everyone thought would live a perfect life. They'd been sensible about it. When Lucas went off to Dartmouth in neighboring New Hampshire and Ellen went to Kenyon in Ohio, they'd decided to date other people, but no one expected they'd do anything but end up with each other. It wasn't to be.

"Hi, Mr. Hawke. Good to see you."

"Jonas," he said. "Call me Jonas."

She smiled, but not happily. "I'm sorry about your partner. I know you were really close."

Jonas shrugged. "He was a king among men." It sounded trite and awkward to Jonas's ear. He changed the subject.

"How are you, Ellen? How's Billy and the kids?"

She frowned, hesitating before answering. "Billy and I aren't together anymore. I thought you knew. He left about two years ago."

Jonas's mouth opened, but nothing came out. "I'm sorry, Ellen," he finally stammered. "I don't keep up with people the way I should."

"No reason why you need to follow all the gossip. It's been hard. William and Karen have it the worst. Teenagers need a father, especially William." She tried to smile.

"I'm sorry," Jonas said again. "Surprised, too. I thought you and Billy were really happy."

She looked at him a long moment, as though pondering whether she should say what was on her mind. Finally, she did.

"I guess I never got over Lucas. They say you never get over your first love, but I think it was more than that. And I think on some level, Billy knew he was second choice."

Jonas turned away so she couldn't see his reaction. He wanted to say something to her, but he didn't know what.

"I'm sorry, Jonas. I upset you."

"No, no. It's okay. I mean, I'm sorry about you and Billy, but you need to be realistic. Even if Lucas had lived and you two had married, you would have had your share of problems, just like everyone else."

She didn't say anything, and he quickly realized he'd said the wrong thing. He had no right to lecture her or judge what was or might have been. "I'm sorry, that was stupid. I didn't mean it the way it sounded."

"It's okay. I know how you meant it." She hugged him and said goodbye, struggling to control her voice, a tear already in her eye.

Jonas continued down the street, feeling like an absolute fool. When had he become so awkward, so unable to relate to people? He used to be sensitive and understanding, with a gift for saying the right thing in a difficult situation. Not anymore.

A tiredness overwhelmed him, followed by a wave of nausea. The Blue Moon was just a few feet away, and he needed to use the restroom. He went directly to it, brushing past a few waves of hello from the handful of surprised patrons. Once inside, he leaned on the sink to get his bearings, then splashed cold water in his eyes until he felt a measure of control. He dried his face and sat down on the toilet for a few minutes before climbing to his feet and walking out.

But he must not have looked that well to Sal Koszciek, the eighty-year-old barber of Beacon Junction, who stopped him at the door and asked if he was okay. He urged Jonas to have a seat, and when the waiter came, Jonas asked for a Diet Coke, but then he looked at the shot glass in front of Sal and added, "And one of whatever Sal's having."

"You okay, Jonas?" Sal asked again.

Jonas nodded. "Been a rough few days," he said. "With the funeral and all."

"Yes," Sal said. "Sorry I missed it. Heard there was a big crowd."

The waiter brought the drinks, and Jonas gulped down half the Diet Coke, careful to avoid looking at the shot glass. Neither man said anything, but Jonas could feel Sal's stare.

Finally, he looked up at him. "I guess I overdid it. Was trying to walk fast and get some exercise, but I need to work up to it." He pushed the shot glass toward Sal. "That's for you," he said.

Sal took it quickly, not drinking from it but moving it farther away from Jonas. The whole town knew about Jonas's battle.

After a minute, Jonas said he felt better and rose to leave. He put a bill on the table to cover the check, but Sal gave it back to him. "I'll take care of it," he said.

Jonas nodded, making a mental note that he owed him a big tip for his next haircut. He had the sense that several pairs of eyes were on him as he left the bar, and after slowly closing the door, he grabbed the handrail to steady himself.

He walked uneasily for a hundred yards or so until he found a bench and sat down. He brought his hands together and put them on his lap to stop them from trembling, a sensation that brought back unpleasant memories. Terrible memories.

Had he really been about to take a drink? He didn't think so. He couldn't say why he'd ordered it. He hadn't even thought about it. The words had just come out of him. Was it a close call or had he been testing himself? It had been upsetting to see Ellen, more upsetting to hear what she said—what she believed—about Lucas. It was as though he'd suddenly been transported back in time, to twenty-four years ago, and he'd reacted the same way he had then. By reaching for a bottle. Only a few hours earlier he had convinced himself that he needed to set a new course, that he'd made a huge mistake to waste so much of his life, and then in almost the next breath, he found himself perilously close to a very wrong turn.

Still, he hadn't taken the drink. That was the important thing. But he knew he had stepped to the edge of a steep precipice. He remembered the AA sessions he'd attended for a few months, until his patience with them ran out. The risk would always be there, they had told him. Obviously. He believed he was strong enough to resist it. But was he?

Yes, he had come close to losing it, but he hadn't given in. He should stop berating himself. There was a big difference between a near miss and a collision. But why didn't he feel that way? Instead of feeling victorious, he felt he'd just been lucky.

He didn't know how long he sat there, but eventually he felt steady enough to head home, and the cool air and exercise did him good. By the time he reached the Sunrise, he was in control enough to keep his emotions hidden.

Emma was already home. It was nearly eight, which surprised him. She made a joke about being ready to call the missing persons bureau, and he smiled.

"Went for a walk, that's all," he said.

"It was a nice night for it. Take me with you next time."

He promised he would.

In the back of the house, a much happier scene was playing out. Ed Riley lay back on the bed and closed his eyes. "Boy, you sure know how to use your hands," he said.

"Who you callin' boy?" Mary Louise teased. "Do I look like a boy to you?"

Ed laughed and kissed her. Their mouths parted, and she nibbled at his lower lip. Then they separated and stared at each other for a few seconds.

"You're still wearing too many clothes," she told him. She had already taken off his shirt and opened his pants, and now she continued undressing him until he was as naked as she was.

He kissed her again and then took a moment to admire her. Her thick red hair had always been her strongest feature, even when she was an awkward schoolgirl, and now it hung down in natural waves that pointed down to her breasts. Her hazel eyes were just a little bit too far apart, giving her nose more room than it deserved, but her smile was wide, sincere, and most important, inviting. There wasn't much talking after that.

Afterwards, they lay next to each other, exchanging the same kind of pleasantries that a married couple might. She lay her head against his chest, her hand moving lower on his stomach in a lazy tease. Their hour was almost up, but she wasn't a clock-watcher. Not when it came to Ed.

He was her favorite client, although she knew better than to tell him that. Let them know you were at all partial, and the next thing you knew they wanted all sorts of special treatment. She'd even known some to think that just because they were regulars, they deserved a freebie now and then. Like at the car wash where you got those cards they punched until you qualified for a free one.

No, Mary Louise knew better than to go down that path. Her rates were set in stone. No exceptions. She had her favorites, but she kept that to herself. Her job was to make each one think he was something special, while somehow making it clear she treated everyone the same.

But she did prefer Ed's company. He was a different kind of client in many ways. Oh sure, he was like the rest in that he'd started coming to her with visions of sexual sugar plums dancing in his head—and Mary Louise always kept up her end of that bargain—but it didn't take long for her to realize Ed was worth keeping. For one thing, he was more mature about the whole thing and let her be herself. Some of the others would make special requests—ask her to wear something particular or play some silly role. Mary Louise would oblige but only up to a point. She was thirty-eight and wasn't going to make a fool of herself or pretend she was some twelve-year-old who'd been called to the principal's office for "punishment." Besides, that gave her the creeps. Her clients accepted her rules or found someone else.

She never had to worry with Ed, who wasn't into games. More than any of her other clients—more than most of the men she had dated for that matter—he treated her with respect, more as a person and less as a commodity he had purchased. And of course, she responded to that, even found it sexy.

Ed was also somebody you could have a real conversation with because he listened. He didn't always have to be talking about himself and what a big deal he was.

She'd been seeing Ed for more than a year. He was in his mid-fifties, with a thin six-foot frame and a too-round face that he tried to lengthen with a tightly trimmed beard that had once been black but now was salt-and-pepper. His hair was a more consistent and more distinguished gray, and his soft facial features made him look as kind as he was. Two years ago, he'd been widowed, and it had taken him a while to work up the courage to approach Mary Louise.

Sometimes she found herself thinking about Ed when they were apart, which almost never happened with other clients. She had begun to feel he treated their weekly encounters as something approaching a date—a weird date by anyone's definition, but nevertheless a date. In some ways, he reminded her of Jonas—basically decent, kind, caring, and intelligent. But he was much more talkative and open with his feelings. With Jonas, she sometimes felt she needed a two-fisted can opener to get at what was really inside. That wasn't the case with Ed.

Ed's wife, Eleanor, had suddenly dropped dead one day of a massive stroke. He'd been devastated, but over time he managed to get back on track, at least in most respects. He was an insurance broker with a good business, and now he was active in town politics.

"A penny for your thoughts," Ed said, pulling her back to the present.

"A penny?" she laughed. "I guess you think the rest of me's worth a whole lot more than my brain."

"That's just all I have left when I finish paying for the rest," he said.

They kissed, and he motioned to the clock and said he'd best get going.

"Not yet," she said, surprising herself. She couldn't remember asking Ed or anyone else not to go when the time was up, but there was something on her mind that she was dying to talk about, just not sure she should. When a woman did what Mary Louise did for money, discretion was sacred, and though she wanted to share her secret with Ed, because maybe as the top official in town he could do something about it, she didn't know how to tell him without violating another client's privacy.

So in the end she didn't say anything, just acted like she wanted to hold Ed a little longer, and after she had, she let him get up and get dressed.

Still, he must have sensed she was troubled. "Something you want to tell me?" he asked, just before kissing her good night.

But all she offered was her standard goodbye. "Be careful out there," she said.

CHAPTER 3

Jonas's son, Nathan, was the only one present the next morning when Delacourt walked into the *Beacon Junction Weekly Clarion*, the small newspaper Nathan ran. Like his sister, Sally, Nathan had benefited from his parents' generosity. They owned the paper but left it to Nathan to make a go of it. That meant being editor, editorial writer, chief reporter, ad salesman, ad writer, and whatever else he needed to be. He had three reporter-helpers, a part-time copy editor and proofreader, and a half-time receptionist, but he did the heavy lifting himself. And he did it pretty well.

Not that it was a great paper. It wasn't. But it kept up with the gossip, spelled most folks' names right, tried to be fair and usually was, and once in a while actually told people something important they didn't already know. It helped that Nathan was born and raised in Beacon Junction, and he was a master of using his editorials to put the feelings of people into words, even the flatlanders who had come over the last couple of decades to try to make the mountains of Vermont their home.

But today he was facing a more difficult task—trying to convince the town to say no to Harrison Health Devices, the largest employer and undisputed engine of economic growth in Beacon Junction.

The company was growing, had been since it won approval from the Food and Drug Administration for an innovative heart stent about two years ago. They had some other new products in the works, too, and the firm wanted to add a big production facility smack in the middle of town.

Harrison was insisting it couldn't put the plant near its headquarters on the outskirts of town because of all the rich cropland there. The landowners were all third-, fourth-, and fifth-generation farmers, and according to Harrison, they weren't willing to sell at a reasonable price. So the company wanted the town to let go of some prime real estate it controlled, with tax breaks to boot, and it threatened to build the plant somewhere else if the town refused. There'd even been hints of heading to Mexico.

Nathan didn't believe the threat of leaving Vermont and had been toying for a week with an editorial calling on the Board of Selectmen to turn Harrison down, a hard sell given that most of the board felt Beacon Junction needed the boost the plant would bring and were afraid to cross Harrison. Nathan would have to show the board that they could win the plant without giving up too much. The key was Ed Riley, the chairman of the board and unofficial mayor, who at fifty-five was twenty years younger than the other men who held voluntary positions on the board.

Nathan was staring at his computer screen, trying to figure out the best course of action, when he heard the front door open and the sound of footsteps on the stairs leading into the big space that Nathan called the newsroom. Everyone else called it the office.

He stood up and introduced himself. Delacourt hesitated and then asked Nathan to repeat his name.

"Nathan Hawke. I'm the editor of the *Clarion*. Can I help you?"

Delacourt shook the hand that Nathan extended and took a second to run his eyes over him. Nathan was tall, even taller than Jonas had been in his youth. He was more handsome than Jonas, despite a slightly crooked nose, the result of a college hockey game. He had a perpetual five o'clock shadow that only made him look naturally attractive, as though he never spent a moment worrying about his appearance. His curly brown hair hung over his forehead, adding to the impression, and he wore a wrinkled white shirt open an extra button to reveal a hairless chest, making him look younger than his thirty-seven years.

"I'm doing a little research," Delacourt said finally, "and I was hoping I could look at some back issues. I couldn't find anything online."

Nathan shook his head and told him the *Clarion* wasn't available on the Internet. "Not much call for it here," he said. But the newspaper had issues from the past several years, since it started using computers, stored on discs. "How far back we talking?" he asked Delacourt.

"When did you go to computers?" Delacourt asked.

Nathan noticed the slight evasion but didn't say anything. "I have the last eight years on CDs. Beyond that, we have printed copies bound all the way back to the sixties. What are you looking for, anyway?"

"Harrison Health. I'm working on a story for a new magazine out of Washington focusing on the medical device industry. I've done a lot of research already, but I was hoping to get more of a local view from some of your back stories."

Nathan grunted. "What do you want to know about Harrison? I might be able to help you find what you need."

Delacourt missed a beat before answering. "It's a profile of Sean Anderson. He's the CEO of Harrison."

"I know who Sean Anderson is," Nathan said. "We did a lot on him when he was appointed a couple years back."

"I might want to go back a little further to learn more about the company."

"Suit yourself." He gave Delacourt a final stare. It would be easier to help the guy if he'd tell him what he was really after, but maybe he was working on some secret investigative story and didn't want Nathan to get wind of it. If he wanted the local view, it'd be a whole lot easier to just ask people. There'd be no shortage of gossip and strongly held opinions. But Nathan didn't say that. If Delacourt wanted to spend the day with his nose crunched up against a computer screen or thumbing through stacks of moldy back issues, that was his business.

Nathan took him to an empty desk and set him up with the CDs. Then he showed him the room in the basement where they kept the old bound issues. "I don't know how they'll be much use, though," Nathan said. "There's no index, and you'll have to look through every one to find Harrison stories."

Delacourt thanked him and sat down at the computer. Nathan went back to work on his editorial. He figured Delacourt already knew about the controversy with the new plant, and if he didn't, he'd find the recent stories about it on the CDs. He wasn't about to mention the editorial for fear Delacourt would alert Harrison, either intentionally or otherwise. Besides, he still wasn't sure what he was going to write.

Delacourt spent about two hours at the computer and then went down to the basement. He was still there at six, when Nathan was ready to leave. When he went downstairs to tell him it was time to go, he startled Delacourt, who immediately closed the volume he was looking at and reshelved it. Nathan noticed the year. 1990.

Nathan asked him if he'd found anything useful. Delacourt mumbled something about it being helpful to know some of the history but said it in a way that made it clear he didn't want to talk about it. There was something about the man's evasiveness that was really annoying. It might be that he was just unfriendly. Or maybe he was trying to hide something.

Either way, Nathan resolved to find out.

It was ten after six when Nathan left the *Clarion* building and headed out on foot for his weekly dinner with his father. It was a fine spring evening, with the sun still shining. He carried a sweater over his shoulders, with the sleeves in the front, European style. It had been nippier in the morning, and he had needed it more then. It'd be cooler again tonight, but it was fine at the moment.

The office was only a few minutes from downtown and soon Nathan reached Maria's, the Italian restaurant where Jonas and Nathan met once a week for dinner. It was a small, family place with one dining room and about twenty tables, never more than half filled.

They were welcomed by John, who bought the restaurant from Maria when she left town with a trucker from Winooski who'd been after her to marry him since they were high school sweethearts twenty-seven years earlier. John asked if they wanted to start with the usual, a large bottle of spring water and an antipasto. They did. Within seconds, a waiter arrived with the water, and before he had filled their glasses, another brought the antipasto. Bread and olive oil soon joined the dishes beginning to cover the plastic red tablecloth.

Nathan complimented his father again on his eulogy, and Jonas shrugged. They exchanged small talk, Nathan asking after his sister, his mother, and life at the Sunrise, Jonas saying fine, fine, fine to each of the questions, much as he always did.

He asked Nathan what was new at the newspaper, and Nathan told him a little bit about the editorial he was working on. They talked over the question of where to put the plant, Jonas saying there would be benefits to the town to have it in the middle of things.

Nathan went on for a while explaining why Jonas was wrong

(traffic, parking, atmosphere), and Jonas played with the salt and pepper shakers, taking it as long as he could.

"I don't know," Jonas said finally. "It could be good for business around here." He waved a hand around the mostly empty restaurant.

"Building it a few miles away will have the same effect," Nathan said.

"But what if he's serious about building in Mexico?"

Nathan shook his head. "We're not talking about making clothes or auto parts. These are FDA-approved products, and it's a lot more complicated to do that overseas. He's bluffing."

Jonas broke a piece of bread in half, dipped it in the oil, and took a bite, letting the silence build. Nathan could tell he wasn't convincing his father and realized it would be best not to push it.

When their dinner arrived, chicken parmesan for Jonas and veal piccata for Nathan, they quit talking and focused on eating for a while. Eventually Nathan broke the silence.

"Had a visitor today."

"Oh?"

Nathan told him about Delacourt coming by the newspaper office. Jonas nodded and told him he'd seen him, that he was staying at the Sunrise.

"What did he want with the *Clarion*?" Jonas asked.

"Said he wanted to read old clips about Harrison for some magazine article he's writing."

"You sound skeptical."

"Never met a reporter less interested in asking questions. Just something odd about the way he acted."

"He say what kind of article?"

"Claimed it was a profile of Sean Anderson, but he was pretty evasive every time I tried to ask anything. And he went down in the archives, back to when Sam Harrison still ran the company. I don't buy his story."

Jonas nodded and thought about Emma's view that Delacourt looked familiar but couldn't see that it led anywhere. When the coffee came, Jonas asked Nathan the one question he knew Emma would ask if she'd been there.

"How are you doing otherwise?" He said. "Heard from Carol?"

Carol had been Nathan's girlfriend until two months ago, but she lived over the state line in Nashua, and the relationship had been unable to survive the ninety-minute drive between their homes.

"No. I don't think I will hear from her," Nathan said. "It's not as though anything's changed. I need to live here for the paper, and she won't give up her job to move."

"Maybe you could find a place in between."

Nathan shrugged. He knew his parents liked Carol and were hoping they could patch things up. "I don't think it would work," he told his father. "Probably too late anyway."

"And you're okay with that?"

"It's still hard," Nathan said. "You wouldn't think it would be. I mean, we never really lived together."

"Still," Jonas said, not needing to say more.

"Yeah. I wish it had worked out otherwise, but I don't know how it could have."

"Maybe you need to start thinking about finding someone else."

Nathan laughed, and then Jonas did, too, realizing that was what Emma was always telling Nathan. Both parents had begun to wonder if Nathan would find someone and start a family before it was too late.

"It's pretty hard to meet people here," Nathan said. "Beacon Junction isn't exactly teeming with single women."

It was still light out when they finished. They shook hands, but then, in something of a surprise, Nathan gave Jonas a hug and kissed him on the cheek. "Thanks, Dad," he said.

Jonas watched Nathan walk away, not sure exactly what Nathan had thanked him for.

———•———

Nathan took the long way home. Talking about Carol had made him a bit blue, and he hoped the cool air and the friendly streets of his hometown would lift his spirits. Nathan had lived most of his life in Beacon Junction. He'd gone to Dartmouth, which was only an hour and a half away, just like his father and brother had, and then spent a year in New York, at the Columbia School of Journalism. After that, he got a job at the *Cincinnati Enquirer*. He hadn't really liked either New York or Cincinnati, and before long, he realized that Beacon Junction was where he wanted to be. On a visit home, he discovered the *Clarion* was up for sale, and he tried talking Jonas into lending him the money to buy it. Jonas said no, then turned around and bought it himself and hired Nathan to run it. That had been six years ago, and Nathan was managing pretty well. He didn't make a lot, and he wondered what he'd do when he had a family to support, but for now, it was enough to get by on, at least in Beacon Junction.

He loved the town, and he wasn't the only native to feel its pull. For every son or daughter who had gone out to taste the world and never looked back, there was another who had stayed or who had gone out and then come back to settle down.

That wasn't as easy as it used to be, however. In the last decade or two, the economy hadn't been kind to this part of the state. Sure, it was okay if you were a dairy farmer or had found a way to take advantage of the tourist industry—skiing in the winter, fishing in the summer, and leaf-watching in the fall. But beyond that, there wasn't much. Beacon Junction was still a small town, as were almost all the towns in Vermont. Heck, there were only six malls in the whole state and only five Walmarts, and it had taken close to twenty years of fighting before they were allowed to move in. So if you weren't much for milking cows and didn't take to smiling at the tourists, Beacon Junction didn't have a lot of jobs to offer. It had once had some manufacturing, but when Wyatt shoes and Sherman paint closed their factories and moved south, it was a big blow. Now, there was just Harrison and a few small manufacturers, machine toolers, and cabinetmakers.

When Nathan got back to the small house he rented, he felt a little better, but the house felt more empty than usual. He took a Rolling Rock from the refrigerator, sat down in front of the TV, and began flipping through the channels. His mind drifted back to Carol, and he thought about calling. But he knew there was no point.

CHAPTER 4

Nathan would never have guessed it, but Sean Anderson, the CEO of Harrison Health Devices, Inc., had bigger problems on his mind than where to locate the new plant. In fact, unless he could put out the fire he faced, there wouldn't be any need for a new plant.

Anderson had been working for several months to keep the lid on concerns regarding Harrison's most successful product, the CARC 2008, a tiny stainless-steel mesh tube less than four millimeters wide. The unique chemical coating on the stent helped prevent new blockages and infections, and it was considered a huge improvement in the treatment of AAA, abdominal aortic aneurysms.

But a problem had developed. The catheter surgeons used to inflate the stent to its operative size of up to twenty-eight millimeters had a tendency to get stuck in the stent. That forced surgeons to break off the tip of the catheter and remove the leftover pieces one at a time. If they didn't do it exactly right, the procedure could lead to complications and infections that could be serious. There were even a dozen patients who had subsequently died, though Anderson and the scientists at Harrison didn't believe the deaths could be blamed on the CARC. Those patients probably would have died anyway, or at least that's what they told themselves. By the time they became aware of the situation, it was too late to gather definitive evidence.

Hospitals were required to tell the Food and Drug Administration if a stent problem led to a death, but none had been willing to draw that conclusion. Harrison, in turn, was required to file a report with the FDA if serious problems were attributed to the stent, but Anderson's top advisers had convinced him that the rule didn't apply because the problems could be blamed on poor surgical procedures, not the stent. It was a gray area, Anderson felt, and he took the path of least resistance. But a couple of employees had voiced concerns, and one of them, Craig Whitney, was beginning to make a nuisance of himself. He'd been pushing for a meeting to discuss the stent, and Anderson had finally relented.

———•———

Craig Whitney took a deep breath as Anderson's secretary showed him into the inner office.

"Craig, glad to finally meet you," Anderson said, barreling out from behind a desk that was bigger than the dining room tables in most of the homes that dotted nearby Route 103.

"Can I offer you a drink?" Anderson said a little too loudly as he shook hands a little too enthusiastically. Whitney declined the drink. This wasn't a social call.

"Have a seat," Anderson said. He pointed to a sofa and two easy chairs. "And don't look so serious."

Craig took one of the chairs, and Anderson settled slowly onto the sofa. He was a big man, six-foot-three, with one of those wide frames that made you want to move out of the way when you saw it coming. A booming voice added to his intimidating presence, and Craig knew he wasn't shy about using it to bully people into agreeing with him. But he could also turn on the charm when he wanted to, and that was the treatment Craig was getting now.

"Relax and tell me what's on your mind."

Craig was about as relaxed as the first time he'd been approached by a drug dealer on his way home from school, a lonely sixth grader in Montgomery, Alabama. He knew it showed.

"I think the problems with the CARC aren't being taken seriously enough," he said, just the way he'd rehearsed it. "We can't dismiss the whole thing as doctor error. And we're withholding data from the FDA. I think we need to put it on hold until we know what's going on."

"Really." Anderson let the single word hang until Craig resumed his speech.

"I've given this a lot of thought. Over a lot of sleepless nights. And I think we're not acting responsibly."

"Craig, I'm not sure how this became your problem. You're not even part of the stent team. It's not your area of expertise."

"I know enough to be concerned. I think we're letting our fears about future sales of the CARC cloud our thinking."

Anderson didn't say anything. He looked at Craig without expression and then glanced down at his hands, which he had folded in his lap. Craig didn't let the silence bother him. He used the time to figure how he should proceed. One thing was certain: Anderson hadn't reacted with horror or even surprise at the suggestion that the company was putting people at risk. But then Craig hadn't expected him to.

Finally, Anderson broke the silence. "Craig, I don't know how much you know about this. I'm sure there's a lot of talk in the hallways, but sometimes the rumors get ahead of the facts. There were problems, but it's far from clear that they can be blamed on the stent. Human error is a more likely culprit. Still, just to make certain, we've made some alterations that further reduce any risk. Whatever happened in the past, I can assure you there won't be any more difficulties."

"How can you be so sure?"

"Well, that's what I mean when I say you're not up to date. We've improved the stent, for one thing, and we've upgraded the instructions and training for all surgeons using it. We're quite confident there won't be any problems going forward."

Craig took that in, comparing it to the more alarmist view he'd heard from a member of the CARC team.

"You work for Madeleine, right?" Anderson asked, knowing the answer before Craig nodded. "Well, she's on board, and you know she wouldn't be if there were any doubt."

Craig shook his head. "But there have been twelve deaths," he said.

"No one can blame any of those on the stent, and even if they could, a handful out of 255,000 patients is far lower than the fatality rate for conventional surgery for AAA."

Anderson looked at Craig in a way that made him feel he was being patronized. Was it because Craig was black? One of the few Harrison employees of color? One of only a few in Beacon Junction for that matter.

"Craig, we do know what the problem was—or what might have been a problem," Anderson said, "and we've changed the design to eliminate it. We've got it under control."

"Then why haven't we leveled with the FDA?" Craig asked.

The expression on Anderson's face changed abruptly. Both men knew that Craig's only leverage was to blow the whistle. No one needed to say it out loud.

"Craig, I appreciate what you're saying, but you've worked here long enough to know what it's like dealing with the FDA. They only want to protect their ass. They'll want to do a big investigation and maybe put a stop to sales until they're one hundred percent convinced of what we already know. They don't care that the publicity—let alone a recall—could kill us, putting a lot of your colleagues out of a job and, not incidentally, depriving a lot of people who need the stent from having it. To say nothing of the fact that the profits from the CARC are what pay for all the other promising research people like you are doing. Even if there is a problem with the implant, it affects a very small minority, and a lot of other patients would die if we took our product off the market. It's far more effective than other stents."

"We don't know that."

Anderson rose abruptly. "Are you sure you don't want that drink? I'm going to have one."

Craig shook his head. He wasn't about to become drinking buddies with the guy, not at two in the afternoon.

Anderson walked over to the bar, picked up a bottle of twenty-four-year-old Glenfiddich and poured himself a healthy dose. He moved over to the window, which looked out over a manicured lawn and garden, with freshly plowed farmland in the distance. After a long ten seconds staring out the window, Anderson straightened one of his suspenders and turned back to Craig. "Do you have a specific recommendation?"

"I think we should talk frankly with the FDA, see what they say, and let the chips fall where they may."

Anderson walked back to the sofa and sat down. When he resumed, his tone was gentle.

"Look, Craig. I appreciate your coming to see me about this, but 'letting the chips fall where they may,' as you put it, isn't the way I define leadership. As head of this company, I have a responsibility not just to you, but to all of the employees, to the board of directors, and of course to our owners and investors. So let's not rush into anything." Anderson rose, indicating he was finished listening.

"Craig, why don't you write me a memo with your recommendations. Then we can talk again. And in the meantime let's keep this between us."

Craig agreed and rose to shake hands, the bigger man towering over Craig's five-foot-eight-inch frame. Craig headed to the door, but before opening it he turned back to Anderson.

"And the patients," he said, knowing he might be crossing a line.

"I'm sorry?" Anderson seemed genuinely confused.

"The patients. You have a responsibility to them, as well." Craig left before Anderson could respond.

Anderson watched Craig leave, then shook his head, more in respect for Craig's guts than in anger. He sat back down on the sofa and lifted his wingtips onto the coffee table. He stayed there for ten minutes, slowly sipping the scotch until it was gone.

It was three-thirty when his secretary buzzed him to tell him that Delacourt had arrived.

———— • ————

Steven Delacourt felt strange driving up to the Harrison building. He'd been a five-year-old kid the last time he'd been there, coming by on a Saturday with his father, who worked there and needed to pick up a few things. They'd run into his grandfather, Sam Harrison, the founder and driving force behind the company. That hadn't been a surprise. Sam spent most of his waking hours at the office, either working with the researchers on some hopeful new product or arguing with the accountants about some cost-cutting moves they thought were essential. It turned out to be one of the last times he saw his grandfather alive. Two months later, Harrison was murdered in his own home.

Delacourt and his mother, Catherine, had moved a year and a half later, after Delacourt's father, Richard Reinhardt, had been tried and acquitted of murdering Harrison, with Jonas Hawke serving as his defense attorney. Catherine couldn't accept the verdict. She believed her husband was guilty, and she filed for divorce as soon as the trial ended. By then, a new CEO had been named—Gary Craver—someone his mother knew well and trusted with the family business. She'd resisted selling after she inherited the lion's share of stock and was glad she had. Gary had built the firm into a more successful enterprise than it had been before, and Sean Anderson had gone several steps beyond that. Today her stake was worth more than ten million.

Catherine was a hands-off owner, a decision that reflected her wish to keep a distance from her father's company and her refusal to return to her hometown. The CEOs who had followed her father often found themselves in Washington and frequently used those opportunities to meet with her at her home in Bethesda to bring her up to date on company affairs.

Catherine had also discouraged Delacourt, who had taken his stepfather's name, from returning to Beacon Junction, but he persuaded her that it was well past time for some member of the family to see the operation. He had used the controversy over building the new plant—what Anderson had described as a minor spat—to argue that now would be a good time. He could visit the company headquarters and quietly take a reading of the town. It was an earnest offer, but one with a hidden motive. After growing up in ignorance of his father, he had developed a strong need to know more about his roots. He wanted some answers, and he rightly sensed that those answers were in Beacon Junction.

Now he was sitting in the small conference room adjacent to Anderson's office, staring up at a portrait of his grandfather, one he remembered seeing as a child. It was far more formal than the family photos Catherine kept around the house.

In fact, Delacourt might have been excused for not even recognizing the Sam Harrison who stared down from the portrait. He'd never seen him like that, not even in photographs. His grandfather, whom he had always called Poppy, had been a garrulous, down-to-earth Vermonter, capable of putting on the clothes and airs that his job sometimes required but never comfortable wearing them. He lived close enough to walk to work. He'd shuck his parka and winter boots and walk around the office in thick white socks, jeans, and a flannel shirt. He always kept a business suit in the office—he never knew when he'd need it—but he often went weeks without putting it on. He was happiest in the lab, working side by side with the other researchers, batting around ideas and challenging assumptions. Everyone liked him, or so it seemed. Obviously, someone disliked him enough to kill him.

The door suddenly opened and Anderson pushed through, a big smile on his face and his hand extended. "Steven, so glad you could come."

Delacourt looked at the extended hand a second before shaking it. He refused the offer of a drink and thought he noticed a look of annoyance when he did. It quickly passed, though, and Anderson asked about his mother and whether the summer heat had settled in yet on Washington, adding that he had to go down again next month for another meeting with the FDA bureaucrats.

"Unbelievable how they can waste a guy's time," Anderson said. "I don't think there's a one of them that has a clue what it's like to run a company or actually make something. All they know how to do is push forms around—forms that someone else has to fill out."

Delacourt didn't respond, and after a pause, Anderson asked if there was anything particular he hoped to see or learn during his visit. "Your mother was a bit vague on the purpose."

Delacourt paused before answering, a very Vermont habit he

had picked up from his mother, and said that he just thought it was time for one of them to see the company operation in person.

Anderson readily agreed—what choice did he have?—and said Madeleine Priest, the vice president for research, was ready to show him around the labs and tell him about their most "exciting" prospects.

Delacourt asked about the controversy over where to put the new plant, and Anderson said there was only minor concern in town and he was confident it could be dealt with. "The usual stuff about traffic and disruption—everybody has to throw in some environmental concerns, too, these days—but we can make some minor concessions and everyone will be happy."

Delacourt complimented Anderson on the latest quarterly numbers and asked about the rest of the year. Anderson assured him things had never looked better.

"The stent is our future. The CARC 2008 is doing well, and we've already made improvements for a new model." Anderson hadn't told Catherine about the problems that were keeping him up at night, and he certainly didn't intend to tell Steven.

They chatted a few more minutes, until Delacourt couldn't think of any more questions, and then Anderson walked him to Madeleine's office. She greeted him warmly, and after Anderson left them alone, she offered him coffee, which he accepted, and took a few minutes to ask about Delacourt's background and interests.

She was a friendly woman in her mid-fifties with an unpretentious look and air. She'd been cursed with uncontrollably stringy hair, a bad complexion, and a nose that was borderline unsightly, but she more than made up for it with her intelligence, warmth, and humor. Delacourt took an immediate liking to her and completely enjoyed the ninety-minute tour. It was packed with useful information, and she gave him time to talk to the scientists and other employees they met along the way. Though one or two seemed uncomfortable and unsure meeting the owner's son, Delacourt got the feeling that most of the staff was happy and that the company hadn't strayed too far from its roots. It had grown large without losing the attributes of an old-time family business.

It was still light when Delacourt got back to the Sunrise.

———•———

A few hours later, Craig Whitney was holding Mary Louise in his arms. He hugged her hard, and she kissed him on the cheek.

"Thanks for seeing me on short notice," he said.

"No problem." She kissed him again, then pulled back and sat down in a chair by the bed. "What's going on?"

Craig had been a client for only a few months. Divorced, about thirty-five, good looking, and smart as hell, with an advanced degree in biogenetics and a good job at Harrison. Of course, you'd have to be damn smart to accomplish what Craig had accomplished, pulling himself up from a very modest childhood in the inner city to go to college with full scholarships and fight his way into the middle class. He'd worked hard and done everything society asked of him, and it had all worked out pretty well—at least until he realized that he and his wife, Kima, had become strangers in the process. They had tried to stay together for the sake of their two sons, but the tension had been too much.

Craig had worried about approaching Mary Louise, not sure how she'd feel about seeing a black man and not having a lot of cash to throw around, but when he saw her ad on Craigslist, he thought it was worth a try.

She'd quickly put him at ease, understanding the tension between his need for companionship and his caution. She rarely saw him more than once a month, and sometimes not even that often, but she tried to accommodate him. She figured it must be difficult for him in Beacon Junction, several worlds away from Montgomery and with so few other blacks in town, none who were single and anything close to his age. Vermont had never had a race problem because it had never had a minority, and while people tried to be kind and welcoming, they almost made him feel uncomfortable just because they were trying too hard to prove how tolerant they were.

Craig asked if he could open the wine. Mary Louise always had a chilled bottle of Chardonnay and some freshly baked cookies for her sessions. He gulped down his first glass and then poured himself another. Mary Louise waited, knowing he'd get around to what was bothering him as soon as he could.

"I talked to Anderson today."

She nodded. He'd already told her about the stent and agonized with her over what he should do. She had urged him to tackle it head on.

"How did it go?"

"Oh, he's slick. He knows how bad it is, and he wants to sweep it under the rug. Tried to convince me it's not a problem but seemed more intent on finding out how much I know, how big a problem I am. Asked me to give him a report on what I'd learned. It's just a delaying tactic."

"What will you do if he won't do anything about it?"

He emptied his glass and refilled it. "I honestly don't know."

She was a little worried about how much he was drinking, so she took the glass from his hand and pulled him over to the bed. They kissed and she began unbuttoning his shirt. He returned the favor, and soon he had something other than the CARC 2008 to occupy his attention.

Later, though, as they lay silently in each other's arms, he sighed, and she knew he was thinking about it again.

"Maybe I can help," she said.

"Talking to you always helps."

"No, that's not what I mean. What if there was a way to put pressure on Harrison without going public."

"That's what I'm trying to do."

"No, I mean what if we got you some outside help? What if there was someone here in Beacon Junction who could lean on Anderson to make sure he does the right thing. It'd be better for the company—and the town—if Anderson took the first step. Less of a scandal."

"Who do you have in mind?

She smiled. "A lady never tells."

———•———

As Craig left, Mary Louise went to the window and watched him go out the back door. He glanced around to see if anyone was looking, and satisfied he was alone, he walked away.

Mary Louise smiled at his caution, then started to get annoyed at how hypocritical the town was. Sometimes folks acted like they were living in an earlier century and the mountains kept them sheltered from the real world. Mary Louise knew otherwise, and when she let it get to her, she could go off, though only to herself, on the hypocrisy of it all. It wasn't as though she lacked for customers.

When she started out, she was living in Brookline, just outside of Boston. A disastrous affair with Danny—the great love of her life who turned into the rat bastard from hell— had left her so deeply in debt that she stopped answering her phone to avoid the collection agencies. One day she found herself sitting at her kitchen table, staring at an advertisement for what was obviously a call girl agency. She decided against it, but she didn't throw the ad away. Days later, she picked up the phone and had a long talk with the very friendly woman who answered. She'd been kind but frank, and above all, practical, and she knew how to ease Mary Louise's reluctance.

"Can I ask you a question?" the woman said after a while. "Have you ever met a guy at a bar and gone home with him and then never seen him again."

Mary Louise admitted she had.

"Well, it's the same thing," the woman said. "Except you get paid handsomely for it."

She agreed to let Mary Louise ease into it, promising the first couple of dates would be with regulars she knew and trusted, so Mary Louise could see if she liked it.

The next night Mary Louise went out on her first call, and soon she was doing six or seven sessions a week. It was a whole lot different than she thought—tough at times, but more like a regular job than she expected.

It still amazed her how few people could believe that it was just a job. Not demeaning. Not something she was drawn to because of abuse or low self-esteem or drug addiction or any of those other stereotypes everyone liked to cling to. In her mind, the whole thing had a lot less to do with sex than with acting. Every client was different, but they all wanted pretty much the same thing—a boost to their egos. Her role ranged from pretending interest in their problems to faking multiple orgasms, and everything in between. She'd arrive, play her part for an hour, and then it was back to the real world, only with a hefty wad of cash in her pocket.

The hardest part was the need for secrecy because it meant she could no longer be open, even with her close friends. Living a dual life became a huge burden. There were also the risks—not only of running into a dangerous customer but also the cops who occasionally ran half-hearted stings. She'd been caught up in one, and though she got off with a light fine, it wasn't an experience she wanted to repeat.

Within a few months, Mary Louise left the agency, which was too demanding and took too big a share of the fee. She placed a discreet ad on the Web: "Petite redhead, mid-20s, available for private encounters. Discretion guaranteed and expected in return." And just an anonymous e-mail address. No name, not even a phony one, and no phone number.

It took less than a year for her to pay off her credit card debts, and she quit seeing clients. But in time she found herself thinking of going back to it. Her more normal jobs, everything from waiting tables to short-order cook to secretary, didn't pay nearly as much and involved a lot more hours. So when her mother had a stroke and ended up in an expensive nursing home, and Mary Louise suddenly needed a lot more money, she didn't have to think very hard about what to do. She decided on a fresh start in a new place. She liked to think someone was looking out for her when she found the Sunrise and moved to Beacon Junction, less than an hour away from the nursing home.

With Sally providing room and board and a modest salary that more than met her personal needs, she figured she could get by with only a couple of clients a week, a small enough number to stay under the radar. She put her ad back up on Craigslist, thinking she'd get clients who would welcome the privacy of getting out of whatever city they lived in. And she was right. Many were willing to make the drive from Boston or upstate New York, but two from towns nearby found her, and soon several of her clients were local, including Craig and Ed. Ed was, in fact, her most regular customer, visiting every week. She smiled for a second, but then the smile vanished as she realized she was daydreaming, thinking what it would be like to go to dinner or a real date with Ed. She did like him, and he liked her. And they were both single. Being seen together wouldn't necessarily pose a problem for Ed, even if someone who knew about her saw them together.

Then she wondered why he hadn't asked her out to begin with. Maybe because he was almost twenty years older. No, that wasn't it. He didn't think of her that way. He was like all the rest when it came to her, wanting only one of two things, her cooking or her body.

She sighed, more loudly this time, and turned the television on to chase the silence away.

CHAPTER 5

The next morning, Jonas called Nancy Hargrave and asked if he could come by. She quickly agreed.

The Hargrave house was on Duncan Street, around the corner from Spruce, where Jonas and Emma had lived for more than twenty years before they bought and moved into the Sunrise. It was in a neighborhood with large stately homes on half-acre lots, close enough to each other to be neighborly but not so close as to be crowded.

On a whim, Jonas went by his old house and stood staring at it for a few minutes. They had moved in when his law practice started to prosper, right after Nathan was born. He still thought of it as having been a happy home, despite the heartaches that marked the later years.

As he stood there, he thought of the days when the children were young and of the family meals they always shared. Dinner was a ritual. Even when he had a big case and was working long hours, Jonas made it a point to be home at six-thirty to eat with the family.

The dinner discussions included Jonas going around the table and asking each of the children and then Emma what their day had been like. And he insisted on a fair amount of specifics. Nobody got by with just an "Okay" or "It was boring."

Jonas did his part, too, talking about his cases in more than a little detail, and that's what usually got the arguments going.

Jonas often lectured the children on his role in preserving and protecting the law, a concept he put on a pedestal, even if he disagreed with a lot of specific statutes. The kids would frequently argue with him, telling him this client or that one was guilty, and Jonas should make him confess or at least drop the case. Jonas loved those arguments, especially the ones with Lucas, who as the eldest took it upon himself to play devil's advocate, a role he relished and that Jonas encouraged.

The ritual of dinner debates continued even when Lucas went off to Dartmouth, but they lacked the same vigor. And after Lucas's accident, dinner was often eaten in silence.

Lucas had been a nineteen-year-old freshman when he and his date, another Dartmouth freshman, went down to Boston to take in a Bruce Springsteen concert. They drove back that night, but as they were cruising north along Interstate 93, their car suddenly veered off the road into a ravine and flipped over. No one could really say why Lucas lost control, but the best guess was that he fell asleep at the wheel.

Lucas's date wasn't wearing a seat belt. New Hampshire was still the only state in the union without a seat belt law. She was thrown from the car and killed instantly. Lucas survived, but just barely. He had a bad head injury, and he was airlifted to the trauma unit at Mass General.

The hospital called Jonas, but Emma was out, and Jonas couldn't find her, so he rushed to Boston by himself. The doctor gave him the bad news. Lucas was alive, though not in any meaningful way. He was on life support and might remain on it indefinitely, having suffered massive brain damage. The surgeon made it clear what he thought Jonas should do, but Jonas wouldn't act on his own. Emma remained mysteriously absent, and by the time she got to the hospital, it was nearly dawn. Together, they made the decision to pull the life support system, and they were with Lucas when he died.

———————•———————

Nancy Hargrave was also thinking of the old days as she waited for Jonas to arrive. Some of the happiest years of her life had been while Jonas and Frank were partners. Not so much at first, when building a practice had meant too much hard work, with long hours and not that much to show for it. But after a couple of years, almost abruptly, they'd made it.

She'd always thought Frank worked too hard, especially after the accident and the heavy toll it took on Jonas. Terrible losing a son like that. She couldn't begin to imagine how she'd feel if anything ever happened to Molly or Michael. Her throat tightened at the thought.

Nancy knew the eulogy must have been hard for Jonas. She wanted to ask him about the case he mentioned, but something made her cautious.

She'd put a fresh pot of coffee on after Jonas called, thinking he'd be there quickly—the Sunrise wasn't far away—but a half hour had passed, and she had finished arranging a plate of pastries and fresh fruit, straightened up the living room twice, and was now staring out the window. It was a pretty day for a walk, and maybe she'd take one a little later.

Nancy had returned to the house the night before, having spent the past two weeks with Molly. Nancy had assured Molly that she was ready, that she'd be fine on her own.

But was she? Last night had been hard. At first she'd been proud of herself, cooking a full meal, knowing that cooking for one was hard but necessary. She made a point of choosing baked eggplant, a dish that Frank never liked, but then she barely touched it. She forced herself to watch television—some silly talking heads on a pseudo news program—and to stay up until it was late so she'd be able to fall asleep. But then she went into the bathroom and saw Frank's toothbrush. That's when she broke down.

Several friends had offered to help pack Frank's things, but she'd said no. She knew that was something she had to do herself, that it was part of the process. After she had a good cry over the toothbrush and even though it was after midnight, she steeled herself and went back into the bathroom with a trash bag, filling it with the offending toothbrush, the shaving paraphernalia, and the other items of Frank's that were still in the medicine cabinet. Fortunately, they had separate closets so she didn't have to deal with Frank's clothing just yet. These old New England houses never came equipped with decent closets, and Frank gave Nancy the master bedroom space while he used the guest room closet.

Still no sign of Jonas. She turned back to the living room and started to straighten up, then realized she'd already done that. She went into the kitchen, took a mug and poured a few inches of coffee and sipped, looking around the empty room, suddenly remembering when it was the center of a family in motion. Had she come back too soon? Molly wanted her to stay longer, but she felt she was imposing. Hal, who was in contention for world's greatest son-in-law, insisted she wasn't, that Molly wanted her company. But that only made her realize that Molly needed to begin the grieving process, too.

———•———

Jonas took a deep breath and knocked twice. Within seconds, Nancy opened the front door, almost as if she'd seen him coming up the walk.

"I hope I'm not intruding, calling on such short notice," he said.

"I'm glad you came." She hugged him, and he put his arms around her gently. He let go before she did.

"I wasn't sure you had come home yet," he said.

She smiled. "It wasn't easy, but I managed to escape from Molly's last night. She's being very protective."

Jonas smiled. "Your kids are wonderful. I'm sure they're worried about you."

She led him to the living room and offered him the coffee. He refused, but when he saw her crestfallen look, he said coffee would be good. While she was out in the kitchen getting the tray, he looked about the room, as though it might give him a clue of what to talk about. He had been there often enough with Emma, but he noticed things now that he hadn't paid attention to before. How formal it was, with the white L-shaped couch and the uncomfortable straight-backed chairs. They were antiques, he thought, like maybe nineteenth-century French, or at least what he thought nineteenth-century French might look like.

When Nancy came back, he told her he liked the room and that it had a comfortable feel, though in truth he didn't feel at all comfortable. She laughed at that and said Frank always thought it was too formal. When she put down the coffee and the plate of fancy little pastries, cake, and fruit, Jonas felt glad that he'd asked for the coffee. He wasn't at all hungry, and if he had been, he would have preferred a glazed donut, but he took a piece of crumb cake to be polite.

He asked about Molly and Michael, and she told him that she didn't think it had really hit them yet. "They're focused right now on taking care of me."

"That's only natural," he said.

"I know, and it feels good to be with them, but I think we also need time to be alone. So the grieving can begin."

Jonas thought it sounded a little too pat, like she'd read it in a book. He thought about when Lucas had died. He and Emma had never been able to share their grief without it being intolerably painful. They'd just look at each other and cry, each feeling even worse because the other felt so bad. That was why he fled, first trying to wrap himself in work and when that failed, turning to alcohol.

After a few seconds of silence, Nancy started to say something, but then caught the painful expression in Jonas's eyes and realized his mind was elsewhere. When he turned back to her, she asked him what he'd been thinking about.

"Nothing, really," he said, but when he saw the look on her face, he realized he was doing it again. Shutting people out.

"I was thinking about Lucas. About mourning. How painful it can be. And how everybody handles it a little different."

Tears came to her eyes, and he apologized.

"No," she said. "I'm glad to talk about it. Everyone else tiptoes around on eggshells, never saying what they're really thinking." She gasped. "It hurts so much."

He'd been sitting in a chair opposite the couch, but now he moved over and sat next to her and put his arm around her. She turned her face into his shoulder and started to sob.

"What surprises me is how angry I feel," she said after a moment. "I don't even know who or what to be angry about. Sometimes I even feel angry at Frank. Like what right did he have to die so soon and leave me like this? Isn't that crazy?"

Jonas knew it wasn't. He'd never had much use for the grief counseling group he attended for a few short weeks—watching other people cry about their pain never lessened his own—but he had learned that much.

"It's natural to feel angry. And whatever you feel, you're entitled to it. It's hard enough without trying to judge yourself."

After he said it, he thought it sounded stupid, like something the grief counselor would say, but Nancy kissed him on the cheek and sat up.

"I wish I could tell you there was an easy way to get through it, but there isn't," he said after a moment. "It hurts like hell. It'll always hurt like hell, but you learn to live with it because there's no choice. It doesn't mean you forget, but you start to accept what you can't change."

"You sound like a minister," she joked through new tears.

"Not hardly. Nowhere near that. You won't hear me quoting scriptures or telling you this is part of a grand plan. Hell, I almost punched out one preacher for trying to suggest that about Lucas."

After a while, she asked him about Emma and the children, and he told her they were all fine. Then he realized she was trying to extend the conversation, and he did his best to elaborate on his answers, telling her what each of them was up to. He wished there were some innocuous questions he could ask her, but even if he'd been good at small talk, there wasn't anything that would work in this situation. He asked her if she needed any help with the estate or anything like that, but she told him the kids had it covered.

"Still, if they want any help, I'd be glad to," he said.

She thanked him again for his eulogy, said everyone had told her it had really captured Frank's personality and that she agreed with them.

"There was one thing I wanted to ask you, though," she said. "That case you referred to. The one you said you shouldn't have handled but couldn't give up."

"The Reinhardt trial," he said. "I put Frank in a bad spot. It wasn't fair."

It took a few seconds before it came back to her.

"That was a tough time for you," she said. "Right after you lost Lucas."

"Did Frank talk to you about it?"

"Not the specifics, but I remember he was worried about you. I think at first he couldn't understand why you didn't let him handle it, but he said he'd never seen you so determined. He figured it had to do with Lucas and your needing to keep your mind occupied."

He looked at her for a moment. "That was certainly part of it, although that never works. You can't really keep your mind off your grief. At best, it only postpones it."

She hesitated. "I think he also thought it was causing some friction between you and Emma, but I think he didn't want to ask you directly."

Jonas was surprised by her frankness. "Well," he said after a moment. "I acted pretty selfishly in those days. It's a wonder Emma stuck with me." He smiled to lighten the moment, and she did, too.

Jonas said he'd best be moving on. Nancy thanked him for coming, and they promised to keep in touch. As he walked down the steps, he made a silent vow to Frank to make sure he did.

CHAPTER 6

The dining room at the Sunrise was the biggest room in the house, with a large table that seated twelve. The room was also the sunniest, bathed in light from oversized windows equipped with hanging baskets of impatiens, hoyas, and lipstick vines.

Emma didn't usually eat with the guests. Mary Louise's breakfasts were wonderful, but they were rich—a French toast cream casserole today—and Emma's petite frame didn't allow much room for extra weight. This morning, however, she had an ulterior motive, and when Delacourt took a seat, she took the one opposite him. She was still sure she knew him from somewhere.

Delacourt mumbled a good morning while he filled his plate and set to eating, stuffing his mouth as soon as it was empty and not joining the conversation between Emma and the other two guests, who had flown out from San Diego to visit their son and his family in nearby Putney. They were planning an excursion to Boston, but the husband allowed as he'd prefer to spend a relaxing day in the Sunrise garden, just reading, with at most a walk around the town.

"What about you, Mr. Delacourt?" Emma finally asked. "More meetings today or are you going to enjoy our town some?"

"A little of both," he said, then changed the subject, asking the California guests whether they'd been affected by the early forest fires near San Diego.

Emma tried to engage him a couple more times but didn't get far. Finally, she got exasperated enough to tackle Delacourt head on.

"I understand you met my son," she said.

He stopped and looked at his fork, which had a big piece of strawberry on it. He stuffed it in his mouth and chewed slowly rather than answer.

"Nathan, the editor of the *Clarion*, is my son," Emma said.

Emma noticed a flush rise in Delacourt's face, and she smiled. "Don't worry, we're not spying on you. He mentioned to my husband that you'd come by."

"I didn't realize you were related," Delacourt finally managed.

"He said you were a magazine writer," Emma continued.

While she waited for a response that never came, she stared at his hazel eyes, the thin eyebrows, and the dimple on his chin. Suddenly she knew who he reminded her of.

After everyone had gone, she went up to the computer. She didn't use it much, but she knew how to do a Google search and eventually she found the confirmation she was looking for.

Jonas came into the room, and she closed the screen quickly.

"You've been busy today," he said. "I hear you had breakfast with the guests." Jonas had gotten up late, having taken until after midnight to read himself to sleep.

She smiled. "Checking up on me?"

"If I'd known, I would have joined you. I can always go for some of Mary Louise's treats."

She jabbed him playfully. "Just make sure they're the eating kind."

He laughed. "So you figured it out yet?"

"Figured what out?"

"Who he is. What he's here for. I know that's what's got your head spinning."

"You think you know me so well."

"After forty-seven years, I reckon I do."

"Well, if I have figured it out, I'm not telling you. You go find your own amusement." And with that, she left the room.

Jonas hesitated a second and then went over to the computer. He opened the browser and clicked on the history button. Soon, he knew, too.

———•———

Jonas spent some time that afternoon working on the downstairs bathroom, which had been leaking a little. He wasn't as handy as Sally's husband, but he was around more and had a lot more free time, so he tried to help out when he could. He drained the bowl, replaced the washers, tightened everything up, and put it back together. He flushed it several times and then tightened it some more, then flushed it and then tightened it again. He had to admit there was still a leak, but he declared it much improved and went upstairs to read a bit, knowing he would drift off into his regular afternoon nap before he got very far.

He found Emma in one of the two reclining chairs in the little nook off to one side of their room. She was reading *Pride and Prejudice* for what must have been the eighteenth time. Jonas couldn't understand her fascination with it. He knew it was a kind of comfort book, one of a few she turned to when she needed an escape, but she'd never been very good at explaining why that was so.

Jonas went over and touched her shoulder. She smiled up at him, and when he settled on the bed and opened the book, she went and lay down alongside him. She put her head on his chest and he put his arm around her. He waited, thinking she was about to say something about Delacourt, but she was soon asleep, snoring softly. He carefully put the book down and closed his eyes, and soon he was asleep, too, snoring not so softly.

They both dreamed of Lucas.

In Jonas's vision, he and Lucas were in court, arguing opposite sides of a murder case. No, they weren't in a court, actually. It was some kind of stadium, with an open roof and a huge crowd of spectators. Lucas was the prosecutor. Jonas couldn't quite remember the defendant or the crime, but he remembered trying to get the confession thrown out, arguing it had been coerced. The judge wasn't buying it. Lucas kept interrupting Jonas's argument, and at one point Jonas lost his temper, called Lucas an impudent, ungrateful son who had turned into a deep disappointment, and threatened to ground him for a week if he continued.

"Irrelevant," Lucas quipped to the judge, who then admonished Jonas for letting his personal feelings for Lucas get in the way and accused him of trying to prejudice the jury.

Mary Louise and Emma had both been on the jury—in fact, all of Beacon Junction seemed to be on it. It was more like the annual town meeting than a trial, and Jonas had been confident that at least Mary Louise and Emma would side with him.

But they didn't. His client was found guilty. Mary Louise told a reporter afterwards that she thought Jonas's case had no integrity.

"Who are you to talk about integrity?" Jonas had said. "You're a whore!" At which point Mary Louise slapped his face, and he awakened.

While Jonas was dreaming of Lucas as the adult he never had a chance to become, Emma was dreaming of him as an infant. He was ill and running a high fever, and she wanted to call the doctor. Jonas told her she was being silly, that all kids got sick and had fevers, and she couldn't run off to the doctor every time it happened. They fought terribly over it, and Emma remembered being so mad she wanted to hit Jonas. Eventually he relented, and Emma went to the doctor the next day, but by then Lucas's fever was down, and the doctor acted like she was a fool for coming in. Back at home, Jonas comforted her and then tried to take her to bed, but she was still furious with him, and she literally locked him out of the bedroom.

Jonas didn't need to wonder why he had dreamed of Lucas or even why he had made Lucas a lawyer on the opposite side. He had long wanted his son to follow in his footsteps, and given how often they liked to argue about the law, it didn't surprise him that they were in a legal setting opposing each other. But why a stadium in front of the whole town?

He was shaken by the seriousness of his disagreement with Lucas and even more unsure what the business with Mary Louise meant. He could still feel the fury that led him to call her a whore but was shocked that he had. He didn't think he ever judged her harshly for what she did, even unconsciously. Now he couldn't be sure. And why had Emma sided against him? Well, he guessed that wasn't so hard to figure. They got along well now, but it hadn't been that way back when Lucas died. And those feelings could never be put completely to rest. After a while, he got out of bed, trying to be quiet so he wouldn't wake Emma, but he failed.

Emma was also startled by her dream, mostly because she hadn't dreamed of Lucas in many months. Then she remembered Delacourt. His appearance in Beacon Junction—now that she knew who he was—couldn't help but dredge up all that old stuff. She felt bad about denying Jonas her bed, even in her dream, and wanted to reach out and hold him, but he had left the room by the time she got that far in her thinking and feeling.

Neither said anything to the other about the dreams. Maybe they needed some time to figure them out, or maybe neither wanted to admit knowing who Delacourt was until it was clear how his visit would play out.

Jonas decided to bide his time. He knew Delacourt was staying at least another day and figured he could wait. Always the lawyer, he wanted more time to prepare for the encounter.

Emma wasn't so patient. She was waiting, sitting on the front porch with her Jane Austen, staring at the page rather than reading it, when Delacourt came back around six. He nodded to her and started for the door, but she called out to him.

"Do you have a minute?" she asked.

He hesitated a second but then walked over and sat down in a chair next to her.

"You haven't been very honest with us," she said right off.

"What do you mean?"

"Acting like you were just visiting on business."

"I am here on business."

"Acting like you've never been here before. When in fact you were born here."

He looked at her, and she stared hard at his face.

"You look a lot like your father."

The words seemed to startle him. "I'm sorry," he said. "I didn't realize who you were until we talked this morning. Your husband was his attorney, wasn't he?"

Emma didn't say anything. She could see he might have a point. Sally's name was the one associated with the Sunrise, and Sally's last name wasn't Hawke anymore. It was a little like her not recognizing Steven Delacourt because his name was no longer Steven Reinhardt.

"You told Nathan you were a magazine writer, and that's not true, either."

"A white lie. I wanted to read about my father's case and didn't want anyone to know."

Emma took that in without speaking. Her guard remained high. What was he hiding? Why couldn't he be more open?

"I wasn't sure how people felt about him," he said, as if reading her mind. "So I didn't want to come out and start asking."

"What exactly is it you want to find out?"

"Everything. What he was like. What people thought of him. Who his friends were if he had any. And the biggie—what really happened."

"You sound like you don't even know him."

"I don't. I haven't seen him since I was eight. I don't even know where he is. My mother forbade contact when I was growing up and frowns on it now. I tried to find him when I got out of college, but I didn't get very far."

"She must have told you about him, though."

He laughed. Emma thought it sounded bitter.

"My mother doesn't like to talk about it," he said. "Says it brings back bad memories and no good can come of it. She wasn't exactly thrilled about my coming here, but I do have some business at Harrison, and she gave in."

He sighed, loud enough so Emma turned toward him.

"She won't talk about what happened," he said. "Not to me anyway. But I suppose if you believed your husband killed your father, you wouldn't find it a very happy memory, either."

Emma took a few seconds to think about that.

"Your father was acquitted, you know."

"I know, but that didn't change my mother's view."

Emma was quiet again. She watched a pair of cardinals flit among the trees in the front yard. They seemed to be looking for something, but she couldn't imagine what.

After a while, Delacourt looked at her. "Do I really? Look like him, I mean?"

"There's a definite resemblance. Same hazel eyes, and the dimple on your chin is exactly the same. Same smile, too, now that I see you have one."

"Did you know him well?"

Emma looked at him to see if he knew what he was asking, but he misunderstood. "I mean, I know your husband defended him, but did you know him personally before that?"

"This is a small town. Everybody knows everybody."

"Well, I'd appreciate anything you can tell me. I only know what I read in the old *Clarion*s and that wasn't much."

Emma rocked a bit, thinking about what she wanted to say, then decided she didn't want to say much until she knew what Delacourt was after. "He was a nice man. Friendly, kind, good looking like you."

Delacourt looked away, taking a minute to think. "Were you glad he was acquitted?" he finally asked. "I mean, I know you were probably glad for your husband, but deep down, did you think he was guilty?"

"I thought he was innocent."

Delacourt asked her why, and she told him that she just didn't see him as a murderer. "And the evidence they had was hardly convincing. Didn't amount to anything but theory."

He thanked her and said if it was okay, he wanted to ask Jonas what he thought.

"Sure, but don't be surprised if he won't tell you much. Then again, he might. You can never tell. But give me a chance to tell him who you are and let him adjust to the idea of talking about it. Those were tough times for us, too."

"What do you mean?"

Emma was already on her feet, and at first she pretended she hadn't heard the question and opened the screen door. Then she reconsidered. "Our son was killed in a car accident a few weeks after your grandfather was murdered." She started to say more, but decided to let it go at that and went inside.

CHAPTER 7

T he breeze tickled Jonas's face as he sat in the rocking chair closest to the porch stairs. He lit his pipe and puffed up the glowing embers before he drew in a mouthful of smoke and then slowly let it out. It was nearing dusk and the street was quiet.

Delacourt was in the house. He'd come in an hour earlier and asked if they could talk this evening, and Jonas had invited him to join him on the porch. Now Jonas wondered what was keeping him. Maybe he's getting his questions together, Jonas thought. Or maybe he's just nervous.

Emma had thought Jonas might refuse to talk to Delacourt, but in a way, he was looking forward to it. He saw it as a chance to make amends of a sort. It wouldn't make up for the mistake he'd made, and he wouldn't admit that mistake to anyone but Emma, but this conversation might be a start at repentance. And redemption.

Still, Jonas was torn about how much to say. He wanted to assure Delacourt that his father had indeed been innocent, but he couldn't be very convincing without telling him what his mother had obviously never told him. He'd try to finesse it, but he knew it would be difficult.

It struck him as odd how he'd spent so many years trying to put Lucas's death and all the events associated with it out of his mind—how he had taken to drinking just for that purpose—but now that Delacourt's return had forced those long-ago events back into the present, he was finding more than a little solace in remembering Lucas. The good times they'd had. The laughs they'd shared. The dreams they'd made together.

It was still painful to think of what might have been, but the memories were also a blessing of sorts, one he had denied himself for too long. Instead he'd given himself over to anger. Anger at Emma. Anger at Lucas for falling asleep at the wheel. Anger at himself for not preventing it. Anger at God for letting it happen—or worse, making it happen. The anger and pain were all he had felt for too long. It was hard to feel much else when someone you love as much as you love yourself—more, even—dies that young. But it had been a mistake. Wasted years. That's all he was left with. He hoped it wasn't too late to change.

———— • ————

Upstairs, Delacourt stared at a yellow legal pad. He figured he'd get only one chance to talk to Jonas, and he wanted to make sure he didn't get flustered and fail to ask what he needed to ask. He had watched Jonas closely these past couple of days, and he didn't seem all that approachable. Something about his manner served as a warning not to get too close. Still, he'd agreed to talk, and Emma had no doubt told him what Delacourt wanted to talk about.

It had been three days since his arrival in Beacon Junction, three confusing days that evoked a mixture of feelings. Walking the streets brought back memories he didn't know were there, not clear memories but vague recollections of feelings he'd had as a child. He couldn't exactly call it nostalgia, more a sense of what life had started out to be and what it might have been had things worked out differently.

He had accomplished a couple of his goals since arriving, but each question that was answered led to more questions.

He enjoyed his visit to Harrison—he was impressed with Madeleine Priest—but Harrison wasn't what really drew him to Beacon Junction, and it wasn't what he wanted to know from Jonas. The legal pad in front of him had one question, written in large capital letters: WAS HE GUILTY? That was the bottom line, he thought.

He didn't remember much about his father. In fact, he couldn't separate what he remembered from what he'd been told, as little as that was. He'd been a distant man, seemingly unfriendly and hard to get to know, according to a close friend of his mother's, the only one he'd ever dared to ask. He had stayed with her one weekend when his mother was out of town, and he got up the nerve to mention his father. At first, she shut him down, much as his mother always did, but then she seemed to realize that it was unfair not to answer him. Still, they didn't talk about the murder, not even close. That was always forbidden territory.

Delacourt was disappointed that Emma had been reluctant to talk to him, but what little she said—being the exact opposite of what his mother's friend said—was enough to make him wonder. Maybe Jonas would say more, but he wasn't betting on it. He'd ask, though, and maybe Jonas had some idea of where his father was. He wanted to meet him, although the thought scared him, and he wasn't sure he'd go through with it, even if he found him.

What other questions would he ask Jonas? Now that he knew about the death of their son, he couldn't help but wonder how Jonas had been able to handle the trial. Maybe he was the kind of man who carried on no matter what. Accepted the things he couldn't change and moved on without looking back that much. That would mean he was a cold man. Or a very practical one. But how else to explain it?

———•———

Mary Louise's room had the best view of the garden, which took up the entire backyard. It was Emma's doing—the garden, that is. She started it when they first bought the Sunrise, marking off a small patch for perennials. It had grown each year, so that now the entire backyard was a tribute to her creativity, with an S-shaped path of grass that let you wander around for a close-up look. There were over one hundred varieties of plants, all carefully selected by Emma, with overlapping bloom seasons, so something would be flowering from the time the tulips and alliums popped up in early spring, such as it was in Vermont, to when the mums and New England Harrington asters finished in late fall. Emma had a little help with the weeding from a couple of carefully supervised high school students, but she did most of it herself. People joked that she wasn't vain about her own appearance but beamed like a proud mother whenever anyone complimented the garden.

Much was in bloom on this late May afternoon, and even in the fading light of dusk the garden brought a smile to Mary Louise's face as she studied it from her window, lifting, at least briefly, the burden of decision.

She knew she didn't have to get involved. Craig hadn't asked for any help. Quite the opposite. He was concerned any fuss would be traced back to him. She knew he was already putting himself on the line, and maybe he knew the best way to handle it. But she did want to help, and she had to admit that a part of her worried that Craig wasn't strong enough to go up against Anderson. She thought she'd be doing him a favor by getting Ed involved. He was less likely to be cowed by Anderson, and as head of the Board of Selectmen, he could have an influence. Anderson couldn't simply ignore him. In fact, Mary Louise thought, Ed might even be able to protect Craig. It would help if Anderson knew that someone else was aware of what was going on.

And in the end, Mary Louise figured, she had to do what was right. The important thing was to stop Harrison from marketing a product that was killing people. That trumped everything, didn't it?

Or maybe she was meddling. What if she ended up getting Craig fired and putting Ed in an impossible situation?

She wanted to do the right thing. She had never really stood up for any cause bigger than herself, and this one had fallen into her lap, as though fate were testing her. Yes, she wanted to do the right thing, and she knew that meant speaking up about the stent. But she wanted to do it in a way that wouldn't hurt Craig or Ed.

Perhaps she should talk to Jonas. He'd have a better idea of what to do. She couldn't tell him the whole story, which would make it difficult. Still, it was worth a try.

———————•———————

Four miles away, Craig sat at his desk in the small second floor apartment that served as home. He'd rented it two years ago, when he moved to Beacon Junction to take the job at Harrison. At the time, he thought of it as temporary, something that would suit his needs well enough until he found a nicer place. But he was always too busy to move, and while he once thought he needed more space to entertain his two young sons when they came to visit, he soon found that his ex-wife made it almost impossible for them to be away for as much as a full weekend. So instead, Craig flew down to Alabama whenever he could to see them there, trying to maintain some kind of relationship. That became even more difficult when Kima remarried. The new husband was nice enough, and the boys liked him, but Craig found himself feeling more and more the outsider, not only in Beacon Junction, but even with his own children. It was hard to watch as Lionel and Barry, now twelve and ten, gradually transferred their allegiance to the new man of the house.

Craig was batting away at his laptop, trying to put the finishing touches on the report that Anderson had demanded. Assembling the evidence wasn't hard, but making the argument that he felt was essential was more difficult. He wasn't a writer. Not at all. He could form a sentence and a paragraph, but they didn't come together with the passion he felt.

Of course, a part of him knew the whole effort was futile, that Anderson just wanted to know how much he knew and how big a problem he would be. Still, he had to follow through and see what happened.

Craig sighed and took another sip of his gin and tonic. No use in laboring over every word. It wouldn't change anything.

———•———

Across town, an altogether different approach to persuasion was under way. Nathan was putting the finishing touches on his editorial. He'd decided to go hard, saying that while Harrison may have its reasons for wanting the plant in town, the town had better reasons for wanting it on the outskirts. He'd spoken earlier in the week with Anderson, who made his strongest pitch, saying he could take the plant away from Beacon Junction but would prefer that it be in town, a move that he argued would help the nearby businesses and prompt many of the new employees to live close by, boosting Beacon Junction's sagging economy.

Nathan wasn't buying it. He dismissed the threats to go abroad or to another state, and he felt the benefits of putting the plant on the outskirts of town would be just as great as putting it in the middle, without the resulting complications. No, Anderson's arguments didn't persuade him. He'd come out against it and see if he could get a majority of the selectmen to agree with him.

He hit the print button and waited for the machine to spit it out.

His eyes caught the desk that Delacourt had occupied, and he noticed that the computer hadn't been turned off. He went over to shut it down and wondered again what had really brought Delacourt to the office. Emma had told Nathan who Delacourt was and what he was supposedly after, but something still didn't feel right. Why all the secrecy? Why didn't he just ask what he wanted to know?

Nathan's mind wandered back to those days of the Reinhardt trial. What a difficult time that had been for everyone. He still didn't understand why his father had insisted on defending Reinhardt so soon after Lucas's accident. They'd all been devastated when Lucas died, and maybe throwing himself into the trial was Jonas's way of dealing with it, but that didn't do much to help the family. They had always looked to Jonas to be the strong one, but in that instance, he had been the weakest, forcing Emma to step up. Nathan still looked up to his father, and eventually they had regained some of the closeness that had been lost, but Nathan could never be as sure of his father as he had once been. His moods were too variable, his attention too fleeting, his good qualities too inconsistent.

Nathan watched the computer screen go dark and retrieved his editorial from the printer. He read it through and left it for Hillary Vance, his proofreader. By tomorrow afternoon, it would be in print. By nightfall, most of his readers would have read it, and by Friday morning, he'd know what their reaction was. He already knew what Anderson's would be.

———•———

Anderson wasn't the least bit worried about the plant location as he sat in his office that night, a stack of papers on his desk and a glass of scotch in his hand. He'd known for a while where the *Clarion* would come down on the plant issue, and he wasn't all that concerned about its ability to sway minds. Besides, he had other options if the town said no. He'd rather have the plant close by where he could keep an eye on it, but there was really no reason why it needed to be in Beacon Junction, and if Nathan and his ilk didn't want it, plenty of others would. In the end, he figured, he'd call their bluff, and they'd back down rather than lose the jobs and the business the town so obviously needed.

No, his concern wasn't the location of the new plant, it was whether he'd have a product for it to produce. Craig Whitney wasn't the only one losing sleep over the CARC 2008. As confident as he'd sounded with Craig, Anderson had his own doubts that he was doing the right thing.

The scientists assured him it was a good product. They honestly believed that. They'd made a mistake—the insertion procedure was too complicated. The newer versions were better, and they had better instructions and training. There was less and less concern about incidents involving the older stents. Any serious complications would have come quickly, and the new version had been used for the last two months. They just had to make sure there were no older stents still out there and no surgeons who didn't get the word. Speaking up now would force the FDA to step in until Harrison could prove they'd made the necessary changes. That could take months. And the CARC 2008 might never recover its reputation.

Which would be a real shame. He knew it was a great

product, and that it really did save lives. No doubt about that. And no one could have foreseen the problem.

No, they couldn't go to the FDA now. Washington would never understand. He had waited too long; the delay would look bad. He had no choice but to cover up the problem. The new version of the stent could succeed and save thousands of lives.

The immediate issue was Craig Whitney. They had to win him over. If they couldn't, they'd have to find some way to silence him. The first step was to find out what he knew. Anderson would get some clue when he got his report. But he had to be ready. There weren't many at Harrison who knew the whole story of the stent and those who did were as invested in it as he was. He'd bring them together in the morning and see what plan they could come up with. He turned to his computer and sent an e-mail setting the meeting for nine-thirty in his private conference room.

CHAPTER 8

J onas wasn't so lost in his thoughts that he didn't hear Delacourt's breathing as he stood behind the screen door, pausing several seconds before opening it and stepping outside. Without saying anything, he sat in the rocking chair next to Jonas and exhaled loudly.

"Pretty spot," he said, looking at the sun sliding down toward the horizon.

"My favorite," said Jonas. He reached for a match to light his pipe. "Smoke bother you?"

"No, not at all."

They sat that way for several seconds, Jonas waiting for Delacourt to break the silence.

"I suppose your wife told you what I wanted to talk about."

"I got the general idea." Then for the first time he looked right at Delacourt. "She's right. You do look like your father. Especially the eyes and of course the dimple. I'm surprised I didn't notice it myself."

"Can you tell me about him? I'd be interested in anything you remember. What he was like. Why he had so much trouble fitting in here. What you thought of him. Anything at all."

"And whether he was guilty."

Delacourt tried to smile, but it came out more like a grimace.

"I was going to work up to that."

"Sometimes, it's best to go right for it."

"I'm interested in the other stuff, too."

Jonas looked at him. "I didn't mean you weren't. Emma says you haven't seen him since you left town and your mother doesn't like to talk about him."

"That about sums it up."

"Well, I understand why your mother didn't want to tell you too much. She was so sure he was guilty. Never could figure out why. You ever ask her?"

Delacourt shook his head. "She never wanted to talk about it. Did you believe he was really innocent?"

Jonas put his pipe back in his mouth and took a puff before answering. The smoke wafted close to Delacourt.

"I think the jury got it right," Jonas said finally.

"Think? Or do you know?"

"Let's just say I'm as confident as anyone can be."

"But they never found another suspect."

"That doesn't make your father guilty, does it? They were sure they had the right guy, and they never looked beyond him. But they were wrong."

They went over the basic facts. How Sam Harrison was killed in his home with his own shotgun. He'd been alone, his wife away, having gone out of town to visit a sister, taking Steven and his mother with her. There was no sign of a break-in, and the police concluded that Richard Reinhardt had opportunity and motive. He would've known Sam was alone, wouldn't have any trouble getting in, and could have reasonably expected his wife to inherit the company.

"It was all circumstantial," Jonas said. "Not a shred of physical evidence. Anybody could have gotten in because Sam never bothered locking his doors, and a couple hundred in cash was missing, so it could have been a burglary that went bad."

"But my father didn't have an alibi," Delacourt said.

Jonas hesitated before saying anything. "Your mother and you were away with your grandmother, so there was no one else in your house that night. Most people in those circumstances wouldn't have an alibi, either."

Delacourt regrouped. "Did you know my parents well? Before the trial I mean."

"Not really. Oh, I knew your grandfather pretty well and your mother when she was a youngster. But I didn't see much of her after she married. I'd run into them from time to time. We attended enough of the same events—town stuff or church stuff, mostly—but it wasn't like we were friends or anything."

"But he hired you to be his attorney?"

"Actually, I wasn't his first choice. He really wanted my partner, Frank Hargrave. But Frank was tied up in another big trial at the time, so he ended up with me. By the time we got to court, Frank's other trial was over, but by then I was too involved in it to let it go. Frank helped a lot, though. An awful lot."

Delacourt didn't seem to know what to say to that, and after a few seconds Jonas went on.

"Your father never really fit in here," he said. "This isn't an easy place for outsiders. Requires a special effort to hold back and listen and try to find your place. People here don't take much to those who barge in without getting to know our ways. Small minded, but it's the way we are."

Delacourt told Jonas about the conversation he'd had with his mother's friend. "She said he felt disliked from day one, that he never made the effort because no one would meet him halfway."

"I suppose there's some truth to that," Jonas said. "But there wasn't any overt animosity, and as the trial proved, a jury of his peers kept an open mind. In the end, that's what he ought to remember."

"She also said he could be ungrateful, that although my grandfather brought him into the business, he criticized him for running it too leniently. Too much like a family and not enough like a business."

"Then he'd approve more of it, now," Jonas said. "They say that new CEO certainly has a different approach. But you'd know more about that than me. You and your mother still own most of it, don't you?"

"She does. I'm just an informal adviser."

"That why you're here?"

Delacourt smiled, no longer sure who was interviewing whom. "Yeah, that's part of it, though I admit I wanted to find out more about my father and what happened back then."

"I can understand that, but you know the best way to find out things is to go to the source. Can't be that hard to track your father down."

"I know. Maybe I will. It's complicated."

Jonas grunted and realized his pipe had gone out again. He took out a match and relit it, which gave Delacourt a chance to work up his courage for the question Jonas knew was coming.

"That was obviously a tough time for you," he said, not looking directly at Jonas. "I guess you proved you could handle it, but I can't help wondering why you didn't cut yourself some slack and let someone else take over."

Jonas didn't answer, and after a minute the silence seemed to unnerve Delacourt. "I mean, from what I've heard, you cut back your practice after the trial. Why hang on for my father?"

"Well, that's my business, isn't it?"

"I'm sorry. I was just wondering if there was something special about the case that kept you involved. But I shouldn't be prying into what must have been an awful time for you."

"Well, that much I agree with. Look, Mr. Delacourt. There's not too much I can tell you. I didn't know your father that well on a personal level—there's others that maybe can tell you more about what he was like as a man, beginning with your mother, of course. I never asked her why she was so sure he was guilty, and believe me, the state worked on her as best they could—within the law, mind you—to provide any evidence she had. Personally, I don't think she had anything but conjecture and, frankly, a lot of hate. By then, their marriage was over, and she was very bitter. Maybe that colored her mind. But all that's for her to say. The bottom line is there was no physical evidence to tie him to the crime and plenty of reasonable doubt. That was all I needed to do my job and I did it."

"I thought the trial broke up their marriage, but you make it sound like it was on the rocks before then?"

The question surprised Jonas. "Well, I doubt she would have suspected him if she hadn't lost trust in him before then. There had to be something going on. But that's really a question for you to ask your mother. Or your father."

There was a finality in Jonas's tone that must have been obvious to Delacourt. He thanked Jonas and apologized again for prying. Then he said he was going to take a walk. Jonas watched him until he turned out of sight. Then he let out a loud sigh, leaned back in his rocker, and closed his eyes.

———•———

But if he was looking for quiet time, it was not to be. Within minutes, he heard footsteps, and Mary Louise sat down in the same rocker Delacourt had just left.

"Evening, Jonas. Mind if I join you?"

He forced a smile and returned her greeting. She was dressed in a sweatshirt and jeans, her hair was pulled back and tied, and she wasn't wearing any makeup. Not working tonight, Jonas thought, then remembered his dream and felt guilty, about what exactly he wasn't sure. When she put her head back and closed her eyes, Jonas stole a closer look. She was a pretty woman and kept herself fit and trim, but she wasn't the knockout that he once assumed high-priced call girls had to be, and she had reached the age when you noticed a certain tiredness around her eyes and mouth. Still, she had a smile and a warmth that were attractive, that made you feel she was glad to be in your company. It always felt genuine, even when she was having a down day.

She must have sensed his stare because she opened her eyes and gave him a smile. "I need some advice."

He smiled back. "Then I better fill my pipe," he said.

She closed her eyes again and waited until she smelled his sweet Scottish blend of Black Cavendish and Latakia.

"I'm thinking of sticking my nose where it doesn't belong," she began.

"That's an easy one. Don't."

"But I think I can do some good, and it's important."

"Why don't you start at the beginning?"

"I'll try, but it's going to be hard because I have to disguise a few things."

"In other words, this is going to be one of those discussions where you want my advice, but I'm not allowed to know what we're talking about?"

"Afraid so. Well, not completely, but it requires client confidentiality. I'm sure you know all about that."

She smiled at her joke and he nodded. "Not sure you're officially covered under that, least not the laws I'm familiar with, but I can see how it's important in your—your business." He looked at her and saw she was enjoying his momentary awkwardness. "How about we call him Mr. X?" he suggested.

"Well, actually it's Mr. X and Mr. Y."

"That makes it interesting already."

"In fact, when you come right down to it, it's Mr. X and Mr. Y and Mr. Z." She laughed. "I'm joking, but it's not really funny."

She sighed and then closed her eyes again. Jonas waited for her to get ready.

"Here's the thing. Someone I care about has a problem. The company he works for is doing something unethical, and he's trying to talk them out of it, but he's not getting anywhere. And I want to get him some help. I have another client who I think might be able to put pressure on the company if I ask him to."

"And they need you as a go-between?"

"They need someone, I think."

"And the risk is?"

"That ultimately the company will figure out who's talking and come down on him."

"And you want my advice?"

"Yeah."

"Mind your own business."

She looked at him and wrinkled her brow.

"I know," he said. "That's not what you wanted to hear."

"Why do you say that? That I should mind my own business."

"Let your client work it out with the company. If he needs advice, he might want to talk to a lawyer before going too much further."

"You're a lawyer."

"I'm retired."

"But it's really important. It's a matter of public concern. Public health. People could die if this doesn't turn out right."

"Well, that would change it. Not necessarily my advice on what you should do, but it certainly raises the stakes."

He stood up, walked over to the steps and leaned on the railing, his pipe clenched between his teeth. She let him think on it a bit and then got up and stood beside him.

"You sure your client can't handle it by himself?" he asked.

"He's trying, but I don't think he can. I think he needs help."

"But he doesn't think so?"

"Not yet, but I think I can talk him into it."

"Well, don't do anything he doesn't want you to do," Jonas said. "And be careful whatever you decide."

After she thanked him and went inside, he stood there a few minutes, trying to think it through. It did feel like meddling, but without knowing what was at stake, he couldn't tell if it was justified. He suspected the public health argument was a little overblown and tried to guess what it might be, but he couldn't.

———•———

The night had descended, but the chill hadn't settled in. Jonas decided to take a walk, but before he left the porch, he heard the screen door open.

"Office hours over?" Emma asked. "I was thinking I'd need to take a number if I wanted to talk to you."

"Too bad I don't get paid for my time anymore."

"But isn't it nice to be wanted?" she teased.

"It's been a while. I was about to take a walk. You want to come?"

As an answer she took his hand, and they set out down the steps. At the end of the walkway, they hesitated, silently debating the direction, and then Jonas took the sidewalk to the right, pulling her along, in the opposite direction from the one Delacourt had taken.

The Sunrise was on an old-fashioned street, with houses of every shape and size. A scattering of red oak, cottonwood, and sycamore trees lined the pavement, and the roots of a few of the older ones had upended some sections of the sidewalk.

All of the houses had well-trimmed lawns, with an honest attempt to dress up the landscaping, though in some cases with limited results. The big trees kept the sun at bay, and too many residents didn't know any better than to try to grow the kind of plants that couldn't tolerate the cool shade. The smart ones stuck to ivy and other ground covers, with hardy holly bushes and nandina for accent. There were no landscaping companies in town, though a few in neighboring jurisdictions would come out if the job was big enough. Some people asked Emma for advice. She was the closest they had to a resident expert, and she would often split and share some of her more mature plants.

They walked in silence for a few blocks. Emma seemed to sense that Jonas wasn't ready to talk, and she made an effort to give him the mental space he needed, but her patience ran out when they reached the green.

"So, what did you tell him?"

"Nothing, really. A part of me would like to put his mind at ease, but a bigger part can't. Or won't. And I didn't know his father well enough to tell him much about what sort of fellow he was. Probably couldn't be objective about it anyway, so I just didn't say much. You're the one who can answer his questions."

"You didn't tell him that, did you?"

"Didn't think it was my place," he said.

"Let his mother answer his questions. It's about time she did."

"You can tell him what sort of person his father was without telling him everything. Let his mother tell him the nasty stuff."

He regretted the phrase as soon as he said it.

"Are you ever going to stop punishing me?" she asked.

"I stopped a long time ago," he said. "I really did."

Emma waited a beat before speaking.

"But you haven't really forgiven me, have you?" she said.

He stopped and looked at her directly. "I can't forget that it happened, and once in a while, it still hurts, but I love you more than I ever did, and that wouldn't be true if I hadn't forgiven you."

She looked at him doubtfully, but all she said was, "I love you, too."

They started walking again. "I'm serious about you talking to him," he said. "He deserves to know about his father, and I don't think his mother's going to tell him."

"I don't know. I don't relish a lot of questions. The last thing I want to do is relive that whole episode."

"It's your choice. Of course, the main thing he wants to know is whether his father is guilty."

"What did you tell him about that?"

"Just that I was confident the jury got it right. Nothing more."

"I told him the same thing."

"The problem is he'll keep pushing on how we know that."

"I don't care. I don't think it's my place to say anything more."

They climbed the steps to the Sunrise and went up to their room, separating to perform their nightly get-ready-for-bed rituals, Jonas spending what Emma considered an inordinate amount of time on flossing, Emma getting out her extra blankets to ward off the cold. Under the covers, there was silence until she asked him if there was a problem with Mary Louise.

"She seemed more serious than usual," she said.

"You were eavesdropping on us."

"No, I wasn't. I just came down to see you and saw you two together. And something about her body language made me think she was troubled. But if you don't want to talk about it, that's okay."

"It's kind of confidential."

"She's not going to leave us, is she?"

"Nothing like that."

They kissed and Emma put her arm over his chest. He took her hand in a lame attempt at a reciprocal gesture. She kissed him again, and he wondered if she was telling him she wanted to make love. They had gotten out of the habit. After a minute she said good night, then turned on her side to face the window. He feared she had taken his lack of a response as a rejection, but he wasn't entirely sure what she had been feeling or wanting, if anything. For that matter, he wasn't sure what he wanted, either. After a minute, he gently called her name to see if she was still awake.

"I'm here," she said.

"Does it ever bother you? What Mary Louise does, I mean."

"Not as long as you stay off those back stairs."

"No, really. Do you ever judge her unkindly for it?"

"I don't think so. I can't understand it. It gives me the creeps, frankly, but I suppose it's her decision, and she seems happy with it. As a job, I mean."

"But if Sally said she was going to do it, you'd do everything you could to stop her."

"Of course. That's different."

He wasn't sure it was but didn't say anything.

"What about you?" Emma asked after a while. "Do you judge her badly for it?"

"No, I don't think so," he said. Then after a pause, "At least not that I'm aware of."

CHAPTER 9

Anderson looked around the room at his top lieutenants, five men and one woman who formed the unofficial working group he consulted on most of his key decisions. On some occasions, he called them together because he genuinely wanted advice and listened carefully to their views. On others, the group had a different purpose—to share responsibility for a critical decision so no single person was left standing out on a limb. He didn't know which category this session fit in. Probably both.

Noticeably absent was Sandra Livingston, the general counsel. Anderson had already spoken with her and would again when he decided on a course of action, but her presence today would have inhibited the free-wheeling discussion he was hoping for.

Anderson began with an update on the CARC 2008, including his conversation with Craig Whitney, and then sat back in his chair. "Thoughts?" he asked after a few seconds of silence.

Don Parker, his tough-minded vice president for operations, was always the first to jump in. "We need to come down hard on Whitney," he said.

"First, we need to know what he knows," said Gordon

Winter, a wiry man never seen by his colleagues in anything but a gray or blue suit, a heavily starched white shirt, and a red tie. He was in charge of marketing and development.

Parker waved him off, saying they couldn't wait. They had to have a contingency plan, and they had to be prepared to play rough.

"Aren't we forgetting something?" It was Madeleine, the unofficial voice of reason among the group.

They all looked at her, with expressions varying from interest to disdain. Anderson had a bemused smile on his face, while Parker couldn't resist rolling his eyes. Winter found the middle road by staring down at his pad, pencil in hand, as though he were ready to take notes. The others also avoided making eye contact.

"Leave Craig Whitney aside for a moment," she began.

"Sure," Parker said, "he's one of yours, so you want to protect him."

"Leave Craig aside for a moment," she repeated. "The real question is the stent and what we want to do about it. Our priority should be deciding whether we're sure we've fixed the problem and whether we're taking too big a chance by not keeping the FDA in the loop."

"I thought we'd already decided," Parker said. "It's your people who created it. You're the one who always defends it. If you've changed your mind, it's damn late to be telling us."

"I'm confident we've fixed it, although to the extent the problem was human error during the insertion procedure, it's impossible to know for sure whether the changes we've made will make it foolproof."

"In other words, you don't have a clue," Parker said.

"In other words, I can't say definitively. What I can say is the fixes we've made should work."

"So going forward, the problem is solved," Parker concluded.

"I believe so, but the FDA might feel it should be involved. We can't be one hundred percent sure until we give it more time to see if the insertions go smoothly from here on out."

"Which is why we shouldn't tell the government now," Parker said.

"Technically, we may be required to," Madeleine said. She looked around, as if she'd suddenly noticed the absence of the general counsel.

"We've been through that," Parker said. "The law is filled with gray areas and our counsel thinks we can defend the way we handled it. I think we all agree we haven't broken—and won't break—any laws." He spoke as though the meeting were being recorded and might be used against them someday in a court of law. Anderson called on those who hadn't spoken, and they agreed there was no need to involve the FDA. It began to look like a consensus, save Madeleine, who remained indecisive.

"It's a troublesome situation," Anderson said, stating the obvious. "Let's all give it some more thought over the next twenty-four hours."

As the meeting broke up, Anderson took Madeleine's arm and ushered her into his office, motioning her to the same chair Craig Whitney had taken less than two days before. "I gather you're on the fence," he said.

"Yes and no," she replied, and they both smiled. "I think we fixed the problem, but I also think that strictly speaking, we're obliged to report the incidents to the FDA. They'll probably be fine with the steps we've taken."

"But it will take time for them to decide. And given the way everything in Washington leaks, that could involve bad publicity that we'll never recover from. Even if we ultimately got a clean bill of health, we'd get slaughtered in the marketplace."

She leaned back and waited for him to continue.

"If we've fixed the problem," he said after taking a breath, "then I think we ought to carry on. If the FDA makes us halt production, people will have to rely on stents that we know aren't as good as ours. To say nothing of what it would do to Harrison."

"Sean, the FDA approval process is there for a very good reason. Sometimes that means people who need a product have to wait, but overall it's worth it."

"Hypothetically, yes, but this isn't a hypothetical case. We know what we're doing. Besides, the FDA process is a mess. We went through all the right procedures the first time, and the FDA wasn't any better at catching the flaw than we were. They're just bureaucrats."

"They're not just bureaucrats," she said. "The reviews are conducted by peer panels, and most of them are pretty damn good. Don't forget I used to serve on one. Besides, there have to be rules or we'd be back in the days of traveling medicine men hawking colored soda water as cancer cures."

"Madeleine, this could destroy Harrison. If we had a bad product that couldn't be fixed, it'd be one thing. But that's not the case."

"You can't be sure. We thought we were right when we went to market in the first place."

"But we learned from our mistakes."

She looked at him to see if his mind was made up and saw that it probably was. Then she asked what he planned to do about Craig. "Want me to talk to him?" she offered.

"No. Not yet, anyway. Let me deal with him for the moment."

She gave him one last look, frowned, and left him to his thoughts.

———•———

As soon as Madeleine had gone, Anderson's secretary came in, carrying a sealed envelope. Craig Whitney had dropped by to deliver his promised report. Anderson asked her to cancel his lunch and have the cafeteria pack him a turkey sandwich and an apple. He was going for a walk and a one-man picnic. On the way out, he saw that the *Clarion* was in the box outside the building, so he dropped in two quarters and put a copy of the paper under his arm. He walked about twenty minutes, his mind going over the morning meeting and his conversation with Madeleine. It reminded him of his days in the military, when he'd been a major in the first Gulf War and had to make tough decisions to put some lives at risk in order to save others. He thought the analogy made sense.

Back on the grounds of the company he stopped at his favorite bench and ate his lunch, letting the *Clarion* and the report sit unopened next to him.

When he finished, he picked up the newspaper and turned to the editorial. Pretty much what he expected. Nathan Hawke just didn't get it. He still thought that if the town denied Harrison the land it wanted, the company would cave and build its plant close by.

So be it, Anderson thought. He'd fight on, pretty confident of winning a vote by the Board of Selectmen, but even if he lost, it wasn't that big a deal. He'd find another site easily enough. No need to lose sleep over that one.

He picked up the envelope and pulled out Craig's report. He read it carefully. Then he read it again. Whitney had it about right, though he didn't have all the latest information and wasn't giving them enough credit for having come up with a solution. But he wasn't harsh or adamant. Firm, maybe, but not adamant. Maybe Madeleine could persuade him they were doing the right thing. Of course, that required bucking up Madeleine, and he wasn't there yet, though he felt pretty confident he could get there.

Anderson thought about the stent. Such a tiny thing, yet so important. A life saver for many patients. And for Harrison as well. Few people realized how tenuous the company's future was. Sam Harrison and his successor, Gary Craver, had run the company as though it were a club, with little concern for the bottom line. That was fine when they had a couple of high selling products to bring in revenue, but Sam Harrison's patents had expired, and the company desperately needed the stent until its next generation of products were ready. It wasn't just lives that were at stake but hundreds of jobs. The whole future of the company.

Maybe he should have kept Catherine Delacourt in the loop, but he doubted she'd understand the risks. Outsiders—and that's what she was—rarely did. You couldn't run a company being a nice guy. The tough decisions had to be made by tough people. That's what he was for.

By the time he returned to the building, he was resolved. And confident he was doing the right thing.

———— • ————

Don Parker was waiting for him and as soon as they were alone, he started in.

"I don't need a whole lot of time to think about this," Parker said. "It would be crazy to tell the FDA anything. I vote for going forward with the improved stent and burying all the reports of problems. Anything else would destroy us."

Anderson nodded. He took no solace in agreeing with his hard-minded vice president. Every chief executive needs an enforcer, and Parker was his, but that didn't mean he liked or even respected him.

"The only question," Parker went on, "is what to do about Whitney, but why don't you let me handle him?"

"And how will you do that?"

"Maybe you shouldn't know."

"No. It's too soon to play hardball. Give Madeleine and me a chance to bring him around."

"Is she on board?"

"Not yet, but I think she will be."

"We don't have much time. If Whitney goes public, we're fucked."

"I know. Let's wait a day or two. I'll get back to you."

Parker got up and left without saying anything more.

CHAPTER 10

O n Fridays, when the *Clarion* came out, Nathan usually took the morning off to sleep in a bit and catch up on errands, so it was mid-afternoon when he finally arrived at the office. He greeted Susan, the receptionist, and she nodded toward his office. "He's been waiting for over an hour."

Delacourt sat reading the new issue of the paper for the second time. "Good editorial," he said by way of greeting. "Good, but tough. You think the town will go along?"

"Hard to tell. What will Harrison do if it does?"

"Hard to tell," Delacourt said and smiled.

"Shouldn't be hard for you. Don't you and your mother still have a controlling stake?"

"My mother does. Anderson's got her convinced that the town can't afford to say no and see the plant be built somewhere else."

"There are other options."

"So you say."

Nathan sat down behind his desk and glanced at the mail for no particular reason.

"I came by to apologize," Delacourt said. "I shouldn't have made up that story about being a reporter."

"Why did you?"

Delacourt shrugged. "I don't know. When you said your

name was Hawke, it threw me. I figured you must be related to the lawyer who defended my father, and I didn't know how that would play out. So I made something up on the spot. I didn't put it all together until your mother talked to me."

"Yeah, she told me."

"Well, I'm sorry."

Now it was Nathan's turn to shrug. "So, you find out what you wanted?"

"Not really. I talked to your father yesterday. Between him and your mother, I've learned a little but not a whole lot. I still don't know whether my father was guilty. It bothers me that they never caught anybody else."

"They probably never looked for anybody else."

"You must have been a teenager back then," Delacourt said.

"I was fourteen."

"And you had just lost a brother in a car accident."

"If you want to ask a question, go ahead and ask it."

"Sorry. It's a bad habit I'm developing. Prying." He put the paper down and folded his hands together, looked out the window and then at Nathan. "I can't figure out your father. He was all broken up about your brother. Never really recovered. Hardly ever appeared in court again and yet he insisted on defending my father. At first I figured they must have been good friends and he did it because of that, but that doesn't seem to have been the case. So I wonder why he didn't let someone else handle it."

Nathan took a few seconds to consider his answer. He didn't owe Delacourt anything. Didn't trust him. Yet he could see how the mystery was eating at him. It'd been eating at Nathan, too, all these years.

"I've wondered the same thing. I know my mother wanted him to drop it, but he wouldn't. A sense of duty is all I can think of." Nathan picked up his mail and then put it down again. "I think he just felt he'd do a better job than anyone else, and that once he'd taken your father on as a client, he shouldn't quit, no matter how much he was hurting. And maybe it helped get him through those days to have something else to put his mind to."

"Did he think my father was innocent?"

"Did he tell you that?"

Delacourt nodded.

"Well, I'd take him at his word," Nathan said. "Not that he wouldn't have done his best in any case. My father loves the law and truly believes everyone should get the best defense possible. Being innocent has nothing to do with it in his mind."

"You really admire him. You must be close."

Nathan sensed the envy. "Not as close as I'd like to be."

Delacourt nodded and then stood up, sticking out his hand. Nathan shook it.

"Well, thanks for your time," Delacourt said. "I'm heading home today."

"Why don't you look up your father? I could help you find him."

"Thanks, but I can do it if I decide to take that step."

"Let me know if you do and what you find out. And keep me posted on Harrison, too. I'd love to break the news that the company's given up on trying to put the plant in town."

Delacourt smiled, said he would, and left. An hour later he checked out of the Sunrise.

———————•———————

Craig Whitney was also leaving Beacon Junction, but only for the long Memorial Day weekend. He was flying down to Alabama to see his boys.

Though it was only Friday morning, the roads were crowded and the drive to Logan took more than two hours. During one slow stretch, he called Mary Louise and told her that he had turned in his report.

She asked again if he wanted her to help without explaining what she meant. He told her he wanted to wait for a response from Anderson.

When he finally reached Logan, it was a madhouse. It took forever to get through security. Everyone acted like they didn't know the drill, whether it was separating liquids into a plastic bag or taking off their shoes. By the time he got to the gate, boarding had begun. He was sweating with the tension when he strapped himself into the seat, only to have the plane sit on the runway for another half hour while they awaited their turn for takeoff.

Craig wasn't a good flier, though he had made the trip enough times that it should have been routine. He felt every square inch of pressure as the plane lifted off and then banked hard to the left. The swallowing of the landing gear into the belly of the plane sounded loud and harsh, and turbulence shook them before the plane reached cruising altitude. It seemed to take forever to get above the clouds and flatten out.

Craig sat sandwiched in the center seat, while next to the window, a fat man spilled over the armrest. Fortunately, a thin young woman sat on the aisle, giving him space to turn. She must have noticed the tension in his hand, and when he looked at her, she smiled kindly. He returned the smile and turned his face into a book, afraid she would try to talk to him.

Eventually, he relaxed enough to begin thinking about seeing his sons. He pulled out a pad and began jotting down little notes, reminders of questions to ask or stories to tell, to make sure he had things to talk to them about. It was silly, but making conversation wasn't always easy or natural, especially after a long absence, and it helped him feel at ease to have a list to fall back on. At one point he noticed the young woman staring at his pad, and he feared she could tell what he was doing. Then he worried she might ask, so he turned toward the window as if to close her out.

Two hours later, he had to suffer through the landing, and although it was smooth, he gripped the armrest with all his might. He couldn't wait to escape into the terminal.

He followed the young woman out and saw her rush into the arms of a young man. They kissed and he turned away. Several of the other passengers were hugged by children, parents, or lovers. Craig took it all in as he moved through the crowd and walked alone to the baggage claim. He was among the first to arrive, which only meant he had to wait longer. They stood around the belt, the others talking easily with friends and family, while Craig stared at the still conveyor.

When he finally got his luggage, he waited in line at the rental car counter and firmly rebuffed all the efforts to shunt him into an SUV and sign him up for all sorts of expensive upgrades, although he was tempted by the GPS system. Once settled in his blue Hyundai Sonata, he drove to his hotel. He'd splurged on a room at the Marriott-Montgomery so he'd have a swimming pool and something to do with the boys besides the usual movie, miniature golf, and the mall.

As soon as he was settled in his room, he braced himself for the call to Kima, but she was warmer than usual, even friendly. She was on her way out, she said, and would be happy to drop the boys off, and within an hour, she had.

Barry, who was ten, wanted to go to McDonald's for dinner, but Lionel, who was twelve, wanted pizza. "You get the tie-breaking vote, Dad," Lionel announced. Craig suggested a little Italian place as a compromise, pointing out that Barry could order a cheeseburger and Lionel could get pizza.

"Do they have Chicken McNuggets?" Barry asked, dashing Craig's hopes for a compromise. He suggested McDonald's tonight and promised they'd do pizza later in the weekend. Lionel grudgingly agreed, but when they got to McDonald's, and Barry ordered a cheeseburger instead of McNuggets and laughed at his successful ruse, Lionel warned Barry he better not complain when the time for pizza came around.

As they dug into the food, Craig asked how school was, how their grades were, who their friends were, and what they did in their spare time. He got the monosyllabic answers he expected and tried to fill the empty space by telling them about Beacon Junction and his own work, and they listened respectfully. No one seemed to be having a lot of fun, but they got excited at the prospect of going swimming the next day. It was a little after eight when he dropped them off at the house. Lionel had his own key and let himself in. Kima shouted a greeting from inside, but didn't appear. Neither did her new husband.

———•———

Steven Delacourt flew out of Logan about the same time as Craig, heading to Washington. The next day Delacourt met his mother for lunch at a trendy Bethesda restaurant that catered to the health-minded set. For each item on the menu, it listed the number of calories, the grams of fat and sodium, and of course the carbohydrate count. But if you could ignore all that, the food was actually pretty good.

Delacourt had suggested meeting at the restaurant rather than at Catherine's home, though he knew the move to neutral ground would tip off his mother to the fact that he wanted to discuss something private, without his stepfather present.

They arrived at almost the same moment, punctuality being a highly prized trait of Catherine's that she had passed along to her only child. The restaurant was about half-full, and they got a quiet table against the wall.

Catherine looked as elegant as ever. Though she'd recently turned sixty, she was trim, nearly wrinkle free when she wore high collars to hide her neck, with a permanent tan and hair dyed a reddish brown down to the roots. She exercised regularly and projected a healthy glow. Even dressed in a simple black skirt and white sweater, she stood out, looking more like Delacourt's older sister than his mother.

Delacourt hadn't been sure what to expect from his mother and was pleasantly surprised to find her inquisitive in the extreme. She hadn't been back to Beacon Junction since she'd moved away and began almost immediately to pepper him with questions about how the town looked, what landmarks were still there, what stores had closed or been replaced, even what roads had been added. There were far fewer questions—none in fact—about any of the people she had known. Although she'd been born there and had spent more than half her life in the town, it was as though she had broken all personal ties, which of course she had.

When she turned her questions to Harrison, she was hungry to know whether the culture of the company had changed, and she wanted to hear his impressions of Anderson.

"He's a slick character," he said. "Tries to be friendly and sincere, but it all seems like an act. At least it did to me." He told her that the company's plan to build a plant in downtown Beacon Junction, if it could be called a downtown, was more controversial than Anderson had implied. He told her about the *Clarion* editorial and the doubts some people had that Anderson would really locate the plant somewhere far away.

"So the *Clarion*'s still around," Catherine said. "Who is the editor now?"

Delacourt hesitated. "Nathan Hawke. He's Jonas Hawke's son."

She stared at him. "Really? You know Jonas Hawke was the lawyer who defended your father?"

"The name rang a bell and I sort of remembered," he lied, not wanting to mention that he had never forgotten the name.

"I met him. He owns the bed and breakfast where I stayed. His daughter runs it, but he and his wife live there."

"Did you meet his wife, too?"

"Yes."

"Doesn't sound like Beacon Junction has changed that much," she said after a while, which Steven took as an effort to shift the conversation. But he wasn't ready.

"I think it's actually changed a lot. I don't remember it that well, but it's obviously fallen on pretty hard economic times. They really need the plant if they're going to have any chance of coming back."

"Well, they can have it if they're not as stubborn as the *Clarion* editor wants them to be. Not surprising, I suppose. The Hawkes were always pretty difficult people."

"How do you mean? They seemed nice enough."

Catherine put her fork down and looked at her son. "Did you talk much to them? Did you ask about the trial?"

"Yes, I asked."

"Let me guess," she said. "He told you he thinks he was innocent."

"Yes. They both do."

She turned and looked at a couple eating at a table nearby. At first he thought she was trying to see if they were eavesdropping, but then he realized she was just avoiding his gaze.

"Did he say why he believed that?" she asked when she turned back to him.

"No, he didn't. Only that he was confident the jury got it right. Said he never could understand why you were so sure he was guilty."

"Oh, he was guilty all right. You can take my word for that."

He looked down at his food and started to take another bite, then stopped. "You've never told me why you were so sure."

"He was my husband, Steven. I wish he hadn't been, but he was. You just have to trust me on this."

"But there was no real evidence. Unless you know something you haven't told me."

"I obviously can't prove it, and neither could the state's attorney, so everyone is free to think whatever they want. But I'm as sure of it as I am of anything."

"Mom, was your marriage in trouble before Poppy's murder? Is it possible you were just so angry at him that—"

"No, it wasn't that." She had raised her voice, and when she realized it, she took a second to calm down.

"Did Emma say anything about your father—or about me?" Catherine asked.

Delacourt raised an eyebrow at the use of Emma's first name. "No. She said she didn't know him very well."

He thought he saw surprise flicker across Catherine's face, but he couldn't be sure.

"Steven, he killed your grandfather. You need to accept that. I know it's hard. No one knows better than me how awful it is to accept that, but you need to do it and move on."

"Mom, I know how strong your feelings are on this, but that's all I know. You don't give me any facts to back it up, and frankly, plenty of people up there had doubts. He was acquitted, after all."

Catherine had stopped eating, and it was clear from the look on her face that she was trying to calm herself. Steven always thought of his mother as pretty, but not right then. There was too much anger in her face. Meanness, even.

"So who else did you meet?"

He named a few people, but none rang a bell with Catherine, and it was clear to Steven that she wasn't all that interested.

"Can I ask you something?" he said after a while, circling back to a question she hadn't answered. She nodded.

"Why did you and Dad get divorced? Was it what happened to Poppy or were you already headed toward divorce before then?"

"Oh, that's a hard question to answer. There's never only one reason. We were happy at first, and especially after you were born, but gradually he changed. Or maybe I just realized he wasn't the man I thought he was. It certainly started a long time before your grandfather was murdered."

She turned her head away and for a moment, Steven thought she was going to cry, but if she was feeling that way, she hid it. "I sometimes wonder if I had divorced him sooner, maybe your grandfather wouldn't have been dragged into it."

"Don't say that, Mom. His murder certainly wasn't your fault. You're speculating—pretty wildly, at that."

The waiter arrived and picked up Steven's empty plate and asked Catherine if she wanted to take the rest of her lunch home, but she said no. When he offered coffee, Catherine quickly said no, as though she wanted to end the lunch as soon as she could. Steven wasn't about to let that happen. He ordered coffee for both of them.

"What did you mean when you said he wasn't the man you thought he was?" he asked when the waiter had left.

"He wasn't caring. Cold. Unwilling to try to adapt to Beacon Junction. Never wanted to make friends."

The waiter brought the coffee and they were silent for a moment.

"Mom," he said finally, "how would you feel if I got in contact with him?"

"After everything I've told you?"

He nodded.

"Why would you want to? Don't you believe me?"

"It's not that. It's not about you. Or your marriage. Whatever he did or didn't do, he's still my father. I want to know him. I don't have many memories left from when I last saw him. I was only a kid."

"Well, you're a grown man now. I can't stop you."

"That's not what I asked. Would it upset you?"

She looked around the room again. It was clear to him that she was trying to formulate her answer, and he gave her time to do that. Finally, she looked at him again.

"If you want an honest answer, I have to tell you I'd rather you didn't. But I'll accept it if you want to go ahead. I trust you."

"Trust me? What does that mean?"

"I'm confident you'll come to the appropriate conclusion."

He shook his head. She didn't understand what he was saying.

"I'm not going to choose sides if that's what you mean," he said. "And unless he chooses to tell me something conclusive, I don't expect to come away knowing whether he was guilty. I just need to meet him. To see him and talk to him. That shouldn't be so hard to understand."

She sighed heavily, then stared down at her untouched coffee.

"Mom, if there's something specific, something I don't know that would change my mind, you should tell me."

"He's an evil man," she blurted. "I've done my best not to talk ill of him to you all these years, which meant not talking about him at all. But I'll let you decide."

"Don't be mad. You know how much I love you. But the way he disappeared from my life was like he was suddenly killed. I never had a chance to say goodbye, and your reluctance to talk made it hard to come to grips with the loss."

"So I see." But then she sighed and softened. She told him she wouldn't stand in his way. He thanked her, then asked if she had any idea where he was. She offered to give him the last address she had for Reinhardt's sister.

"If you find her, I'm sure she'll know where he is," she said.

Catherine called him a few hours later with the phone number, and that night Delacourt spoke to an aunt he hadn't seen since he was seven. It was an awkward conversation. He filled her in on his life, what he was doing, and where he'd gone to school. She told him about his cousins and what they were up to, though Delacourt barely remembered them. She asked about his mother and whether she had remarried, and Delacourt told her she had, without going into any detail.

Then he asked about his father. "Do you think he'd mind if I tried to get in touch with him?"

There was silence on the line, and for a minute, he thought she hadn't heard him.

"I'm sorry, Steven. He died two years ago. From cancer."

He felt the disappointment well up, but it quickly turned to anger. "You should have told us he was sick," he said.

If his aunt caught the edge in his voice, she hid it. "Your mother made it pretty clear she didn't want to hear from him or us again. He was a broken man after the trial. He never recovered from it."

"He was my father. I never knew him. I should have been told. Didn't you think I'd want to know?"

He heard her sigh. "The truth is I did think of it, and when he got real sick, I asked him if I should call you or your mother. He wanted to see you, but I guess he thought you might refuse, and he didn't want to risk the rejection. And by then he was so weak, I think he didn't want you to see him that way. I'm sorry."

He was about to hang up, when she said there was one thing he ought to know about his father if nothing else. Delacourt waited.

"He was innocent, Steven. Believe me, he didn't kill your grandfather. I know he made some mistakes, but he didn't kill your grandfather. No matter what your mother thinks."

"What kind of mistakes?" Steven asked. But she had already hung up.

He lay down on his bed and put his arm over his eyes. He wanted to cry, but that didn't make sense to him. He hadn't known his father, hadn't even been in touch with him, so how could he cry for him?

But he did cry, for himself if not for his father, for having waited too long, for having not cried when he first lost him twenty-four years earlier.

Chapter 11

Nancy awoke to the buzz of a lawn mower next door. *It's so early,* she groaned. Then she remembered it was the middle of the afternoon. She had flopped onto the bed to rest a minute and had fallen asleep. That was happening more often lately.

She went down to the kitchen and put on another pot of coffee. Somewhere in the back of her brain a warning bell sounded over how much caffeine she'd been having. She'd even bought a bottle of No-Doz the other day for quick hits. But she ignored the bell. It wasn't as though she was getting hooked on heroin, after all.

The phone rang and she knew before she reached it that it was her lifelong friend Marcy.

"Just checking in," Marcy said. "What are you up to?"

They talked for a while and Nancy, after some hesitation, agreed to meet for dinner. After she hung up, she regretted it. Marcy had lost her husband three years ago and now considered herself an expert on the grieving process. Knowing she'd get quizzed on whether she was making progress in getting rid of Frank's things, Nancy headed for his study, her coffee mug refilled for fortification.

She didn't understand why everyone was so eager for her to clear the house of Frank. *It's only been a month,* she thought. Do they think I won't live every moment missing him just because I've sent his suits to Goodwill? Still, she set about going through his desk. She needed to gather up all the financial papers anyway. Molly and Michael didn't want her to waste any time in converting all the accounts to her name. As if it mattered. Frank had made it ridiculously easy, keeping an up-to-date master list, part of a file he labeled "In case . . . ." It was short for "In case Frank gets hit by a bus." It was funny when he first showed it to her, much less so now.

She started looking in the files, but gave up quickly when she saw they were stacked with old statements. She couldn't see any use for them but figured if Frank kept them, he probably had a reason. She'd keep them for a while. She supposed she should have taken a bigger role in dealing with the family's finances so she wouldn't feel so dumb now, but she wasn't interested then and nothing had changed just because Frank was dead. Besides, she knew he had left her in good financial shape. Good shape for what? What did she need money for beyond keeping a roof over her head? She didn't even need much in the way of food. Wasn't ever hungry. Maybe she should call Marcy and cancel dinner. No, that would only make her think she needed more attention, not less. Better to go and get it over with.

She tried looking at the files again, but soon stopped and closed the drawer. She thought about Jonas's offer to help. Pretty superfluous. Molly and the partners at the firm were handling probate, such as it was. She supposed Jonas's offer had been pro forma, as Frank would have said, but something told her it was more than that. She knew Frank and Jonas had been close, talking regularly even after Jonas retired. The relationship had morphed into more of a real friendship, less of a relationship dominated by talk of work. She supposed that Frank still told him about the cases the firm was working on and that the law was still the biggest thing they had in common, but she knew how much Frank looked forward to seeing Jonas. And Jonas had seemed really lost, both on the day of the funeral and on his visit to the house. She opened the center desk drawer and reached under it until she found the key taped to it. It would open a locked box in which Frank kept his private journals. He had told Nancy about the key and suggested she hold on to the journals for a few years before tossing them. He told her they contained personal notes on the cases he was working on— musings to himself that he didn't feel comfortable putting in the office files where any of the other attorneys could see them.

She unlocked the box and was surprised at how little was in it. On the front of each journal were the years it covered, usually five or more. She opened the top one and started reading, but quickly lost interest. Most of the notes were too cryptic, especially if you weren't familiar with the cases, and there were whole months with no entries. Still, she wondered why he needed them and whether other attorneys did the same thing. She might mention them to Jonas, if only to see how he reacted.

Then a thought occurred to her and she started looking for the book that covered the Reinhardt trial. Was it '89? Or '90? She looked through both years, but there was nothing on the case.

She closed the box and locked it, though she wasn't sure why. She put the key back in the drawer, not bothering to hide it.

She looked around the study for something else to do there but couldn't find anything so she went upstairs to the guest room where Frank kept his clothes. She had already purchased several boxes that stood awaiting assembly. After a couple of false starts, she managed to fold one into shape and turned to the closet. She grabbed the handle of the door, hesitated slightly, and then opened it.

She clenched her teeth to fight back the tears and pulled out the first suit. Maybe it's too soon for this, she thought. She sat down in the upholstered chair, then quickly realized sitting and staring would be worse. She got up and looked at the clothes. Should she take the suits to the cleaner first? She usually did before giving something to Goodwill, but there were a lot of clothes here. It would cost a fortune. And she'd have to cart the clothes back and forth more than she wanted to. No, she'd give them away the way they were.

She pulled one down and folded it carefully and placed it into the box. They were just suits, she told herself, let's not get maudlin. So many of them, though. She decided she didn't have to do this all at once. She'd give away the summer suits now. No one would want the heavier stuff until fall anyway. That decided, she packed one box with five suits, three of them the blue Frank favored, and added a couple of extra pairs of slacks and some sport coats.

She put a second box together and put several pairs of shoes in the bottom of it. Would that be enough to satisfy Marcy? Oh what the hell, she was on a roll. She turned to the chest of drawers. She opened the top one and found several unopened packages of new socks, underwear, and handkerchiefs that she had bought for him. Obviously he didn't think he needed them. She'd save the socks and handkerchiefs for Michael, but nothing else would fit.

She moved down to the second drawer, feeling she should keep going. Sweaters, neatly folded and stacked, were quickly moved to the box. Polo shirts, khakis, and jeans soon followed.

Then she saw it.

A large manila envelope. It had been opened and closed so many times that the clasp had broken off, and it was taped shut. It was hidden amid some old flannel shirts Frank wore for working in the yard.

She pulled it out and looked at it. She sat down on the chair again, the envelope on her lap. She fingered the tape. She thought about what might be inside. He had hidden it, so whatever it was, he hadn't wanted her to know. She should respect his wishes. She should throw it in the trash unopened. Yes, that's what she should do. But she couldn't move. She sat there, the envelope on her lap as the room darkened. She looked at the clock. Time to shower and get ready to meet Marcy. But the weight of the envelope kept her from getting up. Throw it in the trash, she thought, and forget about it. To open it would be as bad as reading someone's diary. It was the same thing.

At five-fifteen, she rose, put the envelope back in the drawer, and got ready to meet Marcy.

———•———

"You need to get your hair done," Marcy told her without pretense. "It's important."

"Marcy, please. I'm not in the mood."

"Even people in mourning need to feel good about themselves. Trust me, I know."

She spoke with the authority and self-confidence of an older sister. She figured a fifty-year friendship entitled her to the same privileges.

They were in the dining room at the Ventura Inn, in what passed for a "nice restaurant" in Beacon Junction. Which meant no television on the wall, white tablecloths, and two forks in the place setting. Nancy was wearing a black pants suit with a navy blue blouse that didn't go with it. She was wearing her frameless glasses instead of her contacts, with only a touch of rouge on her cheeks. Her curly hair was longer than usual, and Marcy was right; there were a few obvious strands of gray.

"You're not eating," Marcy said.

"And you keep stating the obvious," Nancy said, but she took a bite of her chicken and chewed it carefully. "Don't push so much. I know you mean well, but it's too hard."

"Sorry. Just don't want you to make the same mistakes I did."

"Everybody's different, you know."

"We're not. You and me, we're the same, girl. Always have been."

Nancy couldn't help but smile. They both knew they were exact opposites, and that's what had kept them friends all these years. Nancy's smile faded, and she gazed off to the wall. Marcy reached across and touched her hand.

"I'm sorry," Marcy said. "You know me. Always trying to make things right by joking around. I wish there were some way to help."

"I know. And it helps to know you're here." Tears welled up in her eyes. "I just miss him so damn much." She got up and left the room.

Marcy sighed and went back to her food while she waited for Nancy to come back. When her plate was clean, she reached across and speared a brussels sprout from Nancy's plate. She loved them and she knew Nancy was going to leave them.

When Nancy got back, she apologized. Marcy shrugged. "For what? Would you rather leave? We could go back to my place if it's easier to be alone."

That sounded like a good idea, and twenty minutes later they were sitting in Marcy's kitchen, sipping coffee. Marcy was trying hard to keep her hands off the apple cake she'd taken out.

"Well, aren't you going to ask me?" Nancy said after a while.

"Ask you what?"

"Whether I got rid of Frank's things yet."

Now it was Marcy's turn to smile. "Nah. I was going to go easy on you tonight. No big hurry."

Nancy actually laughed. "Serves me right for listening to you. I packed three big boxes today."

Marcy gave her a high five and then got up to refill the coffee cups.

"I found something," Nancy said, softly enough to get Marcy's full attention. She sat down and looked at Nancy, waiting.

"An old manila envelope. Hidden in his clothes. Taped shut."

Marcy waited. Then finally, "What was in it?"

Nancy told her that she hadn't opened it, that she didn't think she should.

Marcy thought for a second and then in her ever practical voice said, "Well, let's consider the possibilities. What's the worst-case scenario? What could be in there?"

Nancy looked down at her hands but didn't say anything.

"That's my point," Marcy said. "You start wondering what the worst is and pretty soon you start assuming that's what it is. Chances are, it's nothing but a few girlie magazines, and believe me, that means nothing. They all do that. You open it, and find that, and you'll feel bad for a couple of days, and that'll be the end of it. But if you don't open it, you'll assume something far worse, and that's not fair to Frank. You're not going to find love letters or anything like that, if that's what you're thinking. I'd bet my life he was as loyal as a Labrador retriever. But no matter what's in there, you're better off knowing and moving on."

"He didn't want me to know what was in there. I don't think I can open it."

"You don't even know that much. Hell, it could be old letters from his father. It could be anything."

Nancy shook her head.

"Nance, trust me," Marcy said. "You can't not open it. Sooner or later you will, so you might as well get it over with. Let's go back there now and do it. I want to be there when you see how silly this is."

"No, I can't do it."

"Yes, you can. And you know you should. That's why you told me. You knew what I'd say."

Nancy told her she knew there was some truth to that, but she couldn't open the envelope. Not now. She thanked Marcy, told her it had been good to see her but that it was time to go. Before she left, Marcy made her promise not to destroy the envelope without talking to her again. "If you do that, you'll never know and will always wonder. The worst of all worlds."

CHAPTER 12

On the Tuesday after his Memorial Day weekend in Alabama, Craig tried to reach Anderson but was told he was in a meeting. He left a message and spent most of the day close to his phone, but no call came. He tried Anderson again before leaving, only to be told the CEO had left for the day.

The next morning he called again and a few hours later, Anderson called back, cold and distant. He said he'd read the report and would talk it over with Madeleine and others involved in the stent, but he made it clear that he thought Craig was ignoring the improvements they'd made. Craig started to argue, but Anderson cut him off saying he'd get back to him. The rest of the week passed without another word.

On Saturday afternoon, Craig called Mary Louise. "He's stalling. I don't know what to do."

"He's got to give you some kind of answer."

"So why delay? Unless he's concocting some new scheme."

"My offer to help still stands."

He asked again what she meant, not seeing how an outsider could do anything he couldn't do himself and not wanting to get her involved. Mary Louise tried to explain that she knew someone in town who could put pressure on Anderson, someone who could work from the outside—without calling the FDA—to support what Craig was trying to do from the inside. If it worked, Anderson would do the right thing, and Craig wouldn't have to blow the whistle.

"But who are you talking about and why would he help me?" he asked.

"Let's just say he'll do it as a favor for me." Craig was silent for a moment. "He's a client, Craig. I can't give you his name, but he's a good guy. We can trust him."

"I don't know. I hate for you to get involved."

They talked some more, but after a while it was clear they were just going in circles. They agreed to give Anderson another couple of days. Craig said if that didn't produce any progress, he'd trust Mary Louise to do what was best, but he urged her to tread carefully, to try to keep his name out of it, and to make sure she wasn't putting herself at risk. She told him not to worry, not that he could pay heed to that even if he wanted to.

When he hung up, Craig paced his small apartment, wondering if he was on the verge of throwing away the years of hard work that had gotten him to this point but knowing he would have trouble living with himself if he did nothing. He had to believe that Anderson would see his way to taking the ethical path. He certainly hoped so. In fact, he had to think that way. If he let himself consider the possible consequences, he might not have the courage to keep going.

———•———

Mary Louise didn't see much use in waiting for Anderson's response. She'd heard enough to know if something was going to get done, she'd have to help it along. She had promised to wait for Craig's go-ahead, but that didn't mean she couldn't prepare for it. She took a few moments to put her thinking in order and went looking for Jonas, who wasn't hard to find.

He was busy wearing out one of the rocking chairs on the front porch.

Mary Louise sat down and looked at the cover of the book he was holding high to double as a sun blocker. "*Crime and Punishment,* huh? I would've thought you knew all there was to know about that," she said by way of greeting.

He finished the paragraph he was on. "It's not that kind of book," he said, but didn't explain further. She smiled at him, and he knew what was coming. "I'm going to need my alphabet again, aren't I?" he asked.

"No, I think we can keep it simple. I just wanted to go over it again. I talked to my client, and he's almost willing to let me contact my other client."

"Almost?"

"I think he'll agree in a couple of days or so."

"Well, that would help a little. But you wouldn't be here if you were sure."

"I wondered if you thought any more about it and had any new advice."

"Other than to mind your own business?"

"Yeah. I don't think I can do that."

"Why not?"

"It means a lot to me. It's hard to explain why."

"Try. It'll help both of us."

She shifted to look at Jonas, then moved her chair so she was almost facing him. "It's hard to put into words. I know what the right thing to do is. I'm really convinced. And I think I'm in a position to make sure the right thing gets done. Maybe by pushing a little. And if that doesn't work, by taking a stand."

"Is it really that black and white? No gray mixed in?"

"I'm tired of the gray area. Hell, my whole life is lived in the gray. I need to take a stand, and this feels like the right time."

"So you're doing it for yourself?"

"No. No. Well, yes, in a way. I do need to stand up for something worthwhile, but this is an important cause. I know what needs to happen. I'm just not so sure how to get there. I don't want to push so hard that somebody I care about—maybe two people I care about—get hurt. That's all that worries me."

He turned away from her and rocked a bit, his way of letting her know he was considering it. "Well, think of it this way," he said. "You're a lucky woman to have people you care about and who care for you. Who trust you. And the very fact that they trust you to do the right thing is important. If your client gives you the go-ahead like you expect, it'll mean that on some level he agrees you're doing the right thing."

She thought about that for a minute without saying anything.

"You know, Mary Louise, it's hard to give advice when I know so little. I'm pretty good at keeping secrets if you want to share this. And if there's anything I can do to help, you know I will."

She gave that some thought. She'd been wondering about asking Jonas instead of Ed for help with Harrison, but she wasn't sure he was up to it. She valued his advice and plenty of people had told her what a great attorney he'd once been. But she hadn't known him then, and she was afraid of what it might do to him if he tried and failed.

She thanked him and started to leave, then turned around and leaned over to plant a kiss on his cheek. He smiled broadly as he watched her go into the house.

———•———

Anderson failed to get back to Craig in the allotted time, and Craig reluctantly gave Mary Louise the okay just hours before her weekly session with Ed.

As always, Ed arrived right on time, on this occasion with a single yellow rose. Mary Louise teased him by accusing him of picking it from the garden, though Emma's bushes weren't in bloom yet. She let Ed open the Chardonnay and offered him a peanut butter chocolate cookie, which she knew was his favorite. "A perfect blend," he joked. "Peanut butter, chocolate, Chardonnay, and you." She moved into his arms and they kissed, her mouth open invitingly, then closing and backing off in a tease she knew he liked.

Though she usually undressed first, tonight she started unbuttoning his shirt, and he began working on her blouse simultaneously. They kissed intermittently until, piece by piece, their clothing lay on the floor, their naked bodies touching.

He leaned down and kissed her breasts, taking the nipple in his mouth. He was a little rougher than she liked, so she gently stopped him. "My turn," she said and kissed his chest, gradually moving down until she was on her knees. He was already hard, had been from the start, and she took him in her mouth.

He moaned softly, ruffled her hair, and then, fearful of climaxing too soon, he gently lifted her up and eased her onto the bed. He took a few seconds to admire her body. She was neither slender nor plump, with long legs and a high bosom. He kissed her all over and gently turned her onto her stomach. He often told her he loved her rump more than anything. It was small and shapely, and it was the part of her he remembered most when they were apart.

After a while she turned over and pushed him onto his back and mounted him. It was far from her favorite position—in fact, she felt almost nothing—but she knew he liked watching her move up and down on him, with her breasts bouncing slightly.

Afterwards she held him in her arms, thinking how to approach what was on her mind, although she had done little else but plan in the last two days.

Then she realized he had fallen asleep. She laughed to herself and lay there a few more minutes, then gently moved so he'd wake up. "More wine?" she asked, pretending she hadn't been aware of his short nap.

He moved to let her up, and she carried both glasses over to the table. He watched her behind as she poured.

"Ed, I wanted to get your help on something," she said when she was back by his side.

"Sure. Fix a parking ticket? A new zoning ordinance? A refund on your taxes? You name it—as long as it's not a business license for this."

She didn't laugh but kept a serious look on her face. He waited for her to speak.

"There's some trouble at Harrison," she began. "A friend of mine works there, and he told me about a problem with one of their products. It's killing people and they won't do anything about it."

Ed swallowed at her words. "That's a pretty serious charge. Is your friend sure?" The way he said "friend" told her that he realized it was a client.

"He's in a position to know and he's seen enough evidence." She told him what she knew, how the company had started to hear reports of problems with the stent, how at first they were rare, but as time went on, there were more, and how soon there was an obvious move to limit who in the company was privy to the information. She didn't know the details, though, and she didn't know about the improvements that the company had made, so her telling of it sounded as bad as bad can be.

"My friend wants them to come clean with the government, but they won't. He doesn't know what to do next."

"And he doesn't want to squeal on the company?"

"He figures they'll know it's him, and he can't afford to lose his job. Not in this economy. He's also worried what it will do to Harrison."

"That makes it tough. I don't know what advice I'd give him."

"Well, the truth is, I was looking for more than advice. I need your help. It's really a matter of public health, and with all the fuss over the new plant, I knew you wouldn't want it kept from people. So I wondered if you might talk to Harrison and tell them they had to go to Washington."

Ed gave her a look as if to say she was asking a lot, but he didn't speak. She took his glass and refilled it. She glanced at the clock and noticed that the hour wasn't up yet and felt a little guilty for using time he was paying for to seek a favor, though Ed didn't seem to take offense. She knew he would do anything to help her if he could.

He began to ask questions about the stent and the problems, and Mary Louise admitted she had few answers. They both began to realize that he'd need a lot more information if he were going to take it up with Harrison, though he had yet to agree to that. In fact, he told her he was leaning against it but stopped short of refusing her outright.

"Mary Louise, I don't know whether this is a good idea or not—my getting involved. But if I'm going to, and before I decide to, I really need to talk to this friend of yours to get a few things straight. Otherwise I can't help."

Mary Louise nodded, but she doubted Craig would be willing. "What about documents? If I could show you some evidence, would that help?"

He told her he'd consider it if he could be sure the documents were genuine and they were conclusive.

She thanked him and pushed him back down on the bed. She glided down to his crotch and covered her head with the sheet. He began to moan, and soon he was hard again. She mounted him and rode him at a gallop until he came. When she next glanced at the clock, the hour was long past.

After he left, she called Craig. There weren't many clients she could call, but Ed and Craig were the exceptions because they weren't married. She asked about evidence, and he offered a copy of his report. She said that was a good start, but she knew Ed wanted company documents to back it up, so she asked for those, too. Craig told her that was a bigger risk and asked if she was sure this was going to help.

"I'm not sure, but we can trust this person. And I think it might work."

Craig told her he'd see what he could do. The truth was he already had the documents and after a sleepless night, he decided to take a chance. The next day, he met Mary Louise at the grocery store during his lunch hour and gave her a copy of his report and photocopies of several documents. Within hours, she had given them to Ed.

All this tore up Ed, who wanted to do the right thing but didn't think he should get involved in somebody else's fight. He studied the documents, and while they looked real, he couldn't be sure. He was no scientist, so he couldn't tell how serious the problem was. He told Mary Louise he didn't think he'd feel right doing anything unless he could speak to the whistleblower, but she said she couldn't do that, that she had to protect client confidentiality, and anyway she didn't think this guy would talk to anyone outside the company but her. That annoyed Ed some. He figured if he got involved, he'd be risking his confidentiality as a client of Mary Louise's, but she insisted people would believe he was drawn into it only because he was mayor.

He wrestled with the problem for a few days, going back and forth. He'd decide it was nothing but trouble one minute and then soften because he knew it meant a lot to Mary Louise, and he liked making her happy. Finally, he did the only thing that made any sense to him. He went to talk to Jonas.

"I got this problem I need help with, only I don't really know what I'm dealing with, and I can't even tell you all that I know about it, which isn't enough," he told Jonas.

"Seems like a lot of that going round lately," Jonas said, not realizing yet how accurate the connection was.

"It involves Harrison," Ed said, and for a minute Jonas thought he meant the controversy over the new plant, but Ed soon set him straight. He told him about the safety questions involving the stent, about how there was a whistleblower who wished to remain anonymous, even to Ed, and how a third party wanted Ed to persuade the folks at Harrison to do the right thing.

Jonas realized he was talking to one of Mary Louise's alphabet players, though he didn't remember his algebra well enough to know if it was Mr. X, Y, or Z. Still, he wasn't so dense as to miss the fact that Ed was one of Mary Louise's clients. He couldn't help asking himself if that would change the way he felt about Ed, but he quickly decided the answer was no. Then he realized that wasn't quite right. He was actually a little jealous.

They spent about twenty minutes exploring the problem, but every time Jonas made a suggestion—like that he should go over the documents with the whistleblower—Ed said he couldn't do that. Finally, Jonas was as exasperated as Ed.

"Well, tell me this, Ed. As best as you can tell, is it a serious public health issue?"

"I think so, but hell, I'm no doctor."

Jonas nodded but didn't say anything.

"I figure my duty is to the town," Ed said, "but I don't know what that means exactly. The town'll be hurt economically if Harrison gets in trouble, especially if we lose the plant. I don't want to be the one to blow the whistle."

"You're not blowing the whistle, though. You're just helping them do the right thing. And if they do nothing and it blows up, the town will be hurt anyway." Jonas had a sudden hankering for his pipe, but he didn't have it with him, so he settled for cracking his finger joints.

"Don't overanalyze it," he told Ed. "You can't guess at the long-term effects. And besides, health trumps the economy. At least in my book."

"Yeah, mine, too. Leastways, it does as long as it's not my job that's at stake."

Jonas smiled, but he knew Ed was only half joking. "I'm sorry I can't be more help."

"No, that's fine. Not your problem, and talking is always a good way of figuring out what you're thinking."

"Ain't that the truth."

CHAPTER 13

D on Parker was the kind of executive employees tiptoed around, afraid of his volatile temper and his too-obvious need to show how tough he was. They mocked him behind his back, accusing him of a Napoleonic complex and joking he stood five-foot-four in his elevator shoes. He was short, but he had a thick neck and broad shoulders, with muscles so well defined, he might be mistaken for a boxer if it weren't for the baby face that had never met anything tougher than an electric razor. He could lose his temper and raise his voice in a controlled, vicious sort of way, and anyone who crossed him would soon regret it. Working for him was grueling, and turnover among his subordinates was the highest in the company. No one quite knew why he had Anderson's confidence, but they figured it meant Anderson needed to have someone around to do the dirty work. Parker certainly filled that bill.

It was mid-afternoon on Thursday, June 12, when his private line rang. He noticed the Boston area code on the caller ID but didn't recognize the number. "This is Parker," he said.

The voice on the other end identified himself as the private detective Parker had hired to dig into Craig Whitney's background. He had completed his preliminary report and had put it in the mail.

"Anything useful?" Parker asked. He'd never met the man, but he'd been highly recommended. As they talked, Parker found himself conjuring up an image of Humphrey Bogart in an old Raymond Chandler movie. It was hard to shake off.

"That depends what you're looking for," Bogie said. "Divorced, two kids, ten and twelve. Live with their mother in Montgomery, Alabama. Whitney goes down there every so often to see them. Last time was Memorial Day weekend. Stayed alone in a hotel and didn't see anyone but the kids. Nothing of note in the divorce records. Haven't looked into his married life in any detail yet."

"What about now? Is he talking to any lawyers or anybody in Washington?"

"Not that I found so far. Lives a pretty lonely existence. Works long days and sticks mainly to himself on his off hours."

"Mainly?"

"Yeah, and that's the interesting thing. The only one he sees is a woman, name of Mary Louise Seaver. She works for a bed and breakfast up there, but she's from here, and get this—she was busted once for prostitution. That was about a year before she moved up your way. Could be she's still in the game."

Parker considered the possibilities. Embarrassing maybe, but beyond that? Still, it was something. Whitney wouldn't want anyone to know, and it was illegal. It was something, but only if she was still a pro and he was one of her johns.

"It's also possible there's more to the relationship," the detective said, as if reading his thoughts. "He met her during the day last week and handed over some kind of big folder, like an accordion file."

That got Parker's attention. He asked the detective to keep digging, to find out whether Mary Louise was still a working girl and to see if she had any connections—any at all—to anyone else at Harrison. And to find out everything he could about their relationship.

That night Nathan had his weekly dinner with Jonas and told him, much to Jonas's surprise, that he thought he'd give up the fight over the new plant's location. Reader reaction to his editorial had been overwhelmingly negative, and his conversations with members of the Board of Selectmen had convinced him it was a done deal. He had nothing to gain by pushing further.

Jonas listened and nodded but didn't say much. He could tell Nathan just needed to talk. He wasn't seeking advice or help because he'd already made up his mind. Jonas was only mildly tempted to tell him about the other problem at Harrison. He knew doing so would require consent from the others involved.

After they parted, Jonas went by the park that was now apparently destined to become the next Harrison plant. He thought about Nathan's decision to abandon the battle and agreed it was the right one. Nathan had stood up for what he believed in but knew he had to give in when it became clear he was in the minority.

Nathan had turned out to be a smart and practical man—principled but not stubborn, strong willed but able to see the other guy's point of view, realistic enough to know he couldn't win all the time. Jonas took more than a little pride in how well the boy had turned out.

That was true of Sally, too, although Jonas had to recognize that he would never be as close to his daughter. He knew that she held an unspoken resentment against him for how he'd behaved after Lucas's death. On some level she had recognized the tension between him and Emma and had taken her mother's side. He supposed that was understandable, though occasionally it ate at him that she felt that way without knowing all the facts. Not that Emma's affair was the main reason for his withdrawal from the family's life, but it was part of the mix. And in recent years he had tried to make up for letting Sally down but hadn't gotten much credit for it.

All this, of course, led to thoughts of Lucas. He had always assumed his relationship with his eldest son would be the most rewarding for him. Somehow he knew that Lucas would have gone into law and that they would have been partners.

Jonas wasn't much for analyzing himself, at least he liked to think he wasn't, but he was aware of how much his attitude had changed in the last couple of weeks. He still had a ways to go, and he often caught himself retreating back into his shell. But there were important differences.

He'd never been so interested in other people and their problems. Since he'd retired, a few had occasionally sought his advice, but not many. He had to admit he was enjoying it, this feeling of importance. For the first time in many years, he felt that he was being asked to help in the way that he had helped so many when he was busily involved in the law.

It was a burden, too, he knew, but a welcome one. He wanted to give Mary Louise and Ed—and indirectly the whistleblower—the right advice. Especially Mary Louise, whom he had come to regard as a real friend.

He thought again about the dream and it disturbed him. Jonas was no fool. He knew his feelings for Mary Louise were complex. She was young enough to be his daughter, and sometimes she played that role, but he knew there was a sexual element to it as well. Heck, any friendship between a man and a woman had some of that, even when there was a generation's difference in their ages. He guessed Mary Louise being a hooker added to it. Whenever they talked, it was never far from his mind. He'd thought lately about talking more directly to her about it—how she got into it, what it was like, and most important, how it made her feel. He wasn't a shrink, but he knew the theories about prostitution and self-worth and how women who were abused as youngsters were more likely to turn to it. He knew Mary Louise had been very young when her father died, and he wondered how that had affected her. He'd like to ask her about all that but never felt it was any of his business. He hoped that if she wanted to talk about it, she'd feel she could, but he knew it'd be hard for her. Maybe he needed to let her know somehow that it was okay. Then again, maybe it was his prurient interest at work. Maybe he was the one who needed her to talk about it and not her.

He wondered for a moment if Emma knew any more of her life story than he did. Emma could keep secrets from him, he thought, then felt bad because the thought had a nasty tone to it, a remembrance of her affair with Richard Reinhardt. He'd come to grips with that, not easily and not quickly, but he was pretty sure, despite Emma's comment, that he had forgiven her. Sure, the surprise visit from Delacourt had stirred it up, but it didn't change anything.

He couldn't blame Emma for the affair. He knew she'd been depressed at the time. The kids had all reached their teenage years and didn't need her as much, and Jonas hadn't been as attentive as he should have been. She'd been caught in a void of sorts, bored and looking for some meaning to her life, and he'd been no help.

After the accident, he'd been even less useful, turning inward and to alcohol. The experts say a tragedy like that can either bring a couple together or push them apart. Neither had been the case with Jonas and Emma. They had just weathered it, too numb and hurt to help each other or drive each other away. Somehow they'd gotten through it.

Emma was reading when Jonas got back. He told her about dinner and Nathan's decision to back off the Harrison plant dispute, but he didn't say any of the important things that were still jangling around in his head.

———•◄———

Things were jangling around for Ed, too, but it wasn't his head that was involved. He was in the back room, lost in the arms and charms of Mary Louise. The secret they shared was changing their relationship, or maybe it was the fact that Mary Louise needed Ed for something other than the plain white envelope with the five fifty dollar bills in it. Another man might have felt used or in some way put upon, but it had been so long since Ed had felt really needed and trusted that he took it in a very different way. To him, it meant he was more than just a customer to Mary Louise. He'd always hoped that was the case, and plenty of times when they talked about their lives and the things that mattered to them, he had let himself think he was special to her, but being asked to help with something so important to her notched it up a bit.

He had begun his visit by telling Mary Louise he had made an appointment to see Anderson, though when she quizzed him on what he planned to say, he had to admit that he wasn't all that sure. He tried to put on an air of bravado, saying he'd wait to take Anderson's measure and play it by ear.

"Which ear?" she teased. "His or yours? Right or left?"

He smiled and kissed her ear, nibbling on the lobe. "Don't worry. It'll be all right," he said.

She wasn't worried. She hadn't yet grasped how complicated all this was, and didn't really understand how much was at stake for everyone involved. It wasn't that she was naive or stupid or anything. She just felt the priorities were clear. To her, it was a simple matter of doing the right thing and letting the greater good triumph. That meant blowing the whistle on another corporation run by greedy men who didn't care about anything but their bonuses and the stock price.

When the hour was up, they dressed and Ed held her tightly, holding on a little too long. She finally broke the embrace and kissed him again. "Be careful out there," she said.

CHAPTER 14

Emma called Nancy in late June to ask if she wanted to join them for a Fourth of July barbecue. Nancy thanked her, but the idea of a crowd was still more than she could fathom. She countered with an offer of a quiet and simple dinner at her house, and Emma readily accepted, but only after making Nancy promise she wouldn't go to a lot of trouble.

It was now more than a month since Frank's death, and while many friends had stopped by the house to pay their respects and see how she was doing, this was the first time she would actually be entertaining anyone, though "entertaining" was not a word that popped into her mind. Jonas and Emma had each visited a couple of times separately, but there was something much nicer about an intimate dinner with the two of them. She wanted the couples that she and Frank had been friendly with to keep her in their circle so she wouldn't always be limited to a one-on-one girls' night out.

She took Emma's advice and prepared a very simple meal of salmon with a sesame sauce, bulgur, green beans, and a salad made with ingredients from the backyard garden that she had been cultivating. For dessert she had a freezer full of choices— for some reason everyone who came by thought she'd be in desperate need of sweets—and she picked an apple pie that

Emma might think she had baked on her own. She was at a loss for what wine to serve—that had always been Frank's job—but the man at the wine store recommended an Italian white something-or-other that looked more expensive than it was. She knew Jonas would stick to club soda, but she wanted the wine for herself, and she figured Emma wouldn't make her drink alone.

Jonas and Emma arrived right at six, carrying a beautiful bouquet of flowers from Emma's garden—tulips, lilies, daffodils, and something Nancy didn't recognize. While she put them in a vase, she asked Jonas to open the wine and fix himself whatever he wanted.

The conversation came easily. Emma took the lead, managing to talk a lot about little things going on in town and at the Sunrise. She told Nancy that Richard Reinhardt's son had visited, that he had lost all contact with his father, and now was eager to learn as much as he could about him.

"Why doesn't he get in touch with him?" Nancy asked, wondering a little about the coincidence. For over two decades she hadn't thought about Reinhardt, but then Jonas had referred to the trial in his eulogy for Frank and now his son was in town.

"That's what I told him he should do," Jonas said. "But he's reluctant."

That led them into a discussion of Harrison and the controversy about where to put the new plant.

"Tell Nathan I'm on his side," Nancy said. "About time someone stood up to them."

Jonas shrugged. "I think he's pretty much given up. He's not getting much support, and he figures the Board of Selectmen have made up their minds."

Over dinner, Emma asked how Michael and Molly were doing, in the kind of serious voice that said she meant how were they coping with their father's death.

"As well as can be expected," Nancy said. "They're spending a lot of time worrying about me, especially Molly. Sometimes it feels like she won't let me alone."

"What's wrong with that?" Emma said. "They're terrific kids. Terrific adults I should say."

"I worry they're using me to avoid dealing with the loss. It's easier to take care of Mom than think about not having a father anymore."

"That's not so bad," Jonas said. "I did the same thing when my father died. It's only natural."

They finished the salmon, and Emma got up to help Nancy clear the dishes. In the kitchen, as they waited for the coffee to brew, Emma again asked Nancy how she was doing.

Nancy shrugged. "It's hard, but it's not like I have a choice. It's going to take a long time, I think."

Emma nodded. "Go at your own pace. Don't let anyone rush you."

Nancy started to cry. She didn't want to, but she couldn't help it. Emma put her arms around her. Jonas appeared in the door of the kitchen, but Emma made a face to indicate he should go back to the dining room.

"I feel so awful. So lonely," Nancy said, her voice muffled by Emma's sweater. "And having people around doesn't help." Emma nodded, and Nancy realized what she'd said. "I don't mean you and Jonas. I really wanted to see you."

"I know what you meant. I wish there was something we could do to help, but I'm afraid it's just something you have to go through. Eventually it gets bearable, but it never goes away. Don't expect it to."

Nancy blew her nose. "I think about you and Jonas a lot. You must have been hurting so badly when Lucas had his accident. I knew that, but I don't think I *really* knew it. Not with the intensity I should have."

"That was different. We had no choice but to get on with our lives because we had two other kids who were depending on us. I suppose that made it easier. Not that we did all that well with it."

They carried the coffee out, and Nancy apologized to Jonas for leaving him alone so long. He could see they'd both been crying, and he didn't say anything for fear his own voice would crack. Being alone in the dining room had made him acutely aware of missing Frank, who on dozens of such occasions had shared the room with him, talking about the Red Sox or the Patriots, while the women were in the kitchen.

Jonas covered his embarrassment by complimenting the apple pie, and Nancy laughed. "I was going to try to fool you, but I can't go through with it." She confessed it had been baked by a neighbor and stored in the freezer.

"That's why lawyers always tell their clients not to volunteer anything," Jonas joked.

As they were leaving, Nancy asked them to hold on and came back carrying a box.

"Jonas, would you do me a favor and look through this? It's some old journals that Frank kept—all office stuff. I think they can be thrown out, but I wasn't sure and maybe you can take a quick look before throwing them away."

"Of course."

Emma and Jonas didn't say much on the way home.

"It's so sad," Emma said, "but I think she's doing as well as anybody can."

Jonas agreed. They both knew she was still at the start of a long and difficult process. They'd try to help, but it was the kind of thing you had to do mostly on your own.

Jonas put the box in the study he shared with Sally. She had a desk she used for the Sunrise accounts, and he had one for his personal and financial papers. It wasn't until a couple of days later that he got around to opening it. He was surprised at first to find the journals. Lawyers were supposed to keep all their notes in the official file, but he soon saw that Frank's comments were mostly reminders to himself, hunches, or ideas that he wasn't sure would pan out. As Nancy had done, he couldn't resist checking the period around the Reinhardt trial and was relieved to find nothing there.

But at the bottom of the box was a large manila envelope, with tape around the seal to hold it together. Paper-clipped to it was a note from Nancy. "Jonas, this may be unfair to you, but I found this hidden in Frank's personal things. I'm not sure he wanted me to see it, so I don't want to open it, but I can't throw it away. He trusted you with everything, so I'm trusting you with this. You don't need to tell me what is in it or what you did with it."

Jonas held it for a moment, wondering why he had any more right to open it than Nancy. But in the end, he felt he owed it to her to take a look. He took a letter opener and sliced through the top. Inside were several letters stored in their envelopes. They were all addressed to Frank at the office and all were from Michael. The postmarks ran from 2008 to 2009, when Michael was away at college. Jonas arranged them by date as best he could—not all the postmarks were readable—and opened the first one. It took only a few paragraphs to understand. Michael was wrestling with his sexual identity, believing he might be gay and planning to explore the possibility. He was worried about how Frank might react but more worried about Nancy. That struck Jonas as a bit odd; it was usually the other way around. But when he read a later letter, he could tell from Michael's gratitude that Frank had been open and accepting, kind and gentle and careful with his advice. Jonas didn't need to read any more. He removed all the envelopes and put them aside, thinking that while he'd like to return them to Michael, there was probably no way to do that without embarrassing him. He didn't know what Michael had decided or done and it was none of his business. What he did know was that it wouldn't be right to show them to Nancy. It was up to Michael to decide what to tell or not tell his mother.

He sat with the big empty envelope for some time, trying to decide how to handle it. Then he got up and pulled down a box of his own that he kept on the top shelf of the closet in the den. In it was the baseball card collection he had kept since he was a child. Frank had been jealous of his cards, especially one of Carl Yastrzemski in his rookie year, which was worth a pretty penny today.

Jonas wasn't about to part with that one, but he did select several others of lesser value, including a team picture from the 1967 season that he had two copies of, and he packaged them into smaller envelopes until the big envelope felt pretty much the same as when Nancy had given it to him.

The next morning, he drove over and gave it to her. When he showed her what was in it, they shared a good laugh.

CHAPTER 15

Ed had been to Sean Anderson's office several times, and he was always a bit overwhelmed by the sheer richness of it. In addition to its size—as big as Ed's living room—it had plush carpeting that always appeared freshly shampooed and ground-to-floor windows that looked out over the lush countryside. Harrison owned a good bit of property, which was always impeccably tended, with grass fit for an upscale golf course and adorning gardens trimmed, pruned, and quickly rid of any plant that didn't look its best. Beyond the property lay acres of farmland, and the corn was already high enough to catch Ed's eye through the window.

Anderson came out from behind the large mahogany desk like a fullback pushing through the line. He gave Ed an energetic handshake and reached out with his left hand to grasp his shoulder. Ed instantly felt a bit shabby. Anderson wore a finely tailored gray suit with a hint of a stripe, a white shirt with gold cufflinks, and a silk tie that had to be from Italy, while Ed was wearing an old blue blazer and gray slacks he'd ordered from Dockers.

Anderson motioned to the large leather sofa, and as Ed took a seat, he offered him a drink. Ed declined and noted the look of disappointment. Anderson settled into the wingback chair facing the sofa. There was a large fireplace, but it wasn't lit on this warm afternoon.

"This is a bit awkward," Ed began. "I wanted to ask you about something that may be none of my business, but some information has come my way and I'm hoping you can put my mind at ease."

"I'll try."

"Can you tell me about this new stent of yours? Is there a problem with it?"

Anderson held his smile, but Ed thought it looked a little too practiced. "Problem? Not sure what you mean. The stent is the best thing that's happened to Harrison in years. It's much better than anything else on the market. Doctors love it. They're talking it up among themselves. Sales are taking off."

"You're sure there's no problem?"

"What makes you think there is? What have you heard? Is one of our competitors spreading false rumors?"

Ed found himself getting annoyed. "Actually," he said, "I don't know who the information came from. It kind of fell in my lap."

"And what exactly did it say?"

"That the operation with the stent doesn't always work. That there are complications. People are suffering, even dying."

"Oh, that does sound like a competitor. Look, Ed, there have been a few isolated problems. There always are with any new device. Some surgeons didn't put it in correctly, but we've made some changes that make it virtually fail-safe."

"How many people were affected?" Ed asked.

"Not many. Not sure exactly."

Ed had not been planning to take a hard line with Anderson at this first meeting. His only aim had been to test the waters, and he'd secretly hoped he'd find there was nothing so he could put Mary Louise's mind at ease. But Anderson was obviously lying.

"How can you not be sure how many people died?" Ed asked.

"Nobody died because of our stent, Ed. We had a very minor problem that was fixed with no serious harm. It's under control. Trust me."

"Can you prove that to me? With real data? For my own peace of mind?"

"Ed, that is privileged information, and the raw data wouldn't mean much to a layman."

Ed got angry at the condescending tone. "I'd really like some answers," he said.

"I've told you what I can. We've got this under control. You can trust us."

"I need more than that," Ed said with a frown, "but obviously I'm not going to get it." He stopped for a beat. "At least not today."

"I didn't mean any offense," Anderson said. He backtracked and told Ed a little more about the modifications they'd made to the stent, but he used a lot of technical language as if to prove his point that this was beyond Ed. Ed listened and then rose to leave without saying anything. Anderson reached out to shake his hand, but Ed pretended not to notice. At the door, Anderson stopped him with another question.

"Ed, I'm curious about one thing. Why would this person have contacted you about the stent? Why did anyone think you'd be involved?"

"They obviously thought I should be involved. I am the chairman of the Board of Selectmen, after all."

"But what does the stent have to do with your being chairman?"

"Harrison is crucial to Beacon Junction's future. You're the one always telling me that. If there's going to be some kind of scandal that would hurt the company and the town, I need to know about it."

"Scandal? There's no scandal, Ed. I assure you of that. Because there's no problem."

"And I guess the person also wanted some help," Ed continued. "If some health hazard was being hidden, it'd be important to make sure the word got out."

"There's no problem, Ed. We've already taken care of what was only a minor issue, but I appreciate your coming to me early. Before you told anyone else."

Ed caught the warning and was pleased that he'd raised enough concern to draw one.

Driving back to town, Ed pondered his next move. He was involved now, and he couldn't let it go. He had a responsibility to the town. And of course he didn't want to let Mary Louise down. She was counting on him.

It was probably time to insist on meeting the whistleblower. The documents had helped, but he couldn't put himself at risk without being sure he was on solid ground. He'd also talk to Jonas again, tell him what happened, show him the documents, and see what he thought.

What surprised Ed the most were the feelings he was beginning to identify. While he was concerned and intrigued, there was something more personal in it. He was exhilarated, like he was doing something important for the first time in a while. He wished that Eleanor were still alive so he could tell her.

As soon as Ed left, Anderson poured a tall Glenfiddich and quickly gulped down half of it. "Damn, damn, damn," he muttered to the window. He hadn't expected this. One more leak in the dike to plug.

Why had Whitney done it? He could have at least waited for his response. He'd read the report and was working hard on doing the right thing.

It had to be Whitney, didn't it? A competitor would have

gone straight to the FDA, not to Ed Riley, so it had to be someone inside. And no one besides Whitney was voicing concern. No one else had come so close to accusing him of hiding the truth and killing people rather than hurt the bottom line.

But maybe that meant it wasn't Whitney. Whitney at least had the guts to confront him to his face. He had the impression that if Whitney was going to blow the whistle, he wouldn't hide behind an anonymous letter to Ed Riley. He seemed to have more character than that, but who knows? People do strange things when their livelihood is at stake. It could be someone else who knew of the problem and was too scared to speak up, someone who may or may not even know that Whitney had been to see him. He ran his mind over the list of people who knew enough to cause trouble. Not many, they'd seen to that. But a half-dozen anyway, and it could be any one of them.

It could even be Madeleine, he realized. No, she wouldn't do that. Not now. Maybe if she ultimately decided they hadn't fixed the problem, but not now, not when she was still part of the discussion and not even sure herself what they should do.

But if not Whitney and not Madeleine, then who?

———•———

An hour later, Anderson had calmed down enough to call in Parker and Madeleine. He told them that he needed to get back to Whitney soon and that he was inclined to open up more of the research and incident reports to him. He was hoping that they could persuade him the problem wasn't as widespread as he feared and that they had taken sufficient steps to fix it.

Parker didn't think it would work, but Madeleine was willing to give it a try. She didn't see there was much to lose. She had been debating with herself whether the steps they'd taken were enough, and a part of her thought that if Craig could be won over, maybe that would put her own mind at ease. Parker thought it was a waste of time but saw some advantage in stringing Whitney along. It would allow more time for his private investigation.

Then Anderson said there was a complication. He told them about Ed's visit. Parker immediately assumed the leak came from Whitney, just as Anderson had, but Madeleine said it didn't sound like Craig, not when he was still trying to work from within.

"Unless that's exactly what he wants us to think," Parker said.

Anderson said he had the impression that Riley didn't have many details, that he was looking for reassurance and didn't have the spine for a big fight. "I think he wants to believe that it's no big deal and so he will."

Neither Parker nor Madeleine was so sure. "If he doesn't do anything," Madeleine said, "the squealer may go to someone else. Maybe to the FDA."

"I don't know," Anderson said. "If he really wanted to stop us, he would have done that first. There's something odd about going to Riley, something that doesn't quite add up."

Parker had no choice but to agree to play it out a while longer, but as soon as he got back to his office, he called the private detective. "I've got another name for you," he said. "Ed Riley."

"Can you send me the employee ID photo?"

"He's not an employee, but it shouldn't be hard to get a photo. He's the chairman of the Board of Selectmen. He's in the newspaper all the time. Some call him the mayor."

Nathan wasn't at the *Clarion* when the call came, but the receptionist handled it, agreeing to send the photo by e-mail for the standard five dollar fee.

Parker got the call as he was leaving for the day. He assumed the private detective had a question about the new assignment, but he was calling to say they already had some information for him.

"You know how you wanted us to check out the girl? Well, we've been watching her place and guess what. Your Mr. Mayor seems to be one of her clients."

"You're kidding me."

"Nope. One of my men saw him there last night, in fact."

"Keep on it," Parker said.

"Oh, no need to worry about that."

———•———

Ed called Mary Louise's cell a little after eight, but she didn't answer. He made himself a salad while he waited for her to call back, then watched the news and a game show that came on afterwards.

He figured she was with another client, and he didn't want to think about it. But that was hard. He had started seeing Mary Louise for one thing and one thing only, but he'd come to accept that there was more to it. His weekly visits were the high point of his existence, and he knew he looked forward to them for a lot more than the obvious. On one level, it was simply to relieve the loneliness. It beat watching the *Wheel of Fortune*, which stared back at him from the screen tonight, for example. But it was more than that. He liked Mary Louise, enjoyed her company. He wouldn't mind just seeing her for dinner some night or going to a movie in Bellows Falls.

Why had he never asked her? He knew part of it was fear that she'd say no, reminding him it was a business arrangement and he had to pay for her time. And even if she said yes, he'd worry that people would see them, assume he was paying her, and laugh at him for being so needy. Or worse, they'd think he didn't know what Mary Louise did when she wasn't cooking breakfast at the Sunrise.

No. Mary Louise was out of bounds. He could never go

any further than he had in that relationship. He'd enjoy her company for an hour each week, but he couldn't think of the relationship going beyond that.

Still, she was the one who had crossed the usual boundary line by asking him for a favor, so maybe she did regard him as more than a client. Or was that only because she needed something? Another man might feel used, taken advantage of, but he wouldn't go there. This was important. At least Mary Louise believed it was important, and she trusted that he'd agree and do something. He'd live up to that trust. Maybe somehow their relationship would grow from it.

He turned off the television and opened a magazine, but he couldn't concentrate. He kept thinking about her, wondering who she was with and if she treated all of her clients as well as she treated him—if she talked to them in the same way or if he really did have a connection with her that went beyond her relationship with the others.

It was almost eleven when she called him back. Any doubt or jealousy he had worked up over the evening melted at the sound of her voice. He told her about his meeting with Anderson, and she asked a lot of questions, though she sounded tired and worn. She didn't believe Anderson, and she assumed Ed was equally skeptical. When she asked what he'd do next, he asked about meeting her source.

"I don't think that's possible," she said.

"That makes it hard, Mary Louise." He tried to explain how he couldn't go too far out on a limb without knowing more, that he had to be sure that the information was genuine and persuasive, and that while he trusted her, he couldn't be sure of the source.

"Mary Louise, I promise not to reveal his name."

"It's not that, Ed. If I introduce you two, he's going to know that you see me and you're going to know that he sees me. I don't know if he's ready for that. And you may not be, either."

"I'm not ashamed of anything," he said, and immediately wondered if it were true.

"I didn't mean it that way," she said. "It's just that you're both entitled to your privacy."

"Talk to him about it. See what he says."

After he hung up, Ed couldn't escape the feeling that it was Mary Louise who was most leery about letting two of her clients meet.

———•———

Ed was right about Mary Louise being upset but only partly right about the reason. When she ended the call, she sat down on her bed cross-legged and put her head in her hands. In a few seconds, she started to cry.

It wasn't the dilemma that Ed had presented her with. She had seen a new client tonight, a difficult one. Some were like that. She'd long ago accepted that some dates were going to be a lot less pleasant than others, and she was glad that she had reached a stage where most of her clients were regulars with whom she was comfortable. She could afford to be choosy and she was. She certainly wouldn't see this guy again, not that she expected him to call.

Over the years, she had learned lots of ways to seize control of the session without clients really objecting. Many of the men who needed her services lacked confidence and wanted her to be in charge, whether they realized it or not. They'd usually had enough experience with women who weren't interested in being with them that they were quick to accept the fantasy Mary Louise offered. They let her be the initiator because they wanted to buy into the notion that she wanted them.

There were a few, though, who had failed in their former relationships because they didn't really like women. Their fantasy went the other way. They needed to be in control, needed to be the aggressor, and on some level wanted to feel like the woman they were with wasn't enjoying what was happening. Humiliation was often an unstated part of it, lying just below the surface or expressed by asking Mary Louise to perform particular acts that embodied it. They weren't overtly cruel exactly, but there was something about their behavior that made Mary Louise think they could get violent at any moment if things didn't go their way. It was scary. And it was demeaning to have to yield to their wishes. If she was scared, she'd cut the session off, although the greater her discomfort with the guy, the more she worried that trying to end the session prematurely would be exactly what would set him off.

That was the way she had felt tonight with this guy. There was something about the way he had touched her that made her feel he was looking for an excuse to get mean. So she did what he wanted.

And afterwards, she stood under the shower for the longest time, first at the hotel and then back at her room, trying to wash him off of her. But she couldn't quite wash him out of her mind. A walk and three glasses of wine hadn't helped either, though eventually she felt strong enough to think she could call Ed and not let on that anything was wrong.

She wondered how the client had gotten her name. He was from Boston and when she had checked him out, she'd confirmed that he worked on a contract basis for a law firm there, though not as a lawyer. He seemed to know all about her, which almost made her think she might have run into him when she lived in the Boston area. He hadn't been surprised when she mentioned living there, desperate for some kind of small talk, not that it did any good.

She had tried to ask how he heard about her, but he ignored the question. She no longer advertised, and she rarely took new clients, but for some reason, when he called, she'd said yes. Now that she thought about it, she realized she'd almost been afraid to say no, that there was that same demanding quality to the call that she'd seen in person tonight. But that's exactly why she should have refused.

She felt the conversation with Ed hadn't gone well, though she wasn't sure why. She could understand his wish to meet Craig, but it was a problem. She knew she was too upset to think about it, so instead she took a sleeping pill and crawled under the covers. She had a fairly simple breakfast in mind and had everything ready. She set the clock for five-thirty, which would still be way too early.

CHAPTER 16

The simple breakfast was a quiche with sausage, fresh spinach from Emma's garden, and Monterey Jack cheese—not the kind of thing you'd think would work, but in Mary Louise's hands, it was scrumptious. Of course it was decorated with blueberries and strawberries and orange slices. Mary Louise's dishes always looked as pretty as they tasted, and the four overnight guests and the six townsfolk who came by ate enough to fix them for the day. Naturally, they oohed and aahed all over Mary Louise, but she didn't respond with her usual graciousness. Nobody really noticed, except Emma, who noticed everything, and Jonas, who more and more noticed things.

After breakfast, Emma went into the kitchen and volunteered to help Mary Louise clean up, which in itself was unusual. Sally was generally the one to help, but she quickly yielded to her mother and went off to catch up on the bookkeeping.

Emma tried a little small talk, but Mary Louise offered only short replies. "Anything I can help with?" Emma asked.

"You can do that pan over there if you want."

Emma reached for it. "Sure, but that wasn't what I meant. You okay? You seem a little down today."

"Oh, sorry. I'm just distracted."

"Something wrong?"

"Just life. Has a habit of catching up with you and dragging you down every so often."

"Well, if you ever want to talk . . . ." She let it hang.

"Thanks, Emma."

They worked silently for a while, but Emma couldn't let go. "You know, Mary Louise, we never talk about your other job, but we could if you ever want to."

A look of near shock took hold of Mary Louise's face, and Emma realized this was the first time she'd ever spoken so directly about the other side of Mary Louise's life.

"One of the drawbacks," Emma continued, emboldened for some reason, "must be not feeling free to talk about it. I want you to know we all think a lot of you and—well, you can tell us as much or as little as you want. That's your right. But if it ever feels like talking will help, I hope you'll feel comfortable."

Mary Louise burst into tears and ran from the room. Emma bit her lip.

———•———

Jonas wanted to approach Mary Louise, too, but when he saw Emma go into the kitchen, he held back and dawdled over another cup of coffee. He was still watching the kitchen door when Mary Louise came out and tore up the stairs. He drained his cup and then went in to find Emma finishing the last of the pots.

"Well, you timed that right," she said.

Jonas smiled and leaned against the refrigerator. "She tell you what was bothering her?" he asked.

"No, just burst into tears when I asked."

Jonas wondered if it wasn't the business with Harrison, but

that didn't seem right, and anyway he wasn't supposed to talk about that with anyone, so he let her go on.

"I think it has to something to do with her . . . ."

"Her freelance work," Jonas suggested. Emma nodded, and Jonas asked if she was guessing or if Mary Louise had said it was that.

"Just a guess."

Jonas expressed doubt, but Emma stuck to her guns. "I think what she does takes a bigger toll on her than she's willing to admit," she said.

Jonas allowed how that was possible but said that the times he and Mary Louise had talked about it, he'd had the feeling she was pretty comfortable with it, that she even enjoyed it.

"Typical male attitude," Emma said. "I suppose she likes some customers and doesn't like others. I can't imagine what it must be like doing intimate things for money. It's got to make you feel ashamed, even violated."

Jonas didn't say anything, letting Emma work through it. "I never really understood why she needs to do it," she said finally. "Sally doesn't pay her much, but she doesn't exactly have an expensive lifestyle. I don't even know what she spends the extra money on."

"She's a private person in many ways," Jonas said. "I'm sure she has her reasons."

"You'd have to have some pretty good ones to resort to that. She doesn't do it for fun. I'll bet that. And I'll bet something happened last night to upset her."

———•———

Jonas spent the afternoon on the porch, reading *The Quiet American*, his teeth clenched around an empty pipe. Every few minutes, he looked up and around and at the front door, hoping Mary Louise would come down. He thought maybe he could help, whatever the problem was, and he hoped she'd feel comfortable enough to seek his confidence again.

But an hour passed with no sign of her, and he got absorbed in the book. When he finally closed it, he let his mind go back to the Vietnam War he'd been reading about. He'd managed to escape the draft, getting deferments first for law school and then as the father of young Lucas, but he had friends who weren't so lucky—one who never came back and one who still bore both the mental and physical scars.

After a while, he grew restless and walked around to the backyard. He found Emma on her knees administering to a group of James Galway rose bushes that had fallen victim to some fungus. They exchanged greetings, but he didn't try to interrupt her. He stood for a few moments and watched as she squirted some kind of spray on both sides of the leaves and then applied a powder. When she moved on to another bush, he ambled on, eventually heading upstairs to take a nap.

———•———

Truth was, Mary Louise had thought about going to find Jonas after her crying spell with Emma but felt conflicted. She'd been touched by Emma's concern and her willingness to broach the usually untouched subject of her being a prostitute, and she was afraid that Emma would take offense if she confided in Jonas rather than her.

Still, she felt more comfortable talking to Jonas. Oddly enough, it was partly because he was a man. Nothing against Emma, but Mary Louise had found over the years that it was usually a mistake to confide in her women friends. They tended to be far more judgmental. Sometimes she thought it was jealousy or their own sexual hang-ups—some just couldn't imagine having sex with a stranger for money. Men could be plenty judgmental, too, but the right men were more understanding than most women ever could be. And Jonas was one of the right men.

Besides, it wasn't her bad experience of the previous night that she wanted to talk about. She'd considered asking Jonas if he could help her find out more about the guy, but then she decided she'd just have to get over it. She sure wasn't going to see him again, and it wasn't as though he'd been violent, though there'd been the hint of it. No, she would be better off focusing on the problem with Harrison, and that was clearly Jonas's area of expertise.

By evening, she'd overcome her reluctance, and when she saw Jonas back in his usual spot on the porch, she went out and eased herself into the seat next to him. She noticed his pipe was already lit, a hint of apple-flavored tobacco in the air.

"You been waiting on me, haven't you?" she began.

"Yep." He smiled. "You took your sweet time."

"I wanted to see if you were really reading that book of yours or just pretending so people would think you're getting smarter."

"I ain't getting any smarter. I reckon I got as smart as I was ever going to be about twenty years ago, and it's been downhill from there."

"My luck. I didn't even know you twenty years ago. And now here I am asking advice from a man long past his prime."

She looked at him with a half smile. She had the feeling that only in the last few weeks had she started to see Jonas for what he could be, what he probably had been. It wasn't just that he was funnier and more charming, he was also far more willing to engage and be serious and show interest in things. She had a sudden realization as to how much he'd been hurting all these years and how it had affected him. On an impulse she got up, walked over to him, and gave him a big kiss on his cheek.

"What's that for?" he asked.

"Because I felt like it. Don't you ever do anything just 'cause you feel like it?"

"If I did, they'd probably arrest me."

She laughed. "Not if you did it to me. I wouldn't press charges. Emma might, though."

"That's for sure." He looked over at her and their eyes met. Something meaningful passed. "Are you okay?" he asked.

"You know, you're the second person who asked me that today."

"I hear you didn't answer the first time."

She looked at him. "You guys have been talking about me."

"Just a little. We're concerned."

"I know. I'm sorry."

"No reason to be sorry."

"I'm sorry that I got you guys worried is what I meant. I'm okay. But I could use a little more advice on that problem I told you about."

He nodded. "Before you go on, I ought to tell you something. Ed Riley came to talk to me the other day. He was looking for advice, too. He didn't mention you, but it was pretty obvious who he meant."

"And they say women can't keep secrets."

She asked him how much Ed had told him, and he told her that he knew about the stent and the unnamed whistleblower. He said he didn't know what Ed would decide but that he was pretty sure he was going to go to Harrison.

"He did go," she told him.

"And what happened?"

"About what you'd expect." She told him that Anderson assured Ed there was no cause for concern, that there had been a little problem, but it was all fixed.

"But you don't believe it?"

"No," Mary Louise said, "and I don't think Ed does, either,

though he's still on the fence. He's seen the documentation, but he says he needs more. He wants to meet the employee I got it from so he can verify it all for himself."

"Seems reasonable."

"I suppose, but my friend doesn't want to. Said he's too uncomfortable about involving outsiders."

"Then why'd he bring you into it?"

"Well, he confided in me, true, but I kinda pushed pretty hard to get myself involved."

"Sounds like you're stuck then."

"There might be another way," she told Jonas.

He looked at her as if he knew what was coming.

"Would you help?" she asked. "I told Craig that you said he should talk to a lawyer, and I think I can convince him to see you if I try."

"But I'm retired."

"You're still smart, though, and attorney-client privilege would still apply." She said it quickly, as though she was proud of having thought of it.

"Well, at least I don't have to think of him as Mr. X anymore." When she looked at him, he said, "You just called him Craig."

"Just like a lawyer to weasel that out of me."

He laughed. "Okay, arrange a meeting with your Mr. Craig."

Mary Louise gave him another kiss on the cheek, said good night, and left him alone with his pipe.

———•———

When she got back to her room, her cell phone was ringing. It was Ed and he sounded nervous. At first she thought it had to do with Harrison, but after some awkward small talk, he asked her if she had plans for the weekend. He wondered if she'd be interested in going to Boston.

"You mean like a real date?" she said. She meant it as a joke, but it hit at the cause of his nervousness.

"However you want to handle it. I know ours is a business relationship, but I thought it might be fun to get to know each other better. I'd expect to pay for your time."

"Oh, Ed, I was just kidding. How about I let you pick up the expenses and we leave it at that?"

"Sure," he said. "But I'd be willing to pay for any private time."

"No, Ed. Let's do this off the clock. It'll be fun."

But as soon as Mary Louise hung up, she began having second thoughts. Was this a mistake? Did she really want this relationship to move to another level? Would they go back to the old arrangement after the weekend? Would she wear the sexy underwear she reserved for clients?

Relax, she told herself. Just be yourself. Have fun.

———•———

The next morning, Craig met with Madeleine, who, despite some doubts of her own, did her best to convince him that the stent was safe, that the problems had been addressed, and that going to the FDA or voluntarily recalling the stent was unnecessary and unwise.

"It would actually do more harm than good," she said, "because it would rob sick people of a treatment they need and that no other stent could provide as well." She told Craig that she was talking to him off the record and was willing to divulge privileged information because she believed in the stent.

She went over the files with him, reviewing the summary statistics but not actually showing him the MDRs, the medical device reports that hospitals were required to send a manufacturer when there was a serious injury. Craig listened and asked a lot of questions. He liked Madeleine and trusted her, but he wondered if she and the other company managers didn't have too much at stake to be objective.

"I understand why you might think that," she said, "but the laws and regulations actually give us a fair amount of leeway to handle this on our own because they know we're in the best position to evaluate something like this. Bringing it to the FDA may force them to act to cover their backs."

"Which may be the best thing."

"Craig, answer one question for me. Do you think we've fixed the problem?" As she said it, she realized that she was beginning to believe it—that talking it through with Craig had helped her convince herself. She wondered if it had worked as well on him.

Craig looked hard at Madeleine, as though he'd find the answer in her eyes. He could see her confidence in what she was saying and thought maybe he should accept it.

"Craig, think about it awhile," she said. "And remember that there is a risk either way. If we're wrong, and we go ahead, somebody might get hurt. But if we're right, and they stop us from using the stent, people who need it will be hurt. There's no sure way. It's a risk no matter what."

At home, Craig read through all the data again and re-read all the reports of problems that he'd been able to get his hands on earlier. All he succeeded in doing was giving himself a headache.

The ring of his cell was a welcome interruption, but when Mary Louise started in on him, he felt he was under pressure from everyone to make a decision he wasn't ready to make. Then she again suggested he talk to this lawyer friend of hers who could be trusted and who wouldn't push him one way or the other. He agreed.

———•———

Ed also decided to talk with Jonas, and he got to him before Mary Louise could set up the meeting with Craig.

They met at Ed's office and Ed began by showing Jonas the documents Mary Louise had given him.

Jonas took his time studying them and asked a lot of questions, but he quickly realized Ed couldn't answer them. The papers looked genuine, and they certainly showed signs of a problem, but it would take an expert to figure out how big a problem and what should be done about it. No doubt such people existed at Harrison, though Ed said he wasn't sure the whistleblower qualified as one. Ed suggested they'd need an independent expert who wouldn't be partial to any particular solution.

"Isn't that what the FDA is for?" Jonas asked.

Ed harrumphed. "The problem," he told Jonas unnecessarily, "is that if any of us go to the FDA, they're gonna be madder than hell that they didn't hear about it from Harrison."

"And why not make Harrison go?"

"Threaten them with exposure, you mean? I can't see any other leverage."

"Not threaten in so many words. Just tell them that you've seen enough documentation to convince you there's a problem that needs to be dealt with. They'll get the message."

"I was probably too easy on Anderson. I could give it another try, but if I go back, they're going to know I've been talking to someone. They'll probably figure it's this fella. He's been complaining to them on his own, so they know he's unhappy."

"Then it's probably too late to protect him anyway."

"Maybe he should go."

"But he already has. You might have more leverage."

"I hate hurting the town. And hurting the company is going to hurt the town."

Jonas put the papers down and looked Ed in the eye. "Ed,

I got to tell you something. Don't be embarrassed or anything, but I know you got these from Mary Louise."

Ed smiled sheepishly.

"She didn't use your name," Jonas said, "but she also asked my advice about the problem, and I couldn't help but put two and two together."

Ed nodded and waved dismissively. "That's all right. I'm not embarrassed. Well, maybe a little. Truth is, it's not what you think. Not exactly anyway. I'm quite partial to Mary Louise. Maybe that's foolish, her being young and beautiful and me being an old fart, but that's the way it is. It's not—"

"Don't talk to me about old farts. And you know I won't tell anybody, so don't worry about it."

"I'll try not to. Anyway, it helps that you know. Because she's a part of the problem. She won't let it rest. If I don't do something, she will. I got to protect her."

"We both do. We can't let this become her problem," Jonas said. "We don't want her sticking her neck out. She's too vulnerable."

"So what next? I guess I go back to Harrison and be a little tougher."

"Not yet, Ed. The whistleblower won't talk to you, but Mary Louise thinks he'll talk to me, as an attorney. Let's see how that goes first. But my guess is that eventually you'll have to go back to Anderson."

They sat silently for a moment while Jonas waited for Ed to accept that.

"There is one other option," Ed said finally. "You could go talk to Harrison."

"Me?"

"Yeah. Everybody around here respects you. They're more apt to listen."

"Ed, Sean Anderson doesn't even know me. My glory days were long over by the time he hit town."

"Well, you could come with me. As my attorney. As the town's attorney."

"Ed, I'm retired."

"That's why you'd do it for free." They both laughed and Jonas left without saying yes. And without saying no.

CHAPTER 17

Two days later, Delacourt returned to Beacon Junction and went directly to the Sunrise. He wasn't surprised to find Jonas sitting in a rocker.

"Afternoon, Jonas. Good to see you again." He stuck out his hand with a smile, and Jonas stood up to shake it.

"I hope you're not too surprised to see me," Delacourt said.

"No, I heard you were coming back."

There was a question in his tone, but Delacourt didn't offer an explanation. He did say he looked forward to talking with Jonas. "Couple of things I need to fill you in on," he said.

Jonas gave him a curious look, but Delacourt just said he'd see him later and went inside to check in.

Delacourt was shown to his room, the Orchid Room, which was a bit of a waste since he wouldn't know an orchid from an iris, although he could have seen both if he'd looked in the dining room. He had to realize the Orchid Room was bigger than the Juniper Room, the one he'd stayed in last time, but he didn't comment on it.

Delacourt unpacked quickly and then went down to the porch, where Jonas was still waiting.

"You're probably wondering why I'm back," he began.

"A bit."

"Well, there's something I found out about my father, and it made me want to talk to you again."

Jonas waited, and when Delacourt didn't respond, he waited some more. Finally, he just got annoyed.

"Well, are you going to tell me?" he asked.

"He's dead. Cancer."

Jonas was taken aback. "Well, I'm sorry to hear that."

Delacourt explained how he found out. "I waited too long to go looking for him."

Jonas didn't say anything. He felt like he should offer condolences. Although Delacourt had said he barely remembered his father, something about his demeanor made Jonas realize he was mourning. But there was something else, too. Maybe hope.

"The thing is," Delacourt continued, "I was wondering if you'd be willing to be a little more open with me about his case now that he's dead. I mean there's no attorney-client privilege to worry about."

"You're wrong there," Jonas said. "Twice, in fact. One, the attorney-client privilege continues even after a man dies. And two, I don't have anything more to tell you anyway."

The hope slid out of Delacourt's face. Jonas felt sorry for him.

"Look, there's only one person who knew for sure whether your father was guilty, and you just told me he's dead. I told you I believe he was innocent. I don't see how I can do anything more for you at this point."

Delacourt nodded and at first Jonas thought he understood, but it soon became clear that he didn't. He began asking about the prosecutor and police and whether the key people involved were still alive. Jonas tried to discourage him. "They won't be able to tell you anything I haven't."

"Maybe I could at least talk to some people who knew him well," Delacourt said finally.

"The one who knew him best was your mother. Why don't you talk to her?"

Delacourt must have picked up on the annoyance because he apologized for nagging and then tried to explain why talking to his mother wouldn't get him very far. "She hates him. Hated him, I should say. There's no getting past her emotions. I need someone more objective."

Jonas asked about other relatives or people who'd been friendly with his father in the years since he'd left Vermont. Delacourt thought of his aunt but said he wanted to know what he was like in Beacon Junction, before his grandfather had been killed.

Jonas filled his pipe and lit it, noting he was a good four hours ahead of his scheduled time.

"There must have been someone in town he was friendly with," Delacourt said.

Jonas didn't respond.

"When I spoke to my aunt," Delacourt said after a while, "she insisted he was innocent, but then she said she knew my father made some mistakes when he was married to my mother. Do you know what they might have been?"

"Why didn't you ask her what she meant?"

"I tried. It was a pretty short and awkward call."

"Well, I reckon we all make mistakes. She could have meant anything."

Delacourt could sense that Jonas had had enough, so he thanked him and got up to leave. But he couldn't resist asking Jonas to let him know if he remembered anybody who was still in Beacon Junction who might have been friendly with his father. He said he was going to be in town a few more days and hoped to do a little more research. Jonas just grunted.

———————•———————

It took only five minutes before Emma appeared on the porch. She knew Jonas was annoyed as soon as she smelled the tobacco, so she sat down and was quiet. He looked at her and then told her matter-of-factly that Reinhardt had died. "Cancer," he said, as though it mattered.

Jonas watched the color drain out of Emma's face before she turned away. After giving her a moment, he briefly recounted the rest of the conversation with Delacourt.

"You talked all that time, and that's all there was."

He smiled at her. "I left out all the repeat questions and all the times I said 'I don't know the answer to that.'"

She looked out at the yard. She knew Jonas well enough to imagine what the conversation had been like. They sat that way a bit, not saying anything, until Jonas finally gave in.

"You know, it's your decision as to whether to talk to the boy. I'll be fine with whatever you decide. You can tell him as much or as little as you want, but he deserves to know about his father. And I can't think of anyone else who can tell him."

She didn't answer right away, just rocked gently, still admiring the view. "Maybe," she said finally. "I'll think about it." They both knew she would talk to him. The real question was how far she would go.

———•———

By the time Jonas and Emma had reached that point in their conversation, Delacourt had arrived at the *Clarion*. Nathan was surprised to see him, but only because he hadn't called ahead. In the back of his mind, he'd somehow known all along that Delacourt would return to Beacon Junction. He had made it clear how important it was to learn more about his father, and whatever avenue he pursued had to lead back to what amounted to the scene of the crime.

Without preamble, Delacourt told Nathan that his father was dead and asked if he could have another look at the old editions of the paper. He'd been rushed the first time, he said.

Only because you didn't tell me what you were looking for, Nathan thought. He told Delacourt to help himself and watched him go downstairs.

Delacourt was still at it when Nathan was ready to call it a day, so he went to find him. "You want to stay, you can. Just twist the lock shut when you leave."

Delacourt thanked him and then showed him a list of names he had made. They were all people mentioned in stories about Harrison or the trial. He asked if Nathan knew whether any of them were still around. Nathan took the list and studied it. A few he knew were dead, but most were unfamiliar and he suggested Delacourt ask at the Sunrise. Delacourt said he would, without mentioning he'd already spoken to Jonas.

"This last name is the only one I know," Nathan said. "Elizabeth's still around."

"Her byline is on most of the trial stories," Delacourt said.

"She was the chief reporter back then."

He told Delacourt where he could find her and left him to the bound stacks. "Put everything back where it belongs when you're finished," he said as he climbed the stairs.

At the top, he paused. "If you talk to her and learn anything interesting, I'd appreciate hearing about it."

Delacourt promised he'd let him know.

———————•———————

Elizabeth Peterson was much younger than Delacourt expected, which made him think there must be a lot of people in town who had known his parents. His grandfather's murder was twenty-four years ago and was a big enough event that people ought to remember it. Why was it so hard to find someone who could unlock the mysteries of that time?

Elizabeth, who had retired early to care for her ailing husband, was in her mid-sixties. She lived alone, in a small, two-bedroom Cape Cod-style house that was typical of whole swaths of Beacon Junction. When he called to ask if she would talk to him about the case, she didn't hesitate. She told him she didn't have many callers and would welcome the chance to talk about the old days.

By the time Delacourt showed up, she'd set out some cookies and had a pot of tea ready. "Sorry, but I don't drink coffee," she told him. He said tea was fine and nibbled at one of the oatmeal raisin cookies while they spoke.

He explained that he'd been looking through old copies of the *Clarion* and had seen her byline a lot. She told him about her retirement and her short career in journalism. She'd fallen into the newspaper job because she'd been a secretary and could take shorthand. "In those days, taking notes was all you needed to be a reporter. Write it down and type it up, and they'd print it," she said. When he asked her why she hadn't liked it, she said there were too many complaints. "People never like what you write about them. Even when you think it's something good, they find fault. Never good enough."

He asked her if his grandfather had been that way. Many of her stories had been about Sam Harrison and the company he founded, but they had all been positive, even glowing.

"No, Sam was different. He was the exception. He was always nice to me, generous with his time and nary a complaint, even when I got something wrong. Once I really got confused about a new thingamajig they were working on, and one of his assistants called to straighten it out. She was a bit curt, and I asked her if Sam was mad, but she said no, that he didn't even want her to call, but she persuaded him they had to set the record straight."

"Everybody seems to have liked him," Delacourt ventured, somewhat cautiously.

"He was one of the nicest men I ever met. It's a shame you didn't get to know him. You were so young when he died."

She said it as if she were telling him something he didn't know. He took another bite of his cookie before continuing.

"Obviously, there was someone who didn't like him," he said.

"And you want to know who that was?"

Delacourt wondered about that for a second. He wanted to know whether his father was guilty, but he hadn't thought too much about who might have been responsible if his father wasn't.

"You covered the trial," he said after swallowing. "Did you think my father was guilty?"

"The jury found him not guilty. I suppose that's all that matters."

"But if you sat through the trial, heard all the evidence, you must have formed your own opinion. I'd be grateful if you'd share it."

"Your mother was pretty convinced he was guilty, but I'm sure you know that. Has she changed her mind?"

"No, but I need something more. She won't talk about it. I don't think she has any real evidence. She sure hated him, but it's complicated, and I don't know that I can separate the facts from the feelings. I'm not sure she can."

"And obviously he still says he's innocent."

"He's dead. Died two years ago. His sister told me she believes he was innocent, so I'm sure he maintained that to the end. But I never got a chance to talk to him about it." He took a sip of his tea. "Or about anything, for that matter."

She told him she was sorry, refilled his cup, and moved the cookies even closer to him. It was the best she could offer by way of comfort. "Have you talked to Jonas Hawke?" she asked.

"Yes. He said the jury got it right, but he didn't give up any secrets. I don't understand why he's so sure."

"And have you talked to Emma Hawke?"

There was something about the way she said it that caught Delacourt's ear and made him cautious. "I talked to her a little, not much. Should I?"

"She knew him pretty well, from what I heard at the time."

Delacourt looked at her, a little confused. Emma had said she didn't know him well. Elizabeth avoided his gaze, and he thought he saw the start of a blush. "Sorry," she said, "I shouldn't be poking my nose where it doesn't belong."

Delacourt tried to hide any reaction and asked if there was anyone else he should talk to. She thought about it and mentioned a few people at Harrison who must have worked with Reinhardt but said she didn't know who his friends were.

"You didn't really answer my question," he said after a minute. "Did you think he was guilty?"

"I thought I could write about the trial more objectively if I tried not to think about that. I don't think I ever decided."

"But as you think back about it now? If you had to guess."

She looked away and stared out a nearby window. After what felt like an extra long time, she looked back at him, staring hard, weighing her words.

"The way I look at it is this. The evidence against your father was pretty flimsy, which is what the jury thought. He had the closest thing to a motive, and he had the opportunity, but I think the main reason they went after him was because your mother thought it was him and they had no other suspects. They couldn't think of anyone else with a reason, and your mother convinced the police that he had one, though I'm not real sure that holds up. And I think that's why the jury found him not guilty."

She got up and began clearing the dishes, and Delacourt realized the interview was over. He thanked her for her time and the cookies and was about to bid her farewell when he decided to push his luck. "Were you suggesting that my father and Emma Hawke might have been romantically involved?"

She looked at him. "I spoke out of turn. I heard they were friends. There may have been someone or other who extrapolated from that, but people had too much respect for her and Jonas to believe anything untoward could have been going on. I think if there was anything, it was just a friendship."

Delacourt thanked her again, but as he walked to his car, his mind wouldn't let go. If they were only friends, why did Emma deny knowing him well?

Dinner at the Sunrise was never planned very far in advance. When they first moved in, Sally was so busy fixing the place up that Emma did most of the cooking, but Sally knew that wasn't fair, and as soon as she could, she tried to take over. That didn't work so well, either.

Eventually, they settled into a routine that meant conferring each morning about who'd be around when and figuring it out that way. They only ate as a group a couple of times a week—Sally's husband got home late, and Jonas and Emma liked to eat early. Besides, both couples valued their privacy, though sharing a house, and living in a bed and breakfast for that matter, put some limits on that for everyone. On occasion Mary Louise would join one couple or the other, but she was always watching her weight and didn't eat very many real meals. Plus she had a little kitchenette in her room.

On this particular Thursday, Jonas and Emma were on their own. Jonas suggested maybe they should go into town for a bite, but Emma said she'd didn't feel like going out and would rather fix something at home. When the time came, Jonas showed up in the kitchen, uncharacteristically offering to help.

"You can make a salad, if you like," Emma said. "But you'll have to wash the lettuce."

That was more than he bargained for, but he decided to be good. He didn't mind the washing; it was the drying that made him feel silly. He could never figure out what was wrong with wet lettuce, though he'd dry it tonight.

Emma was seasoning some turkey cutlets that she planned to serve with rice pilaf and broccoli with sesame seeds.

"Would you rather have a baked potato?" she asked. She knew he would, and when he hesitated, she said she'd do it in the microwave so it wouldn't take any time at all.

The large kitchen had plenty of counter space and they worked side by side, not saying much. At one point when Emma turned her back to him, Jonas pinched her backside lightly, and when she laughed, he pretended not to know what it was about.

When he finished slicing the cucumber, he decided to approach her more directly.

"I'm sorry about before."

"What do you mean?"

"The way I told you about Richard Reinhardt being dead. I should have been a little gentler."

Emma sighed. "Jonas, it was fine. Not your fault he's dead. And there's not much anybody can say that would make a difference now."

He nodded, but she wasn't looking at him.

"Just the same, I'm sorry," he said.

At that, she turned and did look at him. She wanted to ask what he was sorry about—she really didn't know—but couldn't summon the nerve. "Thank you," was all she said.

Almost instantly her thoughts drifted back to the night of the accident, how she had finally made it to the hospital, so frantic about Lucas but still worrying in the back of her mind what Jonas would say about her being missing, what he might be thinking, and how much he knew. She found him in the waiting room outside the OR, sitting and staring at a wall, his cheeks wet with tears. They hugged and he told her that she had just missed the surgeon.

"How is he?" she asked. He shook his head and said Lucas would probably never regain consciousness and that if he did . . . . He couldn't finish the sentence. She broke down completely then, and he just held her. The doctor reappeared, and Jonas asked him to tell Emma what he'd already told him. Then, together, they had made the only decision that made any sense.

Jonas didn't ask where she'd been, didn't say a word about trying to find her. Not that night and not during the awful days preparing for and then living through the funeral. She often wondered about that—how much of his silence was because he couldn't bear any more pain and how much was because he didn't want to make her shoulder any more. Either way, she was immensely grateful. She couldn't have dealt with both her grief and Jonas's anger. But somehow she never told him that.

The silence lasted for a month before Jonas broke it with a question. "I don't care who he is. I just need to know one thing," he said evenly. "Is it over or are you planning on leaving?"

She assured him it was over and tried to tell him how sorry she was and how it had been stupid and had never meant anything important to her, but he shushed her with a wave of his hand. "All I need to know is that it's over."

But he left the house that night, not wanting to share the same space with her, and he'd come home as drunk as she'd ever seen him, but not as drunk as she'd grow accustomed to seeing him in the weeks that followed.

Eventually, when she saw he was still planning to defend Reinhardt, she realized she had to tell him who her lover was. That had sobered him up, but only for the duration of the trial.

"You're awfully quiet," Jonas said as he placed the salads on the table.

"Just thinking," she said.

"Have you been in touch with him at all since the trial?"

The question surprised her. It never occurred to her that he might be wondering.

"No, Jonas. Not a word. I wouldn't have done that without telling you, but I never had any inclination."

Jonas filled his plate, cut his potato, and proceeded to smother it in margarine.

"Still, it must be a bit of a shock to hear all of a sudden that he's dead," he said.

"This whole thing has been a bit of shock, to be honest. And scary, too."

"Scary?"

"I'm so afraid of Delacourt digging around. I'd hate for the kids to know."

Jonas hadn't considered that, oddly enough.

"Well, I suppose it's possible they'll find out, but they're grown up now. They'll understand."

She almost laughed. "You can't believe that. They'll be shocked, and you'll probably be glad, at least on some level."

"No," Jonas said, shaking his head vigorously. "I wouldn't be glad. How can you say that?"

She saw the hurt in his eyes. "I didn't mean it the way it sounded. I just mean that it would be too embarrassing to tell the kids." Embarrassment—mixed with shame—was actually her overwhelming fear when she thought about revealing her secret. And it bothered her that her fear overpowered any grief that came with knowing Richard was dead.

Jonas put down his fork and knife. He was almost done, and Emma had barely taken her first bite. He glanced out the window. From the small breakfast nook off the kitchen, he could see into the back garden. Even from a distance, Emma's handiwork was impressive.

"I'm sorry you have to go through this," he said finally. "If there was something I could do to prevent it . . . ."

She shook her head. "No, I'll just have to see what happens and deal with it."

"I'll do what I can to help," he said.

She smiled and set about eating a little more.

"Can I ask you something?" she said and waited until he nodded. "Did Frank know? Did you ever tell him?"

He shook his head. "No. It's not something a man wants to brag on to his friends," he said. He tried to smile, but it didn't work. "And besides, he would have insisted I give up the trial, and I wasn't going to do that."

"But now you wish you had given it up."

He lifted his head and looked at the ceiling. "I wouldn't exactly put it that way. I realize defending him wasn't the right thing to do, but I'd be lying if I said I wouldn't do the same thing all over again, given the chance. I was selfish and unprofessional, and ultimately I hurt Reinhardt. But I'd probably be selfish and unprofessional again. That makes me a good deal less than a good man."

She got up and went behind him and put her arms around his neck. He touched her wrist and neither of them moved or spoke.

CHAPTER 18

Ed was a little nervous at first, but Mary Louise soon put him at ease, and the drive to Boston passed quickly as they talked about things they never had a chance to explore in their one-hour sessions in bed.

Mary Louise sounded really interested in the insurance business, asking about his clients, their problems, and how he helped solve them. He never thought of insurance as a particularly noble calling, but Mary Louise said he was wrong about that. She told him that when she was a little girl, she made fun of the short, little bald man in the soiled suit and white shirt who came to the house to sell a policy to her father. "He was the original nerd, right down to the pocket protector he wore." But two years later a heart attack killed her father, and the insurance money saved the family from a life of poverty. She always felt guilty for the way she made fun of the salesman.

"No one ever made me feel like a hero before," Ed joked, but when she didn't laugh, he stole a glance. She was facing straight ahead, her chin raised, her eyes focused on some spot in the sky.

"It must have been hard losing your father when you were so young," he said after a few seconds.

"Yes," she said, her voice sounding weak, distant. When he looked at her, she turned toward the side window, and he realized she didn't want to talk about it. He didn't press her. He knew a thing or two about grief, and before long, his thoughts turned to Eleanor. He couldn't help wondering what she'd think if she knew he was on his way to Boston to spend a weekend with another woman, one he regularly paid for sex.

They rode in near silence until they got close to the city, when Mary Louise asked if they could take a detour to Peabody, the working-class neighborhood she grew up in.

"I'd love to," he said and meant it.

She showed him the house her parents bought shortly after she was born and the nicer one they moved up to when she was eight, the one where her father had his heart attack. Her mother moved from it as soon as she could sell it, and Mary Louise showed him the somewhat more modest home where she and her brother spent their teenage years. The mood lightened as she pointed out favorite hangouts and the spot where she first kissed a boy.

He asked her if she was as beautiful then, whether she was popular, a cheerleader, president of her class, a good student.

"No, no, no, no," she laughed. "Well, popular enough, but that was probably because I had boobs before most other girls."

"I have a feeling it had more to do with the way you treat people."

"You mean giving the boys hand jobs?" she said, not letting him get serious.

He knew her mother was in a nursing home, but she never talked much about her brother, and he asked her if he still lived in the area.

"No, he took off first chance he got. Last I heard he was in Montana working on a ranch, something I still can't picture. He never liked the city, so maybe it makes sense. He dropped out of high school, got a job at Home Depot, and as soon as he put together a little money, he headed west, deserting Mom and me. Like all the other men in my life," she joked. "I was only fifteen and I haven't seen him since. For a few years, he called at Christmas, but not anymore."

The late June day was perfect, a coolish sixty-five degrees with a brilliant blue sky, so they decided to buy a picnic lunch. She took him to a park she knew but was disappointed when she saw it. "They used to keep it up better," she said, shaking her head at the beer cans and plastic bags that overflowed the trash bins and littered the picnic area.

He found a blanket in the trunk, took her hand, and they walked into a wooded area until they found a clearing where they could sit on the ground.

He asked to hear the rest of her life story, but she insisted it was his turn and made him describe growing up in Beacon Junction.

"It was a lot different then. Everybody worked at the Dixon Mill, not Harrison Health Devices. There was also the shoe factory and the button factory, and Beacon Junction was much bigger and much more blue collar. I think the population was almost double what it is today. And it was younger. There was more to do. But it was a still a small town. I knew all my neighbors. They all had kids my age. It had a real family feel to it."

"I think it still does," she said.

"It's not the same."

His father was an accountant at Dixon, a gentle man who never raised his voice or lifted a hand toward Ed or his two brothers. All three went to the University of Vermont, but only Ed came back to Beacon Junction, happy to make it his home.

That had a lot to do with Eleanor. They were high school sweethearts, and it almost killed him to go off to the university while she went to the community college in Bellows Falls.

"Want to know a secret?" he said, and Mary Louise nodded eagerly.

"It wasn't until Christmas of my senior year of college that I got up enough nerve to even put my hand under her blouse."

Mary Louise smiled but wasn't at all surprised. She just hoped he wouldn't want to compare notes. She'd lost her virginity the night of her junior prom. "I bet she was beginning to worry about you," she said.

He nodded. "She asked me afterwards what took me so long." They got married soon after he graduated.

He was silent for a moment, and she reached over and took his hand. He knew that she wanted to hear more about Eleanor. A part of him wanted to tell her what a great marriage they had and how much he still felt the loss, but at the same time he was afraid of spoiling the afternoon. He also didn't want to let the two relationships intrude on one another. They were separate and should stay that way.

But Mary Louise's curiosity wouldn't let it go, and she began to ask questions to draw him out. What kinds of things did they like to do? Did she like her work as a dental assistant? Did she have a lot of friends? What kinds of movies and books did she like?

He answered tentatively at first, uncomfortable trying to reduce Eleanor to words, but gradually he opened up, telling her how he and Eleanor had been inseparable, soul mates and best friends. "We had fun together, whatever we were doing."

The catch in his voice told Mary Louise everything she wanted to know. Well, almost everything.

"You never wanted to have kids?"

"Oh, we would have wanted them, but children were never a possibility for us. Eleanor had some serious problems as a young girl. Little tumors in her uterus. Benign but terribly painful. She had what amounted to a hysterectomy as a teenager. All her life she had to take hormones, and there were always problems getting the balance right. But we managed."

"Did that affect your sex life?" she asked. Many of her clients were eager to tell her of their wives' failings in bed. Ed never mentioned the subject, but Mary Louise had always been struck by his lack of experience.

He shrugged, a little surprised at the bluntness of the question. "I don't know. That was our one weakness, and I never knew why. It wasn't awful or anything, but it was never that good. Not even in the beginning. She never wanted to do it as much as I did, but that didn't interfere with the relationship."

"Still," she said, finding that hard to believe, "there must have been times when it was hard for you. Didn't you ever—"

"No," he said, smiling a bit. "I can't say I never thought of it. I guess you could say I lusted in my heart," he joked. "But Eleanor was my first and only. Until I got up the nerve to approach you."

She squeezed his hand in response.

"God, I can't believe I'm telling you all this," he said. But in truth he had learned some time ago that even when he decided not to tell certain things to Mary Louise—usually some failing that he was afraid would make her think less of him—his desire to share with her inevitably trumped any reluctance. It was another sign of how much he missed his soul mate and how his feelings for Mary Louise were growing.

"I'm glad you did," Mary Louise said. "I wish I'd known Eleanor. Though if I knew you both a long time ago, I might have tried to steal you away."

A tear came to his eye, and she leaned over and kissed him. They lingered, and it became a long, hungry kiss.

They packed up and headed back to the car. She took the wheel and resumed the tour of her old haunts, the apartments she lived in, her favorite restaurants, the community college she attended. Along the way, she told him more about her past, describing her life as a young single, though nothing about her relationships with men. She even recounted her career history, from waitress to junior bookkeeper to apprentice cook to call girl. She went through the list matter-of-factly and without explanation, as though it were a typical career ladder.

They checked into the hotel around four, unpacked and lay down on the bed to rest. She wondered if he'd want to make love now, but they both fell asleep within minutes. They woke an hour later, showered, and dressed for dinner.

He had picked a fancy spot to impress her, and when they arrived he was almost embarrassed. Too obvious that he was showing off, he thought. In truth, the whole weekend was stretching his budget, especially the five-star Ritz-Carlton, which was costing him $425 for a single night. But she seemed to enjoy it, and he loved being with her. He noticed other men staring at Mary Louise, and he felt proud.

She looked stunning, wearing one of those little black dresses that was cut low. He had trouble keeping his eyes from darting down to her breasts, and at one point she caught him and laughed. "It's not as though you haven't seen what's down there," she joked.

"I know. It's hard to explain. I guess it's part of the anticipation."

Still, he spent most of the evening looking into her eyes. They were more alive, more inviting than ever. She had teased her hair and was wearing extensions, and she laughed when he asked her if she was growing her hair longer. She told him she'd take them off later, then smiled and added "along with everything else."

She didn't have what he'd learned to think of as classic cheekbones, not the kind that had given Eleanor a lovely but somehow unapproachable look, but Mary Louise had such a happy face and a ravenously sexy mouth. For that matter, he thought everything about her was uncontrollably sexy, but he knew that had more to do with the memories of his hours with her and what they'd done together.

Suddenly, he wanted dinner to be over. She sensed it. In fact, she felt the same way. They decided to skip coffee and dessert, and he asked for the check.

Back in the room, he bolted the door, and she went into the bathroom. He took off his tie and his shoes and suddenly felt a little awkward. The feeling evaporated, though, when the bathroom door opened and Mary Louise walked out naked. There was no shyness in standing there in front of him. She let him get a good look and moved into his arms, and they kissed. She started to undress him, but he stopped her.

"I want this to be your night," he said, and, when she looked at him puzzled, he led her over to the bed and made her lie down. He kept his eyes on hers as he removed his shirt but left his pants on. He climbed down next to her and kissed her softly. Their tongues touched, and he nibbled her lips, then pulled away. He told her to close her eyes and he kissed her eyelids, her cheeks, and her earlobes. He moved gradually down her body, smothering her with kisses and caresses. When she reached out to pull him close, he stopped her and insisted she lie still, her hands by her side.

"You're always thinking of my pleasure when we're together," he said. "Tonight I want you to be completely selfish. This night's for you."

She smiled and spread her arms in a gesture of luxuriousness and let him continue. He took his time, kissing, teasing, caressing, moving downward then back up, kissing her everywhere. He turned her over and gave her a gentle massage, lingering on her buttocks. Then he turned her back over and started all over again. Finally he moved down her stomach. His tongue found moistness, and he took pleasure in that. She groaned. He paused and invited her to guide him. "I'm very good at taking direction," he said.

"I don't think you need any."

"No, really, help me make this night special."

She moved his head slightly and her groans got louder, much louder. She lost track of how many times she came, and when she was finally exhausted, she gently stopped him.

He lay down beside her, and they kissed. After they'd rested for a while, he undressed and got under the covers. When she reached down for him, he took her hand away.

"I meant it," he said. "This night was for you."

She smiled and closed her eyes, and soon she fell fast asleep.

———•———

When she woke two hours later, he was propped up on an elbow, staring at her.

"Were you watching me sleep?"

"Uh huh."

"That's a switch. Usually it's the guy who falls asleep." She regretted it instantly, hating herself for reminding him how much experience she had. He saw her self-chastisement.

"It's okay. Really," he said. Then after a pause, "Can I ask you something?"

She braced herself for the question she hated, the one everyone wanted to ask: Why and how had she come to rent out her body?

"Were you ever married?" he asked.

She smiled at her mistake. "No," she said. "Never."

"Seriously in love?"

"Define love for me."

"The way I feel for you."

It surprised her. She didn't know how to respond. He wasn't asking if she felt the same, but the question was implied, and she didn't want to go there. Not because she knew she didn't love him, but because she honestly didn't know whether she did.

"Are you sure it's not just infatuation?" she said, trying to keep the tone light. "Do you really know me well enough to be in love with me? Even if being in love with a whore was acceptable in polite company?"

"Don't use that word. You know I don't think of you that way. I don't."

She hugged him. "I'm sorry. If there was ever anyone who let me forget it, it's you. When I'm with you, you let me be myself. No games, no airs. I'm almost able to forget how we met. And today was one of the best days of my life," she said, surprising herself and simultaneously thinking it was really true.

"What makes you think it's infatuation?"

She paused before answering, not wanting to say anything that might hurt him. "Don't take this personally, but sex tends to take over a man's head. I think most men have trouble separating it from love. And to be honest, when you told me today about your life and your love life, I realized I might be the only woman you've ever had good sex with. And that can influence a guy."

"Hey, I'm not nineteen anymore, in case you haven't noticed. Guys do change when they get older."

"I don't mean it that way. You are different. In a very special way."

"But you still haven't answered my question. Were you ever seriously in love with someone?"

She hesitated, but he'd been so honest with her. "Yeah, there was someone I thought I was in love with, but I was a fool. I didn't realize what a bastard he was. We dated for a year before I found out he was married, if you can believe that. He lived in another town and said he traveled a lot, but I should have picked up on his evasions whenever I suggested one of us move so we could live together."

"What did you love about him? Can you say?"

She looked at him and took a second to think about how to answer. It was a question she had asked herself hundreds of times, often coming up with different answers.

"He was charming," she said. "Oh, so charming. And I thought he was successful and had a big career, though that turned out to be a lie. And he was funny and witty and smart."

"And there was chemistry," Ed said, eliciting a smile.

"And there was chemistry. I can't deny that. He wasn't my first, but he was my awakening. I guess no one forgets that."

"So what happened? How did you find out he was married?"

"I didn't. His wife found out about me. Called me up one day screaming. It was awful."

"I'm sorry," he said, and he really was.

She looked down at the bed. "The whole thing really threw me into a depression. So much so, that I had to take some time off of work, which I really couldn't afford. By the time I went back, I owed twenty-seven thousand dollars on my credit cards, and each month I fell further behind. The interest was impossible, and I almost went bankrupt. Becoming a working girl was my only decent option," she said.

"But you managed to pay it off?"

"Yes, but that wasn't the end of my financial problems. Just when I got out from under, my mother had her stroke. I tried to take care of her on my own, but it was too much. I had to put her in a nursing home. We could have gone on Medicaid, but have you seen the kind of place they put you in? I couldn't do that to her. So she's in a top-of-the line facility. And that's not cheap, believe me. So that's why I'm still seeing clients."

"You're an amazing person. To take care of your mother that way."

"If you say anything about a whore with a heart of gold, I'll punch you out."

He laughed softly. "Is it awful? Being a working girl, I mean?"

She smiled. "Not when I get to meet people like you." She would have liked to have told him that there were lots of aspects of it that she enjoyed. It sure beat a lot of other jobs she'd had, and if you could afford to be choosy and keep control, it wasn't bad at all. But she didn't.

"God, what am I doing?" she said instead. "You take me off for a fun weekend and I give you the sad story of my life. What a drag I am!"

He shushed her. "No, I asked and I'm glad you told me. I want to know everything about you. I really do love you."

She kissed him, and a moment later slid her hand down his chest, then farther. He was soft, but not for long. And this time he didn't stop her.

They slept late and made love again in the morning. On the ride home, neither said much. It was as if they knew the weekend had changed their relationship and were pondering that, not sure exactly what it meant or what lay in store.

CHAPTER 19

Anderson called another meeting to discuss the stent the next morning. This time, it was Madeleine, Parker, Gordon Winter, and the key people involved with the stent from research, government relations, sales, and marketing.

Madeleine understood why Anderson had been calling almost daily meetings; he wanted reassurance that he was doing the right thing. She'd never seen him so unsure of his course of action, and she didn't fully understand it.

She and Anderson had worked together before—at a big pharmaceutical firm in the 1990s. He'd been a vice president and like most of the other key people there, he understood that making money was the only thing that mattered if you wanted to get ahead. That made some sense to her at a big public company, where you always needed to show stronger profits than the last quarter in order to keep the stock price rising. She fell victim to the peer pressure as well, but when Anderson took the job at Harrison and invited her to join him, she hoped it would be different. This was a much smaller operation, a family business with a friendlier, less driven mentality. She thought that would change the way Anderson operated, but instead he'd changed Harrison, at least until now.

The stent controversy was a real test. She had no doubt he

was worried and less certain than normal about which way to go. Parker was clearly pushing him in one direction, and he was looking to Madeleine for balance. The problem was, she didn't know. One day she felt confident they'd fixed the problem and the next she worried they were in over their heads. What she wanted to do was put everything on hold until they had more time to collect evidence and analyze all of the problems. Unfortunately, that wasn't an option.

The meeting started on a neutral note, with the researchers presenting the data in their scientifically dispassionate way, and the salespeople saying they weren't hearing any concern from doctors. The discussion, boring even to Madeleine, dragged on about thirty minutes before Parker interrupted.

"I think it's pretty clear that we don't have any real problem here. We go forward with the improved version and better instructions, and we'll be fine. Anything else would cost us valuable time, keep the stent from helping patients who need it, and hurt the bottom line."

"Anyone disagree?" Anderson asked. He looked around the room, but no one rushed to object. Madeleine didn't think they would after Parker had been so forceful.

Anderson was about to adjourn the meeting when Sarah Egan, a young woman in marketing, spoke up. "I agree that this is a tempest in a teapot, but if the FDA gets wind of what we're keeping from them, there'll be trouble. Is it worth that risk?"

Parker glared at her. "That's nothing to worry about," he said.

"But they could sanction us," she said, her voice wavering with nervousness under his unpleasant stare.

"Not going to happen," Parker said. "There's plenty of leeway in the regs. We're not breaking any rules."

An awkward silence followed and Sarah retreated, turning her eyes down to her notebook and not saying anything more.

Anderson thanked everyone and dismissed them, but as was

the custom, the vice presidents hung around afterwards to talk among themselves.

"Who was that?" Parker demanded.

Winter came to her defense. "She's okay. Young, but a hard worker. You don't need to worry about her."

"Just the same, if she were working for me, I'd have a word with her."

Winter stared hard at Parker in a rare moment of courage. "Well, she doesn't work for you, so it's none of your concern," he said.

Anderson intervened to ask if they were all in general agreement, and they said they were. That left the question of how to deal with Craig. Madeleine said she thought he was coming around but that maybe another meeting with Anderson would help.

Anderson asked Madeleine to arrange it.

"Want me there, too?" Parker asked.

"No, we'll handle it," Anderson said, and Madeleine breathed a silent sigh of relief.

Parker decided to push further. "You're going to tell him that we're going ahead, right?"

———————•———————

That night Anderson sent his secretary home early, closed his office door, and poured himself a double. He stood at the window, sipping slowly, admiring the view, and thinking about the pending meeting with Craig Whitney.

Anderson had no great animus toward Craig. In fact, in a way, he was beginning to appreciate the fact that he had become such a pain. It forced Anderson to give the whole matter more thought, and he was beginning to see that as a good thing, as anguishing as it might be in the short run.

Like Madeleine, he let his mind run back to his time with his previous employer, and like Madeleine, he knew that would have been an easier, clear-cut decision. As managers of a big public company, the shareholders always came first. They demanded it, and as the ones who put up the money, he supposed they were entitled to preferential treatment.

He knew that he had applied that approach to Harrison out of force of habit rather than necessity. Catherine Delacourt didn't demand heaps of profit every year. He remembered when she interviewed him before he was hired, remembered how surprised he was when she told him her goals and they included things like improving the health of Harrison's customers and letting them live more normal lives, as well as providing employees with meaningful, rewarding jobs. For Anderson, those had always been means to the end, not ends in themselves. At the time he dismissed Catherine's talk as lip service, but gradually, and especially as he learned more about the company's earlier days, he realized she was sincere.

But how to apply that lesson to the dilemma posed by the stent? That was harder. The people who were supposed to know were telling him that the problems had been solved, and there was nothing he could do about past mistakes. There was certainly nothing to gain by going back and revisiting the whole thing with the FDA. Those guys were clearly more of a problem than a solution. Telling them would set the company back and hurt both patients and employees. He believed that. He did. And if he were going to adopt Catherine Delacourt's goal of helping patients as his own, he'd have to assume she'd support him. Which wasn't the same as briefing her and letting her decide.

That turned it back to a practical problem: How to convince Craig to go along? He wasn't sure they could, and that if they did, that would quiet Ed Riley. But he sure as hell had to try.

———•———

On Thursday afternoon, Jonas met Craig on neutral ground, at Cindy's Country Kitchen. Jonas got there first, ordered coffee, and was toying with the word puzzles on the paper placemat when Craig entered. Mary Louise had told him Craig was black, which made him pretty easy to spot, and Jonas gave him a friendly wave. Craig also ordered coffee, and when the waitress mentioned that the cook had just taken an apple pie out of the oven and it was still hot, they both ordered a piece with vanilla ice cream on top.

"Thanks for meeting me," Craig said when the waitress left.

"Glad to." Jonas told Craig that he'd seen the documents that he'd given Mary Louise but wanted to hear about the whole problem from the beginning, in Craig's own words.

Craig began with an explanation of how stents were used to hold arteries open for patients with certain kinds of problems. He told Jonas why Harrison believed the CARC 2008 was better than the others on the market and how it had become popular with surgeons. He said the stent had been in use for more than a year when Harrison heard of a problem with the catheter occasionally breaking off during the procedure. At first, it seemed a fluke, but then there were too many reports to dismiss out of hand. He explained how the company had made improvements—in the stent, in the catheter, and in the instructions that doctors received.

"But you're not satisfied?" Jonas asked.

"I don't know what to think anymore. At first I was pretty sure we had a serious problem and were wrong not to report it to the FDA. But it's turning out to be more complicated."

He told Jonas about his meeting with Madeleine, whom he

said he trusted. "She's pretty sure that the fixes have solved the problem," he said, "but I'd feel a whole lot better telling the FDA and letting them decide."

"But telling them could open a can of worms."

"Exactly. Leaving aside the fact that we probably should have told them right away, they might shut down production until they sort it out. That means bad publicity, and we may never recover. It could be the end of Harrison."

"What about the people who are walking around with the old model inside them?"

"A good question. The fixes were made a few months ago, so the chances are that any bad insertions would have come to light by now. No way to be sure, though."

Jonas nodded and dug into his pie, which had arrived a few minutes earlier and was no longer warm. Jonas asked Craig to go over the timing again. Exactly when did Harrison become aware of the problem? Why did the problem not show up when the stent first went on the market? How many reports were there before the company began to act? Whose idea was it to fix the stent but not tell the FDA?

But most of Craig's information was sketchy and came secondhand. He wasn't directly involved, and by the time he heard about the problem from a friend in another department, the improved stent was already widely used. When Jonas asked who would have been aware of the very first reports and who would have made the decision to ignore them, Craig said he had to assume it went to the top, but he had nothing to back that up.

Finally, Jonas asked Craig what he planned to do next.

"I was hoping you'd have a suggestion."

Jonas shook his head. "I'm afraid you have to figure that out for yourself. It sounds like you have a pretty good idea of what factors are loading up each side of the scale, and now you have to decide which way it tips."

Craig said he wanted to do the right thing, but it was no longer that clear to him, and he was a little worried about the impact on his career. He said Mary Louise was pushing hard, harder than he wanted, but he agreed with her that there was no point in wasting more time if they were going to blow the whistle.

"Don't let Mary Louise decide this," Jonas cautioned.

They went over the options again, and Jonas volunteered to take a look at the FDA regulations if that would help. He said he could also do a little research on how vulnerable Craig was personally, but Craig was less interested in the rules and legal issues than in the moral implications. He said he still wasn't sure what to do, that he felt he was playing with people's lives, including his own.

Jonas figured that was exactly right, but he didn't say so.

Before they went their separate ways, he asked Craig if he had access to the names of everyone who had been treated with the stent. Craig shook his head. "No. I'm sure the company knows which doctors used it, but probably not the individual patient names, other than those they got complaints about."

Jonas nodded, wished Craig well, and asked him to keep in touch.

* * *

Craig's meeting with Anderson and Madeleine came early the next morning and went better than Anderson expected. Craig wasn't belligerent. He listened carefully to what they had to say, and then asked a lot of pointed questions, showing he'd given careful study to the data Madeleine had given him. Anderson responded with all the assurance he could muster, and Craig seemed genuinely grateful that they were taking the time to try to answer his concerns.

After about twenty minutes, Anderson felt they had covered

the ground, and he couldn't resist asking what Craig thought and what he planned to do.

"I'm not sure what to think," he answered. "It does sound like you've looked at this closely. A part of me feels this is too big, that we ought to let the government decide, but I know they're not necessarily smarter than we are. I'm still worried, though. It will be awful if more people die because we're making the wrong decision."

Madeleine put her hand on his forearm. "I don't think that's the case, Craig. I hope you know I'd tell you if I thought otherwise."

Anderson sensed his moment. "Craig, it may well be that we didn't handle this right in the beginning. We've obviously made some mistakes. But the important thing is to figure out what's the right thing to do now. What's going to help the most people going forward."

Craig nodded but didn't say anything. Then he stood and thanked them again, shook hands with Anderson, and then after an awkward pause, reached out to shake hands with Madeleine.

After he left the room, Anderson looked at Madeleine as if asking her whether she thought they'd won him over.

She shrugged. "We'll have to see, but I think he'll let it ride at least a while longer." She got up to leave, but as she reached the door, she turned and finished her thought. "But nobody else better die."

Anderson briefed Parker over lunch, saying he was pretty confident Craig could be persuaded, that he was bending, and they'd keep working on him.

Parker didn't buy a word of it, and when he got back to his office, he slammed his office door behind him, not caring who heard. They were so timid he wondered how they'd made it this far. He had half a mind to let them crash and burn, which was where they were headed if they thought they could use persuasion to keep Whitney quiet. He wasn't about to wait any longer and he wasn't about to tell Anderson what he was up to. He realized there was a chance that Anderson would discover what he was doing, but he was willing to risk it. *If he has any sense, he'll thank me for giving him plausible deniability,* he thought.

He pulled out his private laptop, a cheap model that he used only when he didn't want his words captured by the company computer system. He attached it to his private printer and began typing. He printed out the note and put it in a plain envelope, the kind you could get anywhere in the country.

When he finished, he contemplated whether this would be enough or if he should send a separate letter to Ed Riley. He decided that could wait. He had more confidence that Riley would come to his senses and back off, no matter what Whitney had told him.

On his way home that night, he dropped the letter in a mailbox in the center of town, far from Harrison headquarters.

———•———

Craig spent the rest of the day in fitful bouts of self-doubt, trying to focus on his work but repeatedly coming back to his discussion with Anderson and Madeleine.

After a restless night, he decided to use Saturday to drive north to see a new part of the state and clear his mind. By the time he returned to the Mountainview Garden Apartments in late afternoon, he had decided to call Mary Louise and tell her he wanted to back off.

On his way into the building, he stopped at the mailroom and pulled out a handful of the usual bills and junk mail without looking at them until he got inside and took off his jacket. That's when he noticed the plain white envelope with no return address. He opened it and removed the single sheet of paper and read it. He immediately felt his face tighten and within seconds, a knot developed in his stomach. He read it a second time. And a third. He looked for a clue of who had sent it, but he didn't have much doubt. He just didn't understand why. He was almost ready to give Anderson his backing. Why would he suddenly do this?

He called Mary Louise. "They're threatening to expose us if I don't back off."

"Who? Expose what?"

"Anderson. Harrison. They know I've been seeing you, and they're threatening to go public about what you do and embarrass me with Kima and the kids if I don't drop the stent thing."

She could hear the panic in his voice, and she tried to get him to calm down. "They're just trying to scare us. They wouldn't dare do something like that."

"It doesn't make sense," Craig said. "Anderson is still trying to win me over, and he had to realize after our meeting yesterday that I'm leaning his way. Why threaten me now of all times?"

Mary Louise let that sink in. Craig hadn't told her about the meeting and his apparent shift in attitude, but she didn't want to press him when he was already upset.

"It has to be somebody from Harrison," she said. "And obviously somebody has been following you around."

"I can't let them expose you."

"Don't worry about me."

"But you could get arrested."

She was tempted to tell him it wouldn't be the first time but thought better of it.

"What about you?" she asked. "How much would it bother you if word got out?"

"I don't know. It'd be embarrassing. And I'd hate for Kima and the kids to find out. What a mess."

"Look," Mary Louise pleaded. "Don't panic. Let's just think about it. You were coming tomorrow night anyway. We can talk about it then."

"I'm not sure I should come. Not if they're watching me."

"What difference does it make now?"

He didn't have an answer for that, so he told her he'd call her tomorrow and let her know.

"Okay," she said. "Be careful out there." But this time it had a hollow ring.

CHAPTER 20

J onas slept in the next morning and by the time he set out
for his walk, the temperature was in the eighties. July had
come in hot and unusually humid, and Emma reminded him
to take a hat. He took the sunblock she handed him but left it
unopened on the table by the door.

He was surprised to notice the lawn was parched. It hadn't
rained all month, and he made a note to water it, hoping it
wasn't too late. But the dry spell hadn't slowed the weeds.
Plenty of crabgrass, chickweed, and some new creation he
didn't recognize.

He wanted to be alone with his thoughts, but along the way
he kept meeting people he knew.

"Hot enough for you?" Ben Fougherty, an old-timer, asked.

"Global warming, maybe," Jonas ventured.

"Hogwash. We've had hot summers before. Tell me about
global warming in February."

The road to the diner also led past Ed Riley's house, and
despite the heat, Ed was out mowing the lawn. Or at least what
was left of it. When he spotted Jonas, he turned off the mower
and came over to chat.

"I talked to our whistleblower," Jonas said.

"And?"

"He's struggling. It's not as black and white as Mary Louise thinks it is. It may be that this is one of those cases when doing the absolutely legal thing isn't necessarily the best thing."

Jonas explained why he thought that, and Ed took a second to absorb it.

"You tell him all that?" he asked.

"Didn't have to. He knows it. And he knows how much is at stake for him. I hope Mary Louise isn't putting too much pressure on him."

"She might be. She called me again about it. When that woman gets a bee in her bonnet . . . ." He shook his head. "Have you told her you're going to go see Anderson?"

Jonas laughed. "I didn't know we'd decided."

"I'll go with you if you want. I'm not sure I'd be much help, but depending on how you want to approach it, it might be good to present a united front."

Jonas thought a moment. "I still need to think it through. Are you sure we ought to get more involved?"

"No," Ed said with a smile. "I'm waitin' on my lawyer to give me some advice. That's what I pay the big bucks for."

Jonas assured Ed he'd be the first to know when Jonas decided. Then he thought of Craig and Mary Louise. "Well, at least the third to know."

It was almost noon when Jonas got back to the Sunrise and called Nancy Hargrave. He asked her how she and the kids were doing.

"They're not kids anymore, Jonas."

"You know what I mean."

She told him they'd been great. Michael had been out to visit again, and Molly and Hal had been spending loads of time with her so she wouldn't be alone. "Frankly, it's almost too much."

They talked a little more and then Jonas asked if she'd mind answering a question. "When Frank had his heart trouble, they put some new stent in, right?"

Nancy said yes, and he asked if she knew what brand it was. She didn't, then added, "That's a curious question," but instead of explaining, he asked for the name of the surgeon who put it in.

Jonas placed the call as soon as he hung up, but the doctor, a fancy cardiologist in Boston, didn't return it until dinnertime. After some hesitation, he said he supposed there was nothing confidential about it. He confirmed he'd used Harrison's CARC 2008. Jonas considered asking whether the CARC might have contributed to the complications, but he doubted he'd get an answer and he didn't know enough about the cardiologist and his relationship with Harrison to trust him. He thanked him and hung up.

———•———

Mary Louise woke up with a new determination. The more she thought about her life, the more she realized she had never taken a stand, and she was resolved to change that. The stent gave her the perfect opportunity. She acknowledged that she didn't really know how bad the problem was and whether it had been fixed, but she knew Harrison couldn't be trusted. Someone else should be making this decision. She didn't have much faith in Washington, but she figured there was no one else.

That led her to break one of her fundamental rules. She called Craig and insisted he keep their date. They had to talk.

Craig acted like a mouse trapped in a maze when he arrived, and Mary Louise knew she was in trouble. Her aim in inviting him had been to buck him up, keep him calm, and stiffen his resolve. She knew he needed that, but it wasn't until he skulked into her room that she realized how much. She offered him a drink.

"I'm afraid I already had one."

"Then give me a hug and let me hold you for a while." She asked him about his kids, the only thing they ever talked about besides Harrison, and he shrugged. "They're okay. I miss them like hell."

"I know this is hard," she began, but then he cut her off by kissing her, hard, urgently, and with more than a little desperation. It felt strange and she didn't like it. It even scared her a little.

"Easy, fella." She tried to make it sound light but wasn't sure it did. Then he stepped back and nodded, understanding he was making her uncomfortable.

"Sorry, I'm just tense."

"Talk to me," she said.

And he did. About how scared he was and how hard it was to keep his emotions in check. How he thought they probably had fixed the stent problem but was angry they were using pressure tactics. How he thought he could get another job fairly easily with his qualifications, but if Harrison let prospective employers know he couldn't be trusted, all bets were off. How he was also worried about his ex-wife and kids finding out about Mary Louise, even though as a single man, it was nobody's business but his own. And how he was concerned about Mary Louise and what would happen to her if she were exposed.

"Don't worry about me. No one cares what I do."

"You can't count on that. There's more than a little bigotry and prejudice in this place. They'll be nice to you as long as you don't get in their face about being different."

She grimaced. "Yeah, the world can suck sometimes." She gave him a kiss, slow and tender. "But don't worry about me.

Worst comes to worst, I can move back to Boston. Let them make their own breakfast." They both laughed, and she tugged on his belt. "Come on," she said. "Let's let off some steam."

But when it came time, he lost his erection, and she realized just how upset he was. She tried to make light of it. "Lie back, relax, and think about the beach," she said and took him in her mouth. He laughed, but it worked. Within seconds she felt a stirring, and she knew how to turn that into something more. She didn't let up until he'd had an exquisite orgasm.

"God, you're good," he said.

She still wanted to talk to him about the stent, to persuade him that they couldn't let it go, but she was afraid of making him tense again, so she kept it light until it was time for him to go. "Be careful out there," she told him, meaning it more than usual.

Afterwards, she sat in the bath and wondered if she was pushing him too hard. She didn't understand all the hesitation. People's lives were at stake, and they had to do something. She lived too much of her life frustrated by the rules other people imposed. They made her sneak around and tried to make her feel ashamed of what she did. The hypocrisy of those in power, whether in government or business, was infuriating, but this time she was in a position to do something about it. If Craig wouldn't act, then she'd get Ed or Jonas to. And if they wouldn't, she'd do it herself. She didn't want Craig to get hurt, but they already had his data on the stent and they could go forward without him. And maybe they could find a way to insulate him from what lay ahead.

Though it was late, Emma was out in the garden, sitting alone on a black, wrought-iron bench. Jonas had bought it for her last Christmas, and he'd found the perfect place for it along the path. There was a half moon out, allowing enough light for her to make out an array of flowering liatris, black-eyed Susans, roses, and some late blooming daffodils and narcissus. A cool breeze brought the various fragrances to her attention.

She'd been sitting like that for almost an hour, trying to figure out what she should do about Delacourt. Which, of course, forced her to think about her affair with Richard.

And Lucas's death.

She knew they were completely unconnected, but she had never been able to think about one without thinking about the other, and in a way that wasn't fair. Not to her, not to Richard, not to Lucas, and not even to Jonas.

What made it hard was that she still had mixed feelings about the affair. She regretted that it had hurt Jonas, had made it so much more difficult to deal with Lucas's death, and had complicated the trial and so many people's lives. And she was still horrified at the thought that Sally and Nathan might find out.

But she didn't really regret falling in love with Richard, however briefly, if, in fact, that's what it was. Falling in love.

She had felt entitled. Jonas was so busy with his career, set on staying in Beacon Junction where there was so little for her, so preoccupied with whatever case he was working on, so unaware of what her needs were. No wonder that when Richard paid some attention to her—a lot of attention actually—she responded. Oh, how she had responded. A smile crossed her face and she felt a tingle in her body. It had been fun with Richard. A lot of fun, even if just for an hour or two at a time when she could be free of the burden of caring for Jonas and the children. She had needed that, had needed something for herself.

Oh, she had been silly. She knew that. Affairs are too easy. A weakness. Of course you can be happier with someone when you don't have real-life burdens interfering with the relationship. Wasn't that what all affairs were about? The fantasy, the lack of reality, the pure escape from the daily grind? It had been a real weakness to give in to it. She knew it was an old and trite story, had even known it at the time, but that didn't stop her from doing it all the same.

She hoped Richard's life had improved after he left Beacon Junction, but she'd never spent much time thinking about it. She was too wrapped up in her own problems. The trial was a huge strain at the worst possible time. Only a parent who's lost a child could know what she went through, and it was compounded by the guilt she had to bear for hurting Jonas and by the concern over what would happen to Richard. It wasn't until the trial ended that she was able to give herself the space she needed to grieve for Lucas.

When she heard Richard was dead, she had felt bad that she hadn't been able to see him one last time, but her biggest concern was what would happen if Sally and Nathan found out, a real fear with Delacourt asking so many questions. It was the reason she didn't want to tell him the whole story.

Was he entitled to know? Would Richard have wanted him to know?

She felt obligated to tell him that Richard hadn't killed his grandfather. His mother obviously hadn't. They'd told Catherine, of course, but she hadn't believed it. She'd hated him so much by then that she couldn't believe he was innocent.

She tried to remember what Richard had said of his marriage, hoping to find a clue even at this late date for Catherine's behavior. But they didn't talk much about their marriages. There was never any thought of leaving Jonas and Catherine to be with each other, and neither ever wanted or needed to speak ill of their spouses. What they felt for each other had nothing to do with their spouses, they kept telling themselves.

Emma stood up to stretch her legs and walked slowly around the garden.

So what was she to do now? She knew she should talk to Delacourt, and she had Jonas's permission to tell him about the affair if she wanted to. That would let her tell him that she knew Richard was innocent because they'd been together the night his grandfather was killed.

But how would he react? Would he be angry that she didn't testify to that alibi at his trial? Would he be angry at Catherine for never telling him? Or would Delacourt be like his mother and think it was all a lie? And most important, would he keep it to himself so that Nathan and Sally wouldn't find out?

She shivered at the thought, or maybe it was the night air. She went inside still wondering what she should do.

CHAPTER 21

The next morning, Delacourt was waiting when Nathan arrived at the *Clarion*.

"Buy you a cup of coffee?" Delacourt asked.

"It's free if we go into the kitchen," Nathan said with half a smile. "That way I won't be beholden to you."

There was no kitchen, but Delacourt followed Nathan to a corner of the big room where a beat-up Mr. Coffee machine sat on a stained table surrounded by Styrofoam cups and a roll of paper towels.

"You ought to fix this place up," Delacourt said. "You could make it a more pleasant work environment."

"Yeah, but then it wouldn't be journalism."

"I heard that was dying anyway."

"You got that right. But I don't suppose you came to give me interior decorating or career advice or because you think we're best buddies. What do you need now?"

"I went to see Elizabeth Peterson," Delacourt said.

"And . . . ."

"She wasn't a whole lot of help."

"Didn't know anything or wouldn't tell?"

"Probably some of both. Sort of like you and your parents." He tried to give it a lighthearted tone but failed, and Nathan kept his face passive.

"Can you be honest, Nathan? How close were your parents to mine?"

Nathan shrugged. "I don't know. They lived near each other, but I don't remember them socializing a lot. My father defended your father, but that doesn't make them friends. That was strictly business. In fact, I suspect if they were friends, he wouldn't have wanted to be involved."

Delacourt didn't say anything, and Nathan went on after a second. "You have to realize those were very difficult times, what with my brother's death. It hit us all pretty hard, but especially my father. He was even more broken up than my mother, if that's possible."

"Which only makes me think it was crazy for him to handle such a big trial when there was so much going on in his personal life."

"You can certainly see it that way, but the other way makes sense, too. The law was his whole life. It was what he could do by rote. Not that he wouldn't be giving the trial the intellectual heft it needed, but it was probably his way of focusing his energy so he didn't spend so much time thinking about my brother. Lord knows, when the trial ended, and he no longer had that distraction, the emotional side got to be too much for him. Much harder to handle."

"Is that when he started drinking?"

Nathan had been staring out the window, but he snapped his head back and looked hard at Delacourt. "Who told you that?"

"It's true, isn't it?"

Nathan looked away again. "Yeah, it's true."

"How'd that make you feel?"

"What are you, a shrink now?"

Delacourt shook his head.

"It was a tough time," Nathan said. "I don't blame him for it anymore. I did at the time, but eventually he got it under control. Stopped completely, in fact. He's been a good father."

Delacourt took that in, realizing he'd asked for the rebuke.

"What about your mother? You know if she was friendly with my parents?"

Nathan shook his head. "Didn't you ask her?"

Delacourt hesitated, but then asked the question that had brought him to the office. "Elizabeth Peterson told me if I wanted to know what my father was like, I should ask your mother. The way she said it—well, it implied they were more than casual acquaintances."

Nathan looked away but didn't say anything, and Delacourt couldn't tell whether he was angry or surprised or resigned.

"That would be news to me," was all Nathan said.

———•———

Delacourt felt bad as he walked from the *Clarion* office to the Sunrise. He hadn't handled that well, probably should have known that Nathan couldn't or wouldn't help and he'd have to confront Emma himself. He was hoping to avoid that, and he guessed that was why he had tried Nathan first. Truth was, he had taken a liking to Nathan. On some level, he hoped they could be friends.

It was only late morning, but the sun had already turned the sidewalk into a hot grill. By the time he reached the Sunrise, his shirt was sticking to his back and his pants were spotted, as though he'd been caught in a rain or had run under a sprinkler.

The porch was as empty as you'd expect to find it in such weather, and the door was closed tight. He realized why when he went inside and was struck by a blast of air conditioning and the smiling face of Mary Louise. He wished he didn't look so rumpled and miserable.

"Hot enough for you?" she said in a way that only someone who hadn't been outside yet could say.

"I forgot it ever got this hot up here. This is more like Washington humidity."

"How about a glass of lemonade? I just made some." She gave him another smile, and he did his best to return it. She really was pretty. Not beautiful, but very pretty. He glanced at her hand and saw there was no wedding ring and wondered if she had a steady boyfriend.

"Lemonade would be great."

Mary Louise let her rump move as she walked away, as though she had no doubt his eyes were glued to it.

When she returned, he thanked her for the drink and emptied half his glass. They made small talk for a few seconds, but when he sensed her trying to leave, he asked if Emma was around.

"I think she's upstairs. I'm headed up there, and I'll send her down if I can find her."

When Mary Louise knocked on Emma's door and said Delacourt was looking for her, Emma looked up from her book at Jonas, who lifted a noncommittal eyebrow. Emma paused for a second and then asked Mary Louise to tell Delacourt she was busy and would catch up with him later.

"I'm not ready yet," she told Jonas. "I'm going to talk to him. I just don't know what I want to say."

———•———

The delay would make a big difference for Emma because late that afternoon Nathan called and asked if she could come by his apartment for a drink. By herself.

"I need to ask you something, and frankly, I'd rather Dad weren't there," he said.

Emma nodded, as though forgetting she was still on the phone.

"You there, Mom?"

"Yes. How about if I come by in an hour or so?"

When she hung up, Jonas looked at her with his eyebrow cocked once again.

"Nathan wants to talk to me. Alone."

Jonas didn't say anything. He didn't have to. He got up and went to her and took her in his arms and held her. He wasn't surprised to feel a tear on his neck.

"I knew there'd be trouble as soon as I found out who he was," she said. "Why did he have to come back stirring things up?"

"It doesn't have to mean trouble," Jonas said quietly.

"What else could it be? He must have said or done something to make Nathan suspicious."

"That's not what I meant. Telling Nathan—whatever you decide to tell him—doesn't have to mean trouble. He's a grown man. It was a long time ago. And most important, he loves his mother."

She wiped a tear away.

"And I love you, too," Jonas said.

"I love you."

They hugged some more.

"I don't want to lie to him, but I don't know how to tell him," Emma said. "I don't know what words to use."

"They'll come to you."

"Will you care if I don't tell him about the night of Lucas's accident?"

"You do what you think is right. I'm sure it will be."

She looked at him and smiled. "You didn't used to be this understanding."

"I didn't used to be a lot of things. I'm trying to be more of them now."

She laughed. And then she cried.

It was too hot to walk and Jonas offered to drive her, but Emma thought that would be too awkward. She drove slowly and took the long way to give herself time to calm down, but she was still tense when she reached Nathan's home. He had rented a little Cape Cod when he expected Carol to move in. He had kept it rather than downsize to an apartment.

"Hi, Mom," he said as he opened the door and gave her a kiss on the cheek. Despite being preoccupied, she walked around the living room as though doing an inspection. She didn't visit often, and she was curious to see what changes in decorating he had made (not many) and how well he cleaned (not very).

The front door opened directly into a sparsely furnished living room, with a couch, a coffee table, and a couple of comfortable chairs. A bookcase with a TV and the various accessories that went with it stood against one wall. It bothered her that there was no hall closet, a total impracticality in a Vermont winter, but he had a hat tree and a boot rack in a corner to make up for it. The floor was bare, which also bothered her. Even if the finish hadn't been worn away, it could have used a big rug to give a homier look and a little warmth.

"White wine?" he asked, handing her a glass of the Pinot Grigio she liked.

She sat down on the couch and took a big sip. Nathan took one of the chairs and tried to make small talk, but she just gave brief answers, waiting for him to get to it. "I suppose you know this fellow Delacourt is back in town," he said.

It wasn't a question and she waited for him to continue.

"He's been asking lots of questions about the old days. Mostly about his father and the trial and why Dad defended him. It got me thinking again about those days, and the truth is, I don't know much about it. He keeps asking why Dad didn't hand the trial over to someone else."

Emma had decided to let Nathan talk before saying anything, to get some idea of what he needed to know and what his frame of mind was. She knew he wasn't there yet.

"I suppose I could ask Dad that question, but the truth is, I have tried a few times over the years, and he always says he wanted to keep his mind off of things, and I'm sure that's true, but I always had a feeling it wasn't the whole story."

He stopped somewhat abruptly and got the wine bottle to refill her glass. She was surprised to find it was empty. She took a sip before she tried to answer him.

"I'm sorry, Nathan. Those were pretty awful times for us. I guess we weren't there when you needed us most."

He shook his head, not so much to dismiss her comment but to say he held no grudge. "I know how tough it was for you," he said. "At least, I think I do. Even I can't really know what it was like for you to lose Lucas that way." He started talking about Lucas and what he meant to the family until he realized he was rambling.

"But there was something else going on, Mom, wasn't there?" he said quietly.

She nodded. "Nathan, this is awfully hard to talk about." And her voice broke. She drank more of her wine, though she knew that might not be so smart.

"I'm sorry," he said. "Maybe it's none of my business."

"No, it's all right. You're probably going to hear about it anyway, and I'd rather you heard it from me." He got up to refill her glass, but she covered it with her hand.

"The simple fact is, I was having an affair with Richard Reinhardt." She started to go on, but couldn't.

Nathan reacted more to the tears coming down her cheeks than her words and went over to hug her. He sat down next to her on the couch. She began sobbing, and he instinctively held her tight, running his hand over her hair. It surprised him how thin it had become, how he could feel her scalp through it. He put his arm around her back and pulled her close, but that only emphasized her frailty. He could feel her ribs, and he loosened his grip so he wouldn't hurt her by holding too tightly.

When she stopped crying, she asked for that third glass of wine, and he laughed as he poured it. "I think this is a world record."

"I think the occasion demands it," she said.

"Mom, it's okay."

"You don't hate me?"

"Why would I hate you? It's really none of my business, and I should never have made you tell me."

"I was afraid of telling you for so long."

"It's all right, Mom. I don't mean to shock you, but I realized a long time ago that my parents were human."

"Don't make light of it. I'm still ashamed of it."

"Please. It's between you and Dad, and you obviously worked it out."

"It took a while."

He nodded. "Just a couple more questions, though?"

"Will I need another glass of wine?"

"No, but I'm driving you home, so feel free if you want one."

She shook her head. "What's your question?"

"Why on earth did Reinhardt hire Dad?"

"He didn't plan to. He asked Frank Hargrave to represent him, but Frank was busy with another case and offered up Jonas. Richard felt he couldn't say no without explaining why. He knew Jonas a little, and of course everyone knew Jonas was the best lawyer around, so he felt boxed in. He just went along with it. And unfortunately, I did, too."

"And Dad knew about the affair?"

"Not when he took the case, but soon afterwards."

"Then why did he keep the case? Why didn't he recuse himself?"

She got serious again and Nathan wondered what other sensitive area he'd stepped into.

"I was with Richard Reinhardt the night Sam Harrison was killed. I was his alibi." She waited a moment for that to sink in. "Your father didn't want me to testify because he didn't want anyone to know. He was too ashamed. He convinced me—and Richard—that the state had no case, that he could get him off without my testimony. And that if he failed, Richard would have plenty of grounds to demand a new trial on the basis of legal malfeasance."

"He was willing to put his whole career on the line that way?"

"Hard to believe now, I know, but back then, neither of us was thinking straight."

"And you went along?" He said it gently, but it still stung.

"It was what your father wanted. I tried to talk him out of it, but there was no moving him. And I didn't feel I could go against his wishes."

Nathan took a minute to absorb that. "Of course Dad was right in a way," he said. "I mean, he won the case without the testimony."

"No, he was wrong. The state couldn't prove Richard was guilty because of course he wasn't. But without my testimony, Jonas could never prove he was innocent, either. And some people, thanks to Richard's wife, remained convinced he was guilty. It wasn't fair to Richard, and when your father realized that, he couldn't forgive himself. But it was too late. That's the real reason he never defended another client in a criminal courtroom."

"But why didn't you tell Reinhardt's wife so she'd know? Or didn't she know about the affair?"

"She knew about the affair. I suppose that's part of why she thought he was guilty. We did tell her that Richard was with me, but she wouldn't believe it. She was convinced we were lying in order to make her believe he was innocent."

"A jury might have felt the same way. Dad may have punished himself for nothing."

"I tried to tell him that, but he wouldn't listen. He doesn't think it matters. He's convinced that what he did was wrong. And that it blemished his integrity forever. At least it did in his own eyes, and in the end, that's the most important thing to him."

Nathan didn't say anything, and they both sat in silence for a few minutes.

———•———

Sally asked all of the questions that Nathan hadn't.

"How could you? Why would you?"

Emma tried to stay calm; she didn't want to get angry or emotional.

"Why are you telling me this now? Did Dad know? How come he didn't leave you?"

Emma tried to put it into perspective, though on Sally's basic question of why, she couldn't begin to explain it to her daughter. "It was a difficult time for me, Sally, and I didn't handle it well. I was selfish, and I made a mistake. I'm not asking you to condone it, but I am asking you to forgive me."

"But how could you do that to Dad? What about his feelings? I thought you loved him."

"Sally, you're acting like a teenager. You're a married woman. Surely every minute with Jake hasn't been perfect. You've admitted that enough times yourself."

"But I never cheated on him. And God knows I'd kill him if he ever cheated on me."

"Look, Sally. I said I made a mistake. I can't explain why. I'm not sure I'd want to if I could. It's really between your father and me, and we worked it out. I'm not saying I wasn't stupid or that I didn't hurt him, but it was twenty-four years ago, and we got past it. Isn't that more important?"

"But for twenty-four years, you've been living a lie."

"Don't be melodramatic."

"How could you not have told Nathan and me?"

"Maybe because I knew you'd react this way." They exchanged glares, and after a few seconds, Emma softened. "Look, Sally, I really didn't think it would have helped you to know. You kids were just teenagers, and it was right after Lucas was killed. I thought you'd be better off not knowing, and your father agreed. And later, when you were old enough, it was even harder because we'd waited. And by then, it seemed less significant and less something we needed to share with you. You're just going to have to accept that."

"How can I accept that? I feel like I don't even know my own mother. Like you're not the person I thought you were. You wouldn't even be telling us now if you weren't afraid we were going to find out from Delacourt."

"Sally, you have a right to be angry—but only within limits. This isn't about you."

"Of course it's about me. You thought so little of me that you went screwing around on Dad."

Emma felt like slapping her, but she didn't want to add to the drama, so she just got up to leave. "We can talk about this more when you calm down."

When she reached the door, she turned and looked at Sally, but Sally had her arms crossed and a stubborn expression. "Or maybe we won't," Emma said in parting.

Chapter 22

Jonas wasn't surprised by the kids' reactions, neither Nathan's calmer acquiescence nor Sally's anger. The initial responses fit their personalities, though he thought Nathan might get a little more upset in time, after he'd had a chance to think about it. He assured Emma they'd both come around to accepting it and that it had been a good idea for her to tell them.

"Best they heard it from you," he said.

"They're both going to want to hear your side of it."

"I know. But I'll wait until they ask. And I'll tell them the same thing you did."

She turned over in bed and lay on his chest.

"I love you," he said.

"I know, but it's good to hear it. You know you've said it a lot more in the last few weeks than in a long time before that."

He laughed. "I told you, I'm a changed man." He closed his eyes and let his thoughts drift back to Frank's funeral and then to the stent. He wished he had Frank to talk to about it, and the irony that Frank may have been a victim of the stent was almost too much to absorb, though the timing would suggest that Frank had received the device after the fixes were made.

"What are you thinking about?" Emma asked after a minute.

"Life," was all he said. He hadn't told Emma much about

the stent issue, and he suddenly realized now would be a good time. It would take her mind off her conversations with Nathan and Sally. And it did, but only for a while.

———•———

In his younger days, Jonas had a lot of trouble with the heat, one of the reasons he liked Vermont so much. In July and August, he suffered, and that was why their home was one of relatively few in town to have air conditioning. It made it hard for Emma, who was always cold. At night, she often wore flannel pajamas and thick socks and doubled up a comforter on her side of the bed, while Jonas slept in a thin cotton night-shirt or sometimes, nothing at all. But as he got older, the heat became less of a problem, and by twilight, it had cooled off enough for him to take a walk. He needed some time to himself. He had a lot to think about.

He was glad Emma had told Nathan and Sally. He always figured they'd eventually find out and have to deal with it, and he was glad they had learned about it from her. Better than from a stranger and certainly better than finding out after Emma and Jonas were dead, which had always been his biggest fear.

There were times in the first few years after Lucas's death that he wanted them to know for the wrong reasons. So they'd feel sympathy for him and take his side. He was glad he no longer felt that way.

He thought about what Emma had said. It was true that he had taken to telling her more often that he loved her, and he knew that was because he thought it more, realized it more. It was part of the reassessment of his life that had begun at the funeral. An attempt to figure out what was important. To rediscover that and live by it. Recognizing and acknowledging what Emma meant to him was a big part of that.

He felt better after he talked to her about the stent. She'd withheld advice but asked good questions. She wondered if he wasn't trying to represent too many different sides in the dispute. "Who's your client?" she had asked. "Nancy Hargrave? Mary Louise? The whistleblower? The town? The FDA?"

He'd suggested maybe he should act as a mediator, not trying to represent any one side but just try to help all the parties reach an accommodation they could live with.

"Maybe," she'd said. "But can you do that? It's very different from the role you always played as a lawyer."

He acknowledged the truth in what she said but told her he no longer had an obligation to fight for one side or the other regardless of who was right. He wasn't bound by that code anymore.

She saw through that right away. "Sounds a little like you want to be the judge. The one who decides what's right for everyone."

As he walked back toward the Sunrise, he couldn't avoid the conclusion that she'd hit the nail right on the head.

———————————•———————————

Sally was sitting on the front porch, in the chair next to what had once been Jonas's regular spot. Her eyes were closed and at first he wasn't sure she was awake, but then he saw her begin a rhythmic rock.

"Evening," he said.

"I've been waiting for you," she said without opening her eyes. He sat down next to her and noticed that she had brought his pipe and tobacco.

"Rough day," he said, not quite making it a question.

"You could say that."

He filled the pipe and tamped it down, then smelled it and put it in his mouth. He didn't light it. "I heard you were pretty hard on your mother," he said after a while.

"You been talking about me?"

"Guilty as charged. Parents do have a tendency to talk about their kids, you know."

"And to withhold big secrets."

"That, too. Usually because they think it's better for the kids not to know."

"Or because they're too embarrassed or ashamed."

He nodded. "That happens, too."

"I could understand your not telling us at the time, but to keep it secret for twenty-four years?"

He struck a match and lit the pipe. He drew on it and let it out, watching the smoke rise. "Once a certain amount of time passes," he said, "it gets harder to go back, especially when it's something you don't want to relive. And it's not as though it was especially relevant to you or Nathan. It concerned your mother and me, and we're entitled to some privacy."

"But you're our parents. We're entitled to know who you are. I keep thinking that Mom's not who I thought she was. I would never have imagined her screwing around on you."

"Watch your language. She's still your mother."

"Dad, I'm not fifteen anymore, and I don't want to be treated as though I am."

"Then don't act like it. Come on, Sally, you're just proving we were right not to tell you sooner."

She didn't say anything to that, and for a while they sat silently, watching the moon grow whiter and rounder. When he finally looked over at her, she was crying.

"You're wrong," he said gently. "Your mother is exactly the woman you think she is. What happened all those years ago doesn't change who she is or was."

"But I had this dream image of my parents' marriage, and it was all a lie."

"Then I'm glad we didn't tell you sooner. There's nothing

wrong with letting a teenager go to bed every night thinking her parents' marriage is perfect. A little silly and unrealistic, perhaps, but it's not a bad way for a kid to grow up." He took another draw on his pipe, but before she could say anything he went on. "And the fact is, your parents do have a pretty darn good marriage, and you should appreciate that."

She reached out her hand and took his but didn't say anything. After a minute or so, he told her it was all right to ask him.

She smiled. "Why don't you save me the trouble and just answer?"

"Of course, it hurt at the time. Hurt a lot. And it took a while to come to grips with it. And of course, the timing was bad. I was already angry enough at God for taking Lucas that it was a little too easy to be angry at your mother as well. But that wasn't fair. And it wasn't smart. We both needed each other, and I made it harder for us to be there for each other."

"I'd say she made it hard."

"Yeah. Well, of course, that's the way I wanted to see it. And I did for a long time. But you're smart enough to know that it wouldn't have happened if I'd been doing my part all along."

"It wasn't your fault, Dad. I don't care what you did or didn't do. She was wrong to have cheated on you."

"Let's just say there are different ways of cheating the other person in a relationship. And assigning blame to only one person is a little too simple."

She shook her head but didn't say anything.

"Anyway," he said after a pause. "You need to go a little easier on your mother. Telling you and Nathan was a pretty hard thing to do. She beat herself up enough over the last twenty-four years, some of it with my help. She doesn't need you doing it now. We've put it behind us, and you should, too. I know you just found out, and it may take some time, but make the effort."

She thought about that and then asked, "Have you really put it behind you?"

"I haven't forgotten it happened, if that's what you mean, but I love your mother more today than when we got married, and I take some of the responsibility for everything in our relationship. Maybe putting it behind us is the wrong expression. Let's just say we learned from it and became stronger—maybe even better people. That's what you should aim for, too."

"Oh, Dad." She reached awkwardly across the chair to touch him and then stood up. He did, too, putting his pipe on the end table, and they hugged.

Sally started sobbing loudly.

———•———

A casual passerby might have mistaken the noises coming from Mary Louise's room for sobbing, but she would have been dead wrong. Mary Louise was in the midst of an honest-to-God orgasm, and she wasn't holding back. She knew being vocal was a turn-on for most of her clients, but this time she wasn't faking it, and she saw no reason not to enjoy it.

One of her clients once asked her if a woman had to love sex to be a call girl. "No," she said. "But it sure helps."

The client who asked didn't really care, but if Mary Louise had been willing to explain it to him, it would have been a lot more complicated of course. She did like sex, and she realized at a young age that she wasn't one of those women who had to be in love—or even care deeply about a partner—to enjoy it. It was different when you were in love, and maybe some would call it better, but that didn't mean it couldn't still be good the other way.

The key to her own enjoyment, she knew, was how relaxed she was. It never happened with a new client or someone who needed a lot of her help and attention. For Mary Louise, and all the women she knew in the business, the goal was just to do your job and move on, without feeling much more than an accountant might feel when the books were balanced. In any given session, she was always focused on making it a good experience for the client—so he'd reward her with a big tip and, more important, call her again.

But tonight she was with a longtime regular, someone she was comfortable with and even fond of. They didn't see each other so often that she felt obliged to come up with new outfits or new moods to keep him interested. They just enjoyed being with each other. And tonight she was really enjoying it. So was he.

She was still feeling good when she got out of the shower, but then she checked her phone messages. The first was from Craig, and she immediately called back, knowing what he would say before he said it. She didn't give him a hard time. She said she understood his decision and she'd do her best to keep him out of future discussions on the stent, but she told him she didn't believe they could drop it. He pressed her, saying it was his head on the line. She started to say no, it was the patients who were on the line, but she caught herself. In the end, she agreed to talk to Jonas before doing anything, but she stopped short of promising to take Jonas's advice no matter what.

She almost forgot to check the second call, then wished she had. It was the client from Boston who had upset her so much. To her surprise, he said he wanted to see her again. That wasn't going to happen, but she wished she hadn't given him her phone number.

Then it occurred to her that she hadn't. She almost always dealt with first-time clients by e-mail, and then she called them, blocking her number from caller ID. She waited until she knew a client fairly well before she gave out her number. It didn't work with the few Beacon Junction clients she had because they knew her on sight, but it did with the others. And because she had her clients' real names and their work phones, they were usually more worried about exposure than she was, especially if they were married.

In any event, she wasn't about to call him back. She hoped that wouldn't lead to harassment, but if it did, she still had the name of the law firm he had done some work for. Presumably she could use that as a threat to get him to leave her alone.

Thinking about his call brought back that night she wanted to forget, and it was nearly midnight before she was able to relax enough to fall asleep.

———•———

Nathan was just finishing up at the *Clarion* the next night when the phone rang.

"You free for a beer? Or a bite to eat if you haven't had dinner?"

Delacourt didn't identify himself, and it took Nathan a second to realize who it was, but he quickly agreed and suggested Sal's Family Restaurant, just outside of Beacon Junction.

Delacourt arrived first, a little before eight, and looked over Sal's, the kind of place that would have been a neighborhood restaurant if it were located in a neighborhood instead of a deserted stretch of road leading to a handful of family farms. It was divided into two rooms, one small, with a bar and not much else, and one much larger, with a couple dozen tables. The lighting was bright, and the walls were decorated with paintings of the White Mountains and a Main Street that could have been located almost anywhere in Vermont.

Delacourt took a table in the big room, which was about half full. The clientele was an odd mixture of men eating, drinking, and talking loudly with their buddies, and several couples in their forties or fifties, tackling hearty dinners of meatloaf, fried chicken, burgers, or the special of the night, fish and chips.

Nathan arrived about twenty minutes later and apologized for the delay. Delacourt was already on his second Bud, and Nathan ordered a Rolling Rock and the fried chicken. Delacourt went for the fish and chips.

"Can I ask you something?" Delacourt said as soon as Nathan's beer arrived.

"Ask away," Nathan said. "I assume that's why we're here."

There was an edge in his tone, and Delacourt was taken aback. "I wasn't planning on giving you the third degree. I was actually thinking we might be friends."

"Sorry. It hasn't been an easy few weeks," Nathan said.

"Same here. A few months ago I got to thinking about my father and thought a trip here would satisfy my curiosity. Before I knew it, I learned he was dead, and still nobody will tell me anything about him."

Delacourt took another drink of his beer, and Nathan waited for him to go on. When he didn't, Nathan gently suggested that what Delacourt needed was a heart-to-heart with his mother. "Can't you get her to talk to you about him at all?"

Delacourt shrugged. "I wish I could. Talk honestly, I mean. But she's so bitter, it's a lost cause. There's got to be another side to him."

He told Nathan that Elizabeth Peterson had pointed him to a few people in town who knew his father, but too much time had passed, and they'd given him nothing but generalities.

"Isn't that the way it always is?" Nathan asked. "How many people know someone well enough to tell you who he really was? Especially when so many years have passed."

"I suppose," Delacourt said, "but there's one person who may remember him better than anyone else."

They stared straight at each other, not speaking.

"Your silence speaks volumes," Delacourt finally said. "They did have an affair, didn't they?"

Nathan shrugged. "I didn't know about it until you hinted at it. Then I asked her."

"Will she talk to me?"

"Please don't ask her. This is extremely difficult for her. It digs up some awful times."

The waitress arrived with their food and asked if they wanted another round of beer. Delacourt did, but Nathan was still nursing his first. When she left, Nathan changed the subject, asking Delacourt if he'd been to see Sean Anderson on this trip. He wondered if Anderson was celebrating his now-certain victory over the plant, but Delacourt said no, he hadn't talked to him on this visit. "Frankly, though, I don't think he was ever very worried about it."

"He understood the politics better than I did," Nathan said.

"And the economics."

"Touché."

There was silence for a moment, and Nathan asked if Delacourt's mother was very involved in company business. Delacourt said she was interested because it had meant so much to her father, but it also reminded her of Reinhardt so she kept her distance.

"Steven," Nathan said, using Delacourt's given name for the first time. "I can understand your curiosity—your need for closure and all that—but maybe it's just not possible and you have to move on."

"Spoken like a man who always had a loving father there beside him," Delacourt said, the bitterness like the lemon he was squeezing onto his fish.

Nathan stopped, his fork halfway to his mouth. "What do you know about my life?" he said.

Delacourt's back straightened, putting more distance between them. "I've met your parents and your sister," he said. "And I've talked to you enough to know how close your family is."

"It wasn't always that way. We've had our losses, too, you know. Don't make us sound like some idealized TV family."

"Your brother? That was a long time ago."

"It doesn't go away," Nathan said, his voice an angry whisper. "And it wasn't just my brother. You have to understand that my brother's death nearly destroyed my family. My father reacted by withdrawing from the rest of us, so in a way it was like losing him, too. And frankly, your father was no innocent bystander. He didn't exactly make the whole thing any easier."

"Why didn't your mother tell me the truth? I can't believe my father meant nothing to her."

"I don't know what he meant to her. I just know it's not fair to get her involved when your own mother won't be honest with you. It's not my family's problem, and you've no right to act like it is."

Delacourt held up his hand in a stop signal. "I don't want to fight with you. I only came to Beacon Junction to look into my father's past. I didn't know it would lead where it did." Then, after a pause: "But I would like to talk to your mother. There's no one else who had any good feelings for him who'll talk to me."

"I'd rather you left her alone. She's suffered enough. Then and now."

"Now?"

"Your showing up forced her to admit the affair to me and my sister. And believe me, that wasn't easy."

"I never intended to make trouble. I just wanted to know about my father."

"But that's the way it worked out. Whatever your intentions, you've caused her a considerable amount of grief."

Now it was Delacourt's turn to raise his voice. "Look, Nathan, all I ever did was ask some basic questions about my father— questions your parents could have answered pretty easily, but instead they lied to me. They didn't give a damn about how I felt, even when they learned my father was dead. It's not fair to blame me because your mother cheated on your father and lied to you about it all these years."

Nathan seemed taken aback by the sharpness of Delacourt's words, but he could see the truth in them.

"You're right. It's not your fault," he said, speaking more

softly in both tone and volume. "The question is where do you go from here."

"I want to talk to your mother. I need to do that."

Nathan shook his head.

"It's not your decision," Delacourt said.

"It's my mother's decision."

"And have you asked her?"

"No." Nathan sighed.

"Did your mother tell you anything about my father?" Delacourt asked. "Didn't you want to know? How the affair started? What he was like?"

Nathan didn't say anything. Delacourt waited, looking around the room, his eyes settling on a family of five. The parents weren't saying much, other than to give orders to one or another of the kids. The parents didn't even look at each other.

Delacourt finally broke the silence. "Help me out here, Nathan. Nobody's telling me anything."

"I can't. I don't know anything about it other than that it happened. I didn't ask her for details."

"Then I have to. Look, Nathan, I'm not here to mess with anybody's head. I'd just like to know something about my father. Now that I know he's dead, it feels more important than ever. I think I have the right to know."

"But why does my mother have to be the one put on the spot? You're giving your own mother a pass. That's not fair."

Delacourt pushed his empty plate aside and took another swallow of his beer. "It may not be fair, but it's not my choice.

"Tell me something," Delacourt said after a few seconds. "Aren't you a little curious about the affair? You were—what? Fourteen? Doesn't it bother you that she did that? It sure as hell bothers me. Don't you wonder why? Don't you wonder what attracted her to my father and what he was like?"

Nathan shook his head, as though trying to clear the image

brought to his mind. "Of course I do, Steven, but it's her decision whether to tell me any of that. I love her too much to put any more pressure on her. Just as you won't put more pressure on your mother. Don't you see it's the same thing?"

Delacourt shook his head. "No, it's not the same," he said, the alcohol fueling his anger and making the words come out louder than he realized. "It's not the same. Your mother's had a free ride all these years. She went back to her loving husband, while my father's life was ruined. She doesn't care at all about what happened to him."

Nathan raised his hand in protest and told Delacourt to lower his voice. Delacourt suddenly realized that some of the other diners were stealing looks at them, but he didn't care. He took the last swallow of his beer and slammed the bottle down on the table to make sure it could be heard.

"I'm entitled to some answers," he said. "And I'm going to ask her for them."

Nathan started to say something but Delacourt stood up abruptly. He pulled out his wallet, tossed two twenty dollar bills on the table and stormed out. Several nearby patrons watched.

Nathan asked for a check as soon as he could get the waitress's attention, but he was forced to wait several minutes for it. He felt everyone was staring, and he tried to act nonchalant, but it was hard. He hadn't accomplished much. Emma would have to deal with Delacourt herself, but he guessed she was strong enough to do that. And maybe she did owe him some answers.

CHAPTER 23

The next morning, when Jonas saw how upset Emma still was, he offered to talk to Delacourt. He had told her a little about his conversation with Sally, and that morning at breakfast Sally had made an attempt to be her usual self with Emma, but Jonas could see they both felt awkward, and he thought he'd try to take this one other burden off of Emma's shoulders.

"Now that you told Nathan and Sally, there's no point in us not being straight with Delacourt," Jonas said. "He knows the gist of it anyway, and this way he'll at least understand why we believed his father was innocent."

Emma thanked him but said he was just delaying the inevitable. "He'll want to talk to me more than ever to find out what his father was really like."

"Probably," Jonas said. "Think of it as a little reconnaissance before you have to deal with him, and who knows, maybe I'll get lucky and get him to leave."

There weren't many places at the Sunrise where one could count on privacy so they met in Delacourt's room.

It was on the third floor, a big L-shaped area with the bed and TV in the longer part of the L and a sitting area with a couch and a little desk in the short part. Sally had decorated each of the rooms individually, and this one was painted dark blue with white woodwork and dark hardwood floors. The bed was a modern yet old-fashioned-looking four poster with a canopy. The night tables were different but looked like they belonged together, and the couch was a light blue print. It opened into a bed so the room could accommodate a couple with children.

The room was normally sunny, but Delacourt still had the curtains closed in the bedroom part. He had hung up the do-not-disturb sign while he waited for Jonas, and the room hadn't been cleaned yet. He apologized for the unmade bed, which struck Jonas as odd seeing how he was the proprietor and all, but he wrote it off to nervousness.

The confusion over who was host and who was guest continued as Delacourt asked Jonas where he'd like to sit. The straighter chair was better for his back, so he took that, and Delacourt sat down on the couch. He had used the room coffeemaker to prepare a pot, but Jonas declined, though he would have liked something to do with his hands. He wished he'd brought an empty pipe to hold and chew on.

"I'll get right to the point," Jonas said. "I gather you figured out a good bit of it anyway without our help. You're going to feel we weren't very honest with you, and with some justification, but I hope you'll be able to understand why it was difficult." He paused, looking for a nod or something, but Delacourt was looking down at his hands, not moving a muscle as far as Jonas could see. So he continued.

"You know, I gather, that your father and Emma had an affair, but what you probably don't know is that on the night your grandfather was killed, they were together. They didn't want anyone to know, and it was their hope—mine, too, frankly, maybe mine even more than theirs—that we could win an acquittal without using Emma as his alibi. We decided we'd use it only if we had to, and we were lucky in that we didn't have to. That's the long and short of it."

Delacourt's eyes opened wider. The affair was one thing, but it had never occurred to him that Emma was also his father's alibi. Nathan hadn't said anything about that.

"I don't understand. What do you mean? You held it in reserve? How could you know he'd be acquitted without it?"

"I didn't know for sure, but the state had a weak circumstantial case, and I figured I could knock big holes in it."

"But you were gambling with my father's life."

"Not really. If he were found guilty, he could blame me for holding Emma back, accuse me of misconduct and incompetence. Any appeals court would have given him a new trial with a different lawyer."

"You don't know that! You were just being selfish. You should have recused yourself. How could you fairly represent him when he was sleeping with your wife?"

"No need to shout," Jonas said firmly but calmly. Then after a second, "Look, I'm not saying it was the most ethical decision I ever made. But I did win the case. Don't forget that."

"So the ends justify the means."

"Think of it this way. Because of Emma, I knew your father was innocent, and I did everything I could to win that case. I did have a personal stake in it, and technically I should have recused myself. But in this case, the personal stake made me more determined than ever to win the case so Emma wouldn't have to testify."

"That's like saying a doctor should operate on his own child because he'd want him to live more than another surgeon might. The fact is, you were emotionally involved, and that could have led you to make a mistake."

Jonas sighed. "You're right in theory, and to some extent, I'm asking you to trust me on this. I'm a good lawyer—was then anyway. There was no one better who could have defended your father. And I had my partner watching over my shoulder every step of the way."

"Did your partner know about the affair?"

"No, of course not."

"If he had, I bet he wouldn't have let you keep the case."

"That's probably true."

Delacourt got up and began pacing the room. He'd been keeping his voice down since Jonas's admonition, but he was still pretty riled up.

"And that's why you kept the case even though your son was killed?"

Jonas nodded, and now he stood, too. He didn't like speaking up to Delacourt.

"When did you find out about the affair?" Delacourt asked.

Jonas was ready for that one. "Not until after I'd accepted the case."

"Is that when Emma told you about the affair?"

"How and when I found out isn't relevant."

"It is to me."

"It was after I had accepted the case and after my son's death. That's all you need to know."

"What about my mother? Did she know about the affair and that they were together the night of the murder?"

"Yes, your father told her while we were preparing for trial. He didn't want her to know, but she was so convinced he was guilty that Emma and I persuaded him he should tell her."

"But she still thought he was guilty." He said it with a puzzled tone.

"She never believed us. Well, she believed they had an affair. In fact, claimed she knew all along he was having an affair with someone. But she accused Emma of lying about that particular night to give him an alibi. That would have been a danger with a jury, too. If I had used Emma as an alibi, it could have worked against him, making the jury think she was part of his motive, that it was all a plot to get Harrison's money and then go off with Emma."

"So again, you were protecting Emma."

"No, I was defending your father."

"But you would have done anything to keep it a secret. That's all you cared about."

"Mr. Delacourt, I'm not going to tell you everything I did was for the purest of motives, but keep a few things in mind. First, your father also wanted to keep Emma out of it. He didn't even want to tell your mother, but we persuaded him to. That didn't help Emma any because we knew there was a chance your mother would make the affair public. Second, your father was acquitted. You came up here wanting to know if he was guilty or not. Well, now you know. And maybe now you should go back where you came from."

Delacourt glared at him. "I grew up thinking he was guilty because my mother thought that, and I didn't know any better. Do you think that was fair to my father?"

"No, I don't, and that disturbs me, but I'm not sure it's entirely our fault. Look, your mother knew about your father's alibi, and she chose to keep it from you. So blame her. She didn't believe it. She was just so convinced he was guilty, she couldn't consider any other possibilities. If you want to blame someone, blame her."

"Maybe she was convinced he was guilty because she knew he was screwing around. Maybe I should blame Emma for that."

"Or him." Jonas gave him a final glare and started to walk out of the room, but before he got to the door, Delacourt called his name.

"One more question if you would."

Jonas waited.

"Did you believe they were together the night of the murder? Do you believe your wife?"

Jonas walked out without giving him an answer.

Jonas, Mary Louise, and Ed met at Ed's office that afternoon. It was the first time Mary Louise had been there, and she was more than a little bit curious. Ed was also eager to have her see him in his more formal work surroundings, and he took care to straighten the office before they came. He even put his tie on, though he hadn't met with any clients that day and wouldn't have usually bothered. At one point, he considered putting away the picture of Eleanor that he still kept on his desk, but that was silly. Besides, he would have considered it a betrayal of sorts, even now, two years after her death.

Ed's receptionist showed them into his office, and Ed came around his desk, reaching out to shake Jonas's hand and then turning and giving Mary Louise a hug. He ushered them to the small conference room he used for meeting with clients, and his receptionist brought in iced tea and a small platter of shortbread cookies and zucchini bread she had picked up at the farmer's market during her lunch hour.

Mary Louise began by recounting her last conversation with Craig and how he wanted out. She told him about the threatening letter Craig had received and how he was worried they'd tell his family back in Montgomery. Worse, he was worried about losing his job and being blackballed as disloyal so he'd never find another one.

Jonas shook his head sadly, but Ed stood up and said he'd be right back. When he returned he handed Jonas a letter. "I got one, too," he said. Then he looked at Mary Louise. "I was going to tell you about it when you called, but I thought I'd wait until we were together."

Mary Louise looked at the letter and said it was very similar to the one Craig got. "Such scumbags."

"Well, this raises it up a notch, that's for sure," Jonas said.

"I can't rightly blame Craig for having second thoughts." Then, after a pause, "What about you, Ed?"

"I don't care about me," he said. "I'm not ashamed of anything I've done, and I don't care what the town thinks."

Jonas sat back in his chair and looked at Mary Louise.

"I don't care, either." she said.

"You have to care," he told her. "What you do is illegal and if you get exposed, somebody's going to have to do something. It may not be the best-kept secret, but it's one thing for folks to look the other way and pretend they don't know. Quite another when it's thrown in everyone's face. You know that, Ed."

"I don't care, either," he said defiantly. "Some things are more important than what other people think."

"You're not listening, Ed. It's not just what people think," Jonas said. "It's the law." He couldn't help wondering how much of Ed's bravado had to do with impressing Mary Louise. A lot, he thought.

"Ed," Jonas continued, "even if they never prosecute johns, you're the mayor, and there'd be pressure to make a big deal of it. They probably don't have a case, not if you're more careful going forward, but it would get you a lot of attention that you don't want. And for you, Mary Louise, it could mean a heap of real trouble. They may not arrest you, but they could certainly make it impossible for you to keep working."

"I could live with that," she said, making Jonas wonder again what it was that motivated Mary Louise to engage in her second career. He had assumed she needed the money, which meant it might not be so easy to quit.

"If I had to, I'd move back to Boston," she said, as though reading his mind. But the comment clearly caught Ed by surprise because he looked up sharply.

"I think stopping these people trumps any personal damage to us," she said. "For once in my life, I want to do the right thing.

And I'd almost prefer to do it publicly. I'm tired of living in the shadows because of what other people think."

The determination in her face matched her words, making Jonas wonder about the cause of both her certainty and her desire to play a role in fixing the problem.

"Even if it destroys Craig?" Jonas asked.

Mary Louise didn't answer right away. "Well, I'd sure rather it didn't, and it makes it a tougher decision if we can't protect him," she said, "but there are lots of lives at stake besides Craig's."

"Would Craig see it that way if I put the same question to him?" Jonas asked.

"Craig was the one who started this whole thing, for God's sake," Mary Louise said, raising her voice. "They've worked him over and made him so afraid he's almost willing to believe they've fixed the stent, but it's the fear talking, not the facts. I understand his situation and I don't blame him, but I don't agree."

"Sounds like you do blame him," Jonas said gently. "How can you be so sure they haven't fixed it? Everything you know about the stent is from Craig. Why believe him before and not now?"

"Because no one was threatening him before."

Ed came to her defense. "Even if they fixed it, Jonas, they haven't kept the FDA involved. It's for them to decide whether it's fixed, not Harrison. They're trying to say the ends justify the means, and they don't. Not even if we could believe them about the ends."

Jonas leaned forward and grabbed one of the yellow legal pads that had been left on the table. In his old-time fashion, he began jotting down the summary points of what they knew to be true and then made separate columns for what they suspected based on Craig's information and what Ed and Craig had been told by Harrison. Then Jonas turned to a fresh sheet and wrote the word "Options."

"Let's see now what our choices are," he said, feeling more than a little of the old exhilaration.

"Drop the whole thing," he wrote and Mary Louise immediately objected.

"No way," she said.

Jonas put his pen down and asked her what exactly she thought they should do.

"Is there some way we can go public without hurting Craig?" she asked.

"Not easily. Whatever we did, they could blame him for opening the whole can of worms. He could go tell them that he'd tried to put the kibosh on it, but they probably wouldn't believe him. Even if they think he tried to stop us, they'd know he tried too late. No way to be sure they wouldn't still fire him."

"But they'd have nothing to gain by doing that once it goes public," Ed said. "It would just be vindictive. And couldn't we threaten them with something so they'd have more motivation not to blame him?"

"Like what?"

"Aren't whistleblowers protected by law? Couldn't they get in more trouble with the FDA if they go after him?"

"Maybe. We could explore that. But if they send an anonymous letter about Mary Louise to his kids, it'd be hard to trace it back and prove anything."

"But how likely is it that they'd really do that?" Mary Louise said. "What would be the point once they'd already been exposed?"

"Not much if they're being rational, but if they feel you've destroyed their company, they may not be thinking so rationally," Jonas said.

"It'd be a risk for Craig," Ed said, "but a reasonable one. Maybe the best we could do."

"Same risk for you," Jonas said.

Ed shrugged. He was willing to take it.

"So how do we proceed?" Mary Louise asked, the excitement showing in her voice.

Jonas thought for a moment. "If you want me to help," he said, pausing long enough for them to both agree, "then I'd like to talk to Craig again. First, though, I need to do a little legal research, but that shouldn't take too long. I don't want to do anything unless Craig fully understands what the risks are."

Ed and Mary Louise agreed and that ended the meeting. Ed thanked Jonas and Mary Louise did, too. Jonas left the room first, telling Mary Louise he'd wait for her in the car. When she caught up with him there, she thanked him again and then kissed him on the cheek.

"You keep doing that in public, and people are going to get the wrong idea," he said, not bothering to suppress a smile.

On the drive back to the Sunrise, Mary Louise kept turning around. When Jonas asked her why, she said she must be getting paranoid, but it seemed like they were being followed. He looked in the rearview mirror and saw a green Toyota SUV. It looked like the plates were from Massachusetts. To ease Mary Louise's mind, he took an unnecessary right turn, and the SUV kept going straight. She laughed at her silliness.

When he reached home and turned off the motor, Jonas turned to her. "Mary Louise, you seem awful sure about this. You know the stakes are pretty high. Be terrible for you and a lot of other people if we were wrong about this."

"We're not wrong. I've never been so right in my life."

———•———

Steven Delacourt spent a restless day, upset and uncertain what to do next. He wanted to confront Emma. He was angry at her, but he was also angry at his mother. Why hadn't she told him of the affair? Why had she refused to believe that his father and Emma were together the night of the murder? Why had she believed his father was guilty?

Despite the heat, he went outside and began walking, paying no attention to where he was going. He got completely lost, wandering into the Dixon Mill section of town, now mostly deserted along with the mill and its employees. There were a few apartment buildings still in use and enough low-wage workers to keep them filled. They had no air conditioning and the windows all stood open, allowing sounds of music or domestic arguments to filter down to the streets, which were filled with young children playing or sitting on the steps in the shade.

One young woman who came out to fetch her kids eyed Delacourt suspiciously, but he asked her the way to the village green, and she gestured roughly. "That way," she said and watched to make sure he followed in the direction she pointed.

He stopped in the BJ Drugstore and sat down at the lunch counter. He figured a cheeseburger would be safe enough, and he ate it slowly, washing it down with two Diet Cokes. He left with a bottle of water and a pack of cigarettes, though he hadn't smoked in years.

Two hours later, he was at Billy Bad's Sports Bar and Grill on Elm Street, playing with a beer, sitting alone at one end of the bar, as far away from the other two patrons as he could get. But after the beer and two whiskeys, he realized he wasn't going to get drunk. He ordered another cheeseburger, but didn't have much appetite. It was still light out, and he wasn't any closer to knowing his next move when he started the walk back to the Sunrise.

He wanted to talk to Emma, but what exactly did he want to know? He tried to recall the years he lived in Beacon Junction when his parents were still together, but it came to him only in bits and pieces. A Sunday afternoon drive to the lake. An embarrassing day at school. A scolding for some silly infraction of household rules. He even tried to remember if there were any nights when his father didn't come home and his mother worried, but he couldn't.

So what would he ask Emma if he talked to her? Was his father really with her that night? How did their affair start? Had they loved each other? If so, why didn't they run away together? What kind of person was his father? Did he speak of him when they were together?

He wanted to know all of those things, but he had little confidence that Emma would tell him, or that she'd tell him the truth instead of what she thought he wanted to hear. His mother let her hard feelings for his father color everything she said about him, prejudicing every memory. Why would Emma be different? One way or another she would twist her answers. He'd have to be a fool to trust the woman who broke up his family.

By the time he got back to his room, he'd made up his mind. He packed his bags and wrote a note saying he'd been called away suddenly and to please put the remaining charges on his credit card. No one saw or heard him sneak down the stairs and drive away.

———•———

The next few days passed quickly for Jonas but were interminably slow for Mary Louise, who kept asking what was happening and when Jonas would decide the next move.

He spent hours back at his old law firm, fueling silly speculation that he might be returning to pick up the mantle following Frank's death. He assured everyone that it was nothing of the kind, that he was helping a friend with a problem and needed to use the law library and the various online reference accounts.

There were dozens of FDA regulations for him to review, but he found few that applied to medical devices. It was easy to see why there might be problems, considering how many devices had come on the market in recent years. There was hardly any supervision after the initial approval, and what oversight there was tended to be much less rigorous than for drugs.

It was clear to Jonas that Harrison had a moral obligation to report any serious problems to the FDA, but he could see enough wiggle room in the way the laws were written to provide at least a possible defense if Harrison felt the problems were the fault of procedure rather than actual failures of the devices. He thought the company was vulnerable for not contacting Washington, but that would probably be a small problem. He didn't see that they were open to much civil liability, not even if people died, because the Supreme Court had ruled in 2008 that medical device makers couldn't be sued if the FDA had approved their products.

The whistleblower laws were a bit stickier. The problem for Craig was that he wasn't really blowing the whistle. If he went to the FDA, he could seek whistleblower status, which came with at least limited protection. But he hadn't gone to the FDA. In what Jonas found a great irony, Craig was putting himself at the mercy of Harrison by keeping his concerns in-house. He had, of course, told Mary Louise, but no court was going to give him much credit for that.

When he met with Craig and explained all this to him, Craig didn't react. He'd already figured out as much on his own. Jonas asked him why he had changed his mind and was no longer pushing Harrison to take the stent off the market. He said he had never been that sure in the first place. He told him about Madeleine Priest and the conversations he had with her, and said he decided in the end that he didn't know enough to go to the government. When Jonas asked him if he regretted telling Mary Louise, he said he did.

"Have you told her that?"

"Yes. Last night, in fact, when she told me it was too late to turn back."

Jonas was taken aback. He thought Mary Louise had agreed to let him talk to Craig before saying anything, but he couldn't quite recall an explicit agreement. He wished he'd been clearer.

"What did she say when you told her that?"

"I don't think she really heard me. I think she's convinced I'm trying to back out because of the threats."

"No one can blame you if that's the case."

"It's not. Oh, sure, it's part of it. It certainly forced me to make a decision, but if I were as convinced as Mary Louise, I'd go ahead anyway."

"It's odd that she's more certain than you are when you're the scientist. Hell, you're the one who raised the issue in the first place."

Craig smiled at that. He asked Jonas what he was going to do, and Jonas asked Craig what he wanted him to do.

"Whatever you think is right, Mr. Hawke. I don't know you very well, but I trust you. Besides, it's pretty much out of my hands at this point."

"It probably is. If this Madeleine is a friend, it might not hurt to go talk to her and tell her you've decided to let it go but that other people know. She's probably already heard about Ed's visit anyway. Can't do any harm to let them know you're no longer part of it. Not sure that it will matter at this point, but it might."

They shook hands and wished each other well.

———•———

That night Jonas had his weekly dinner with Nathan and both looked forward to it with a mix of anticipation and trepidation. Jonas had called Nathan after Emma told him about Reinhardt, just to thank him for being so understanding to his mother. Nathan was surprised by the call. It was hardly the kind of thing Jonas was known for, but he was also touched.

The call had lasted only a minute, and they hadn't discussed the substance of Emma's confession. They both figured they would tonight, though neither knew who would bring it up or where it would lead them.

At any rate, Nathan had a lot of news to share with Jonas, and that kept the sensitive subject of Emma's affair at bay.

"I called Carol," he announced as soon as they were seated. Jonas raised an eyebrow but didn't say anything right away.

"We decided to get together this weekend. Maybe start seeing each other. No idea whether it'll go anywhere and still no idea how to deal with the distance thing."

"What brought this on?"

"Hard to say. I guess I was just missing her and called her to talk. It turned out she was missing me, too, so we decided maybe we should give it a try. I don't know. We'll see." He took a sip of his water. Jonas did a little calendar sorting in his head and realized that Nathan must have made the call a day or so after talking to Emma.

"This didn't have anything to do with what your mother told you, did it?"

Nathan seemed surprised. "Why would it?"

Jonas let it drop and said he'd always liked Carol and he hoped they could work something out.

"I know," Nathan said. "I hope so, too."

Their salads came and they stopped talking for a few minutes while they ate. Both seemed far away in thought.

"Had an interesting development at the paper today," Nathan said after a while. "An anonymous letter."

Jonas stopped his fork in midair.

"It was like a high school kid would send," Nathan said. "Telling me that Ed Riley was seeing Mary Louise and the *Clarion* ought to tell everyone so they'd be run out of town."

"I don't suppose you brought it with you."

"Sure did. I didn't want to leave it in the office, but I never got a chance to go over to the safe deposit box."

He took a plastic bag out of his pocket. "I know that's dramatic, but I thought if it gets nasty, well, who knows, maybe at some point, it could be useful if there are fingerprints, although I doubt there are any."

It was flat in the bag and Jonas could read it without taking it out. It referred to Mary Louise as a whore and mocked Ed for "having to pay for it." Jonas handed it back in disgust.

"What are you going to do?"

Nathan shrugged. "Nothing. I don't see that there's a story in it for us. They're both adults, and there's no reason to think it affects how Ed does his job as mayor. He's not even married, and he sure as hell never ran on a family values platform."

Jonas breathed a silent sigh of relief. "What about the fact that prostitution is illegal?"

"I'm not a cop. Not my job to expose everybody who runs a red light, is it? How's this any different? Because he's the mayor? Some might go with it for the prurient interest, but not me. That's never been the *Clarion*'s thing. And I wouldn't do that to Mary Louise if I could help it."

Jonas smiled. "Sounds like the right decision to me," he said, feeling a little pride creep into his voice. "But I have to tell you there may be a little more to this, and there may come a time when you do want to get involved in the bigger issue."

Nathan leaned forward. "What bigger issue?"

"This isn't the first of these I've seen. Ed Riley got one, too. And another one of Mary Louise's—patrons—got one, too. It's tied to a mess they got involved in. Someone's trying to scare them off."

"And I bet that explains why you've been so busy—and down at the law office so much."

Jonas smiled. "You newspaper guys know everything that goes on."

"I wish." He pushed his empty salad plate to the side. "So what's it about? What's the big issue?"

Jonas leaned back. "I'm sorry. I can't tell you, at least not yet. There may come a time when it's appropriate, but for now I'd have to counsel my clients not to talk to you. And of course, I can't."

"Your clients? Are you serious?"

"Unofficial clients, but clients. Let's just say I'm advising them a little at this point."

"And here I am sharing all my secrets."

"I promise you'll be the first to know."

"I better be."

Their dinners came and the conversation moved on to other things, but soon there was nothing left to talk about but Emma.

"Anything you want to ask me?" Jonas said by way of introducing the subject.

Nathan smiled and shook his head. "Not unless you want to talk about it."

"You look at me any different tonight? No horns on my head or anything?"

"It's none of my business, Dad. It's between you and Mom."

Jonas sat back and looked his son in the eye and saw that he meant it. He felt the pride again. This was quite a young man he'd brought into the world.

They paid the check and left the restaurant, but Jonas suggested they walk a while, signaling to Nathan that the conversation wasn't over.

"I'll just tell you a few things," Jonas said as soon as they were alone. "You know those were tough times for us for a lot of reasons. Sometimes I'm amazed when I look back that we worked through it. And we did work through it, even came out stronger on the other end. My drinking was a far bigger problem—probably far less excusable than anything your mother did. That's because it hurt you and Sally as well as your mother. Her affair didn't, and it'd be a shame if it hurt you or your relationships with her at this late date. And if you get a chance, you might tell that to your sister. Gently, mind you, but it'd be good for her to hear it from you if you can see your way to it."

Nathan said he'd already talked to Sally, though briefly, and knew she was upset but that he was sure she'd come around.

"I think so, too, but I hope it doesn't take too long."

"I'll do what I can to help."

"I know you will." Jonas turned and started to say good night, but Nathan took his father in his arms and gave him a hug. They stood there like that not saying anything.

"I'm very proud of you, Nathan."

"No, Dad, I'm the one who's very proud of you. And very lucky to have you as my father. Don't think you let us down. If you stumbled, it was perfectly understandable, and more important, it was temporary. We'd never hold that against you."

Jonas walked away before he started to cry.

CHAPTER 24

Sean Anderson was feeling good, like a man who'd been wandering for days lost in the woods and suddenly discovered what looked like a way out. The brush was clearing, and he could move forward again, confident of the direction he was taking.

For one thing, Craig Whitney had backed off. He'd told Madeleine that while he still had doubts, he could see that maybe they had fixed the stent problem and that it was better to focus on the future than dig up mistakes from the past. He made her promise to tell him if new problems arose, and she told him if they did, she'd be the first to blow the whistle.

There was still some uncertainty about Ed Riley, but weeks had passed without any contact, and Anderson was pretty sure he had persuaded him that the rumors he'd heard were inaccurate. Even if Riley might be inclined to push, he had to know it could backfire and do more harm than good for Beacon Junction.

Another indication had been the Board of Selectmen's unanimous vote to give Harrison approval to build the new plant in town. In the end, there'd barely been any debate, which must have rankled Nathan Hawke. Put him in his place, that's for sure.

Anderson related all this at a meeting that morning with

Parker, Madeleine, and Winter. Madeleine and Winter congratulated Anderson on a job well done, while Parker just gave him one of his smirks, as though he knew it all along. He was a strange one, Anderson thought, useful in many ways, but impossible to fully trust. You always had to be sure his interests were the same as yours and then not ask too many questions.

Anderson was now back in his office, standing at the window and enjoying the view of the Harrison campus. The grass was a little parched, he noticed, and wondered if the groundskeepers were watering enough. The unusually hot and dry summer had sapped the local water supply, and there were new guidelines in place on usage, but they were voluntary and Anderson didn't want the grass to die because of them. He'd speak to someone.

He went out to tell his secretary, but before he could say anything, she told him he'd had a call from Jonas Hawke, who wanted to set up a meeting. She said the name as though he should know it.

"Is he related to Nathan Hawke?" he asked.

"He's Nathan's father."

"He work for the newspaper, too?"

She laughed, which was rare. Betty Flaherty, who had been with Harrison for thirty-two years, was very prim and proper. "No," she said. "He's retired now. He's a lawyer. Was quite well known in his day, all across the state."

"What does he want with me?"

"He said he was doing a little volunteer work for the town, that he wanted to follow up on that matter Ed Riley brought to your attention awhile back. Said you'd know what he meant."

Anderson told her to call him back and set up a meeting as soon as possible, even if it meant canceling other appointments. He turned and started to walk back into his office, the dry grass a distant memory.

———•———

"Afternoon," Jonas said, "thanks for seeing me so soon."

"Betty said you made it sound important."

Jonas looked in Anderson's face, letting him know he knew that was a lie. In fact, he'd been intentionally casual with Betty, whom he'd known for years. They both went to the First Congregational Church, and Betty had been chairman of the bereavement committee when Lucas was killed. She'd been extremely kind.

Anderson gestured to the couch and chairs, told Jonas to have a seat, and asked if he'd like a drink.

"Bottled water would be great," said Jonas, who, in truth, thought the tap water in Beacon Junction was as good as it got. Jonas looked to the couch but then caught sight of the little connecting conference room, a more neutral site, and asked if they could sit in there. "I got some papers I'd like to spread out and it might be easier." Jonas had brought a briefcase, but there wasn't anything in it except a yellow legal pad and a few notes. Anderson wasn't the only one capable of a little game playing.

Anderson reached into his private bar and pulled out a bottle of water and two glasses, showing no signs of pique. "I hope you don't mind if I have something a little stronger. Ice?"

"No, thanks."

Anderson poured himself a little scotch and carried both glasses into the conference room and put the lights on, shoving the dimmer to the brightest setting.

"What can I do for you, Mr. Hawke?"

Jonas made a show of taking out his legal pad and two pens and placing them on the table before answering. He pulled a pair of reading glasses out of his suit jacket, which he had declined to take off, and put them on. They were half-glasses that allowed him to look over the lens at Anderson, who showed no outward signs of annoyance at the slow pace. Jonas admired his control.

"Well, Mr. Anderson—"

"Call me Sean."

"Ed Riley asked my advice on that matter he discussed with you, and I've agreed to offer my services."

"Does that mean you're acting as his attorney? Or the town's attorney?"

"Well, I'm retired now, and I don't expect any remuneration for my time, but I'm still a member of the bar and licensed in the state of Vermont to practice."

"I'll take that as a yes."

Jonas waved his arm around the room. "It's just the two of us," he said. "You're not under oath and there's no one taking down your words."

"Mr. Hawke, exactly what—"

"You can call me Jonas. Seems only fair if I can call you Sean."

"Mr. Hawke, what exactly do you want from me?"

"Is the CARC 2008 safe?"

Anderson sat back in his chair. "As I told Ed, there were some problems in the beginning. Mostly due to doctor error in inserting the stent. We've taken steps to improve the instructions and to make the stent almost foolproof, even for incompetent doctors."

"Is Dr. Sydney Meyers incompetent?"

"I'm sorry?" Anderson said, with genuine confusion in his voice.

"Dr. Sydney Meyers. He's a cardiologist. Was president of the American College of Cardiology and is on the faculty at the Harvard Medical School. He put a CARC 2008 in Frank Hargrave, who was my partner for twenty-five years, and within days Frank was dead. I'm just wondering if Dr. Meyers is one of the surgeons you describe as incompetent?"

"So this is personal?"

"No, this is legal. I'm just questioning your assertion that the only problem was incompetent doctors."

Anderson shook his head and sat back in his chair. "Look, I'm sorry about your partner, but I don't believe the stent was responsible for his or any other deaths. If there'd been a problem in his case, we would have known about it."

"So there *were* problems."

"I said there were a few problems with the actual insertion of the stent, not with its performance. In any event, we've made improvements to be super-sure. We wouldn't be selling the CARC if we didn't believe it was safe, and the FDA wouldn't have approved it."

"Wouldn't be the first time the FDA approved something that turned out wrong."

"No, it wouldn't. But the point is we are selling an approved product which is of huge benefit to thousands of people. It has probably saved countless lives."

"Didn't save Frank Hargrave," Jonas said, leaning forward.

"And I'm sorry about that, but I can't bring him back to life, and I don't accept any responsibility for his death."

"I guess that means you won't be willingly compensating his widow."

"I won't be compensating his widow willingly or unwillingly. Are you familiar with *Wyeth v. Levine*, in which the Supreme Court ruled manufacturers can't be sued for medical devices approved by—"

"I'm very familiar with it, thank you. I'm also familiar with the Safe Medical Devices Act of 1990, and subsequent amendments, which require you to report all serious problems with any of your devices to the FDA. If there's new evidence calling into question the original approval—if you lied about the data and got approval under false pretenses, for example—your immunity under Wyeth might be null and void."

"There is no evidence calling into question the original approval."

"Have you reported the problems to the FDA?"

"Our communications are confidential, but we've been very careful to follow the law. As I've told you repeatedly, we don't believe there were any deaths attributable to the stent."

"You don't believe there were deaths?"

"All reports we have involving the death of patients who had the CARC 2008 have been examined, and in every case, we believe the stent played no role in the subsequent death."

"But according to my information, you didn't report the problems."

"The 'problems,' as you call them, were mostly with the procedure, not the stent. The FDA regulations give us a lot of leeway on that."

"They do?"

"It's a gray area that allows us to use our expertise and judgment."

"The regs clearly state you have to report serious injuries to the FDA. I don't see much gray area in that. And even if what you say were true, how would it look to the public to know you were sweeping the problems under the rug?"

"We're not hiding anything. We've taken extra steps to make it easier to use the stent so there won't be any more problems. If I thought there was any purpose to disseminating additional information, I would. The greater risk is panic. Look, Jonas," and here he lowered and softened his voice. "We're not villains. We're trying to do what's right. We *are* doing what's right. Yes, we might be vulnerable to bad publicity, but the end result would be for people to stop using a stent that I'm absolutely sure is better than anything else on the market. It has saved thousands of lives."

"It didn't save Frank Hargrave's life."

"So you said. Twice now. Look, I'm genuinely sorry about that, and if Mrs. Hargrave is in need, maybe we could do something for her unofficially, as long as it didn't set a precedent or suggest we were responsible."

Jonas sat back and glared. "I'm not looking for a bribe."

Anderson raised his hand as if to say he was sorry. "I didn't mean it that way."

"And while you're at it, enough with the threats. If anything makes me think you have something to hide, it's those."

"What threats? What are you talking about?"

Jonas tried to judge whether Anderson was lying. He didn't think he was. He reached back into his briefcase to pull out the note Ed Riley had been sent. Then he hesitated. If Anderson wasn't responsible, he didn't want him to have the information it contained about Ed and Mary Louise. He left the note where it was.

"Ed Riley got an anonymous note threatening to expose some embarrassing information about him if he didn't back off. Another anonymous note about Ed was sent to the *Clarion*," Jonas said. He had decided earlier not to mention Craig in any context.

Anderson's eyes widened at the mention of the *Clarion*. "Does the *Clarion* know about the stent?"

"The note didn't say anything about the stent. It was aimed at hurting Ed, not Harrison, which was why the evidence points to you being the source."

"Have you told your son about the stent?"

"No," he said, "Not yet."

"Can I see the notes?"

"No. If it didn't come from you, I don't want you to know the nature of the threat. Suffice it to say they contain a threat to make some personal information public."

Anderson stood up. "I need another drink. You sure I can't get one for you?" Jonas shook his head and sat thinking until Anderson returned.

"Jonas, you may be right. The threat may have come from here. But I promise you it was without my knowledge or consent, and I promise to get to the bottom of it."

Jonas nodded and Anderson asked what he could do to persuade Jonas that the stent's problems had been fixed. Anderson asked if Jonas knew Craig Whitney, and when Jonas didn't say anything, he said Craig had been the strongest critic at first but had been won over. He said if Jonas didn't know him, he would encourage Craig to tell him everything he knew.

Jonas said he might take him up on that, but in the meantime he'd appreciate it if Anderson could tell him the whole story: When did they first get reports about problems, and how had they handled them? How many incidents? How many deaths? What improvements had they made? What testing had they done to be so certain the fixes were all that was needed?

Anderson answered each question carefully, frequently consulting his files and showing Jonas actual reports and data. After an hour, Jonas's basic questions had been answered, but he kept coming up with new ones, mostly because he wanted to keep Anderson talking. As a lawyer, he rarely had the chance to question someone like this, one-on-one without an opposing lawyer present, and with no one taking down every word. That of course meant Anderson wasn't under oath, as he would have been in a formal deposition, but this was more valuable. Jonas felt he had an unusual chance to read his opponent, to try to gauge how honest he was being, and how much of the story he was holding back.

At first Anderson had been cautious, measuring his words, even stopping to make two calls that Jonas assumed were to an attorney. But after three scotches, Anderson was talking more freely and Jonas was beginning to like the man. He had known some very good liars, and he was smart enough to know it was impossible to tell for sure, but he still trusted his instinct, and he liked what his instinct was telling him.

"Honest to God, Jonas," Anderson said after two and a half hours of talking about the stent. "Some may feel we were wrong not to tell the FDA, though I'm confident we can defend our decision not to. But I really wouldn't keep selling the stent if I weren't as sure as possible that we'd fixed the problem and that we were doing more good than harm for our patients. No job means that much to me."

"What's the risk to the people who have the earlier version still in their bodies?"

"None. As I've said, the only problems came at the time of the procedure, not weeks later."

"Are there any defective catheters still out there? Mightn't a doctor be unaware of your improvements?"

"There's only a slight risk of that. We've sent new instructions to everyone."

"How can you be sure they got them?"

"We worked very hard to do this right."

Jonas sat back, and the two men looked into each other's eyes. Jonas couldn't read much beyond exhaustion at the difficult conversation.

"Frankly," Jonas said, "I'm inclined to believe you, though I think it should be up to the FDA to decide. You should have told them."

"We don't see it that way. Going through those channels would have caused unnecessary delay and maybe even panic, denying the stent to new patients and causing immeasurable economic harm to Harrison and Beacon Junction."

"The anonymous notes," Jonas reminded him. "They had to come from Harrison."

Anderson sighed. "They probably did. But they didn't come from me or with my authorization. How about I give you my word that I'll track it down and fire the person responsible? I already have a pretty good idea who it is."

Jonas nodded again. "Do that and let me know. I'm going to think on all of this. I won't do anything without telling you in advance."

"What about Craig Whitney? Do you want to talk to him?"

Jonas nodded. "Probably. And maybe your head of research, Madeleine Priest."

It was dusk when Jonas climbed into the Explorer and realized he should have called Emma to tell her he'd be late for dinner.

———•———

The next morning Anderson fired Parker. He didn't bother confronting him about the anonymous threats because he had no proof and didn't want to argue.

"We just have different styles of operating," he said. "I'm not comfortable with your approach, and I don't want to worry about you doing things I don't approve of."

"What approach are you talking about?"

"The black-and-white-do-whatever's-necessary-no-matter-who-gets-hurt approach."

"You used to be pretty agreeable to that."

"True enough, but I'm not comfortable with it now."

"You disappoint me, Sean. I never thought you would be so easily intimidated."

Anderson offered a far more generous severance package than Parker's contract required and a promise of a good recommendation in exchange for Parker's silence on all matters having to do with Harrison, and especially the stent. The bonus portion of the severance would be paid out over time, so that it could be canceled if Parker violated the agreement.

"And that means you call off any outside investigations you may have started. Cease and desist with all efforts to influence how this plays out."

"I know you're going to regret this someday," Parker said. But he accepted Anderson's terms.

Anderson then called Madeleine and told her about his conversation with Jonas.

"What do you think he'll do?" she asked.

"He's a hard man to read. I think he heard me, and he'll think about it." He told her that Jonas's partner had the CARC 2008 and had died. "Can you find out what the cause of death was?"

She said she'd try and Anderson gave her Dr. Meyers's name.

Next Anderson called Craig and asked him to come by. Craig was visibly nervous, so Anderson moved immediately to put him at ease.

"I think I owe you an apology. I gather someone at Harrison has been sending out anonymous threats over the stent. I'm guessing that you may have been the target of one of them. If you were, I want to assure you that I knew nothing about it, and I promise it'll stop now. The last thing I'm interested in is any retribution."

Craig nodded, thanked Anderson, and got up to leave, but Anderson wasn't finished.

"I got a visit yesterday from a lawyer named Jonas Hawke. I won't ask you if you know him, but I suspect that one way or another some of his information came from you. In any event, I told him that if he wanted to talk about it, he was welcome to call you. My hope is that you now believe we've fixed the stent problem and that you'll help me convince him of that. But I'm not asking you to say anything to him you don't believe. Do what you think is right."

Craig nodded. It was a lot to absorb. "I'll do what I can to help," he said.

Now it was Anderson's turn to say thanks. They shook hands. "I'm sorry I made this so difficult for everybody," Craig said. "I was just trying to do the right thing."

"I know," Anderson said. "It doesn't matter now. All that matters is how it turns out. I had my own doubts at times, but I really think we're correct on this. I only hope they let us go forward with our plans."

Chapter 25

B ehind the Sunrise, in the center of the garden Emma had created, stood a small gazebo that Sally's husband, Jake, had constructed. Mary Louise and Ed had taken to sitting there on quiet afternoons, surrounded by an array of late blooming astilbe, both red and yellow, a low row of spirea, and alternating beds of marigolds, celosia, blanket flowers, dusty miller, and melampodium.

The gazebo, being in the back, was not what you'd call public, but the move from Mary Louise's room to the outdoors was still a significant statement of how their relationship had changed, with them spending more time together just to talk and share each other's company without sex or an exchange of money. They still had the other kind of meetings, and Mary Louise knew that their dual-level relationship couldn't go on much longer. If nothing else, she had to deal with Ed's declarations of love, which had become more frequent. She still hadn't responded directly, but on this August day, Ed seemed determined to give her no choice.

They started the visit talking about the situation at Harrison. Jonas had filled them in on his meeting with Anderson, and Craig had told Mary Louise about the assurances that the anonymous threats would end with no harmful consequences.

She remained as determined as ever to make the issue public and didn't understand Jonas's ambivalence. He was still "mulling" it, as he put it. Ed sided with Mary Louise, but she suspected it was because of their relationship rather than out of a genuine conviction.

There was a light breeze, and Ed suggested they go for a walk. She agreed, though they rarely let themselves be seen alone together in Beacon Junction. Since Boston, they'd shared several other outings but always to some far-off place to protect their privacy.

When they reached the end of the block and turned the corner, Ed took her hand. She smiled but couldn't help asking him if he was sure he wanted to be seen holding hands.

"Yes, I'm very sure. In fact, I've been thinking a lot about us lately. Mostly about how I don't like having to sneak around and how I don't think it's fair to either of us."

She heard the catch in his voice and suddenly knew what was coming. Her reaction was close to panic.

He turned to look at her and took her other hand. "Mary Louise, will you marry me?"

A tear came to her eye, and she dropped her reserve long enough to give him a long kiss and a longer hug.

But she didn't answer him.

"You don't have to give me an answer now," he said. "I know it's all happened very quickly, and I know it's complicated. Just promise me you'll think about it."

She told him how flattered she was and that of course she would think about it. "But have you really given it enough thought?" she asked.

"Of course I have."

"Ed, do you have any idea what it would be like for you if this small town—filled with people you grew up with—found out you were going to marry me?"

"I don't care what anybody else thinks or says. I only care about you."

"You have to be realistic and honest with yourself about this. There'll come a time when it gets to you."

"Some things are more important."

He said it with such certainty that it only convinced her he hadn't thought it through.

"I love you, Mary Louise. I want to spend the rest of my life with you. That's all that matters."

"Oh, Ed, I love you, too," she said for the first time, and then bit her tongue wondering whether it was true. "I wish it were all that simple."

"It can be," he said. "If we both want it to be. I don't want to have to share you with anyone else." He promised to give her time and not rush her decision, and as if to prove it, he changed the subject as they continued their walk. But soon they were silent, both lost in their own thoughts.

Back at the Sunrise, she invited him up to her room and they made love. For the first time, he didn't offer to pay.

———•———

Nathan waited until Tuesday to invite Sally for lunch, knowing that was generally a slow day at the Sunrise so she'd be less likely to turn him down. They met at Cindy's. Nathan ordered a bacon cheeseburger medium rare, and Sally tried the special of the day, vegetable lasagna.

"Mary Louise's cooking, it's not," she said after the first bite. "But it'll do."

Nathan was considerably more enthusiastic about his burger, having already wolfed down several bites. The French fries were pretty good, too, especially with the extra salt. He was lucky to have inherited his father's genes and still had a boyishly thin frame. Not even a sign of a paunch. Sally, on the other hand, had been watching her weight all her life, struggling to stay within reach of an average figure.

"So how's Carol?" she asked.

"She's good," he said. "Really good. I didn't realize how much I missed her."

"Yes, you did. That's why you called her."

He smiled. "Yeah, you're right."

"So what are you going to do?"

"We're trying to figure it out. Might try a compromise. Maybe move there but keep my place and spend a couple nights a week here so I won't lose touch with the town. See how bad the commute is."

She told him that sounded expensive. "Maybe we can find a bed for you at the Sunrise."

"Oh, I think that place is full enough without me."

"What, you don't want to move back in with Mom and Dad and Sis?" she joked. "I might even have Mary Louise's room free."

"She's leaving?" He remembered the note he'd received.

"Not sure, but Ed Riley asked her to marry him."

"No shit. And she accepted?"

"She's thinking about it. I think she might if it weren't for fear of how people will talk."

"I didn't realize you guys were such good friends."

"Actually, she mostly confides in Dad. And of course, he won't say much about it."

"Dad? Are he and Mary Louise that close?"

"Oh yeah, real close." Then she looked at him and laughed. "That's a strange thought, isn't it? Although maybe it'd serve Mom right."

He smiled. "Frankly, that's what I wanted to talk to you about."

"So I figured. Big brother wants to give little sister a lecture."

"It's not like that," he said. "But from what I hear, you've been a little hard on her."

She was silent and when he looked at her, a tear fell from her eye, right down into the lasagna.

"So she's human," he said. "Those were pretty rough days for them."

"For them? What about for us? And don't forget, she was cheating on him before Lucas died. What was so rough then?"

"Maybe it's none of our business," he said, but without much conviction.

She sighed and took a sip of her water. "I just feel so betrayed. So deceived. She wouldn't have even told us if Steven Delacourt hadn't shown up."

He put down the French fry he was holding, wiped his fingers on the napkin, and reached across to take her hand but didn't say anything.

"I'll be okay," she said. "I just need some time to get used to it. It feels like if their marriage—which I always thought was perfect—was in trouble, then what chance is there for the rest of us?"

He didn't know what to say to that. "No one can know what anybody else's marriage is like. Not even the children. Nobody has a perfect marriage, but there are some damn good ones. It takes a lot of work. Look at Carol and me. We're not even married yet, and it feels like we've been through a hundred crises already."

"Yet? Are you thinking of getting married?"

He smiled sheepishly. "I guess. A little. Have to see how this new arrangement works out."

That got them onto more neutral ground, and they finished lunch without talking anymore about their parents.

When Sally got back to the Sunrise, she went looking for Emma and found her in the garden, putting powder on a rose bush that still had a little rust. She asked her if she wanted to go shopping at the new Macy's that had just opened up in Brattleboro.

"Kind of a long drive, isn't it?" Emma said.

"That'd be good. Give us a chance to talk."

Emma said she'd be glad to, and they made a date for the next morning.

———◆———

When Emma got back on Wednesday, it was late afternoon and she was exhausted, but it was a happy exhaustion. She found Jonas in the bedroom, reading *Anna Karenina*.

"I thought you were supposed to read trashy books in the summer and save the heavy stuff for winter," she said.

"Maybe that's why I've read the first five pages four times already." He put the book down. "So how'd it go?"

"Good. We had a nice time. A nice talk."

He could see she was tired and didn't press. She shook off her shoes and lay down on the bed.

"How about you?" she asked. "You decide how you're going to save the world?"

"Maybe. I spent a good part of the day with Ed and Mary Louise, talking it through again, but it's beginning to feel like we're saying the same things over and over."

Jonas and Emma had been talking about it a lot, too. He had told her all about his meeting with Sean Anderson, his talks with Craig, and a meeting he'd had the day before with Madeleine Priest.

All his life he had treated Emma as a confidant and sounding board. He'd never been one of those men who could leave work at the office, and when something was bothering him or he had a big decision to make, there was no one he wanted to talk it through with more than Emma. She wasn't a lawyer and couldn't provide the same kind of advice as Frank Hargrave, but she knew Jonas and his sense of right and wrong. The very few times he kept her out of his thinking, he came to regret it.

"Is it strictly up to you, then?" she asked. There had always been a question as to what Mary Louise would do if Jonas decided not to make the problem public. Would she act on her own?

"She says she trusts my judgment, but I think that's easy to say in the abstract."

"And Ed?"

"I think Ed thinks we should let it rest and see how it plays out. But he's so smitten, she could probably talk him into taking on al-Qaeda by himself if he thought it would get her to marry him."

Emma laughed. "I guess he really is in love with her. I must admit it still surprises me that he wants to marry her."

"You mean why buy the cow when the milk's free?"

"Hardly free," she said, laughing. "And no, that's not what I was thinking. I just have trouble seeing the two of them together living happily ever after."

He thought about that for a while and how relationships were so unpredictable. It reminded him of Emma's morning with Sally.

"So are you and Sally friends again?"

"I think we'll get through this. She's hurt. And I understand that. I think it shook her up, made her question what she can trust and what might be phony."

"That's harsh. There's nothing phony about us."

Emma shrugged. "Did you know she had lunch with Nathan yesterday? She thinks he and Carol are going to make it work this time. She said he's even thinking about marriage."

"Really? I hadn't realized they were moving that quickly."

"Me, neither," she said, then after a pause: "But what about Harrison? Which way are you leaning?"

"First, I should tell you that Dr. Meyers called. Priest got in touch with him and Meyers said it wasn't the stent. Frank got some unusual infection that had nothing to do with the procedure or the stent."

"That's one case."

"Yeah, I know. I took the opportunity to ask Meyers about the whole issue, but he wouldn't say much. He uses the stent a lot and never had a problem and didn't know anybody who had. Said Madeleine Priest told him about the improvements they'd made, and he thought that was all to the better. She didn't confess to any errors on Harrison's part."

"So that wasn't much help."

"Took Frank out of the equation. Certainly doesn't answer all the questions, but he did make me feel a little better. And he explained why the Harrison stent was better than most. Said not every doctor agrees, but it's his first choice. I asked him plum out how he'd feel if it were taken off the market, and he said he'd be disappointed if there wasn't a good reason."

"That enough for you?"

"Not by itself, but it's a weight on one side of the scale. There is evidence that they've improved it and that it wasn't terrible to begin with."

"And on the other hand?"

"What they did seems wrong. There were serious injuries. The intent of the law is pretty clear. They were supposed to tell the FDA about the problems, and they didn't. But at the same time, the FDA might have been fine with their plan to fix the problem. And there's no civil liability on their part so it's not like anyone's losing a chance to recover damages. Supreme Court fixed that."

He got up off the bed and walked over to the window, a habit he had when he was nervous about how Emma would take what he was about to say. But he turned back to her before he continued.

"Anyway, I'm going to let Anderson handle it his way. It's not the way I generally like to do things, but considering the harm that can come from doing it by the book, this is one time I'm inclined to forget the book."

He could see the words hit her like a gust of cold wind.

"You're disappointed," he said.

She didn't say anything.

"I didn't know you felt that strongly," he said. "You never gave me an opinion before."

"It's the words you used," she said finally. "It's exactly the phrase you used when you told me you didn't want to use me as an alibi for Richard Reinhardt."

He sat down on the bed. "Oh," was all he could say as he spread out next to her.

"I'm sorry," she said. "I didn't mean it the way it sounded."

"No, you're right. It's the old ends-justify-the-means argument. Only it assumes we know the ends, and sometimes we only think we do or only partially do."

"It's okay," she said. "You should follow your instincts. Just be sure."

"No," he said again. "You made an important point. It's thinking I'm smarter than the law again. I won't do that. Not again."

"We all do it sometimes. We'd never think of turning Mary Louise in."

"That's different."

"Is it?"

"Yes. Whole 'nother matter, though don't ask me to explain why," he said with a smile. "I'll tell Anderson tomorrow that he has to tell the FDA or I will."

She turned toward him and put her head on his chest, but he lifted her chin and kissed her. They both opened their mouths slightly and held the kiss. Within a few seconds he reached down and began unbuttoning her blouse. She laughed in nervous embarrassment, but he didn't stop.

"It's been years since we made love in daylight," she said.

They stopped and undressed, each a little shy about what age had done to their bodies, exposed fully despite the drawn shades.

They made love tenderly and lovingly. Like two people who had lived and loved life together. When they finished they held each other tight.

"We ought to do that more often," Emma said.

"You're right," he replied. "As usual."

CHAPTER 26

Mary Louise was ecstatic. No other way to describe it. "Oh, it feels so good to have you on our side," she told Jonas. "I know it's the right thing to do."

Ed was nervous about the consequences, but any reservations he felt were overwhelmed by the joy he took in seeing Mary Louise so happy. "I trust you, Jonas."

Craig was ambivalent, perhaps disappointed, and still worried that the fallout would destroy Harrison and cost him his job.

Anderson was devastated. "Jonas, please. This is a mistake. We fixed it. There's no need to do this."

"It's not for us to decide, Sean. You need to bring the FDA in and let them handle it."

"But that will do more harm than good."

"Maybe, but the law is the law and it says you have to report serious injuries. You didn't do that."

"But we had a good reason. We knew what we were doing. Our intentions were good."

"Sean, that's my point. Your intentions don't matter. No one's above the law. We all have moments when we think we know better, but it's not up to us to pick and choose which laws we obey. We may think we can predict the outcome, but we can't. Eventually, you get in trouble if you think you can, even when you have the best of intentions."

Anderson gave up after that. "Give me a few days to put things together and go to the FDA," he said. "It will be better for everyone if we offer it up instead of having you go public."

Jonas gave Anderson a week, telling him he would tell the *Clarion* and let them break the story after that. Nathan agreed to hold back that long, and he let Anderson know he would call the FDA for comment in a week and write the story after he had their reaction.

"What about Delacourt?" Nathan asked Jonas. "Does he know about this? I should call his mother for comment."

"I'll mention that to Anderson," Jonas said. "Best if they hear it from him if they haven't already."

Jonas's last call was to Nancy. He knew it would reopen wounds just beginning to heal, but he thought she should hear it from him before the news went public.

"I don't think it had anything to do with Frank's problems," he told her after he had explained it all.

"But how can you be sure?"

"Well, we can't be certain, but the timing is wrong. Plus Dr. Meyers said it was an infection unrelated to the stent."

"But you wouldn't expect them to admit it."

Jonas sighed to himself. "Well, the FDA's going to investigate. I'll make sure they know about Frank and take a look at it, but I really don't think they'll find a connection."

She thanked him, but it sounded tentative. He made a mental note to follow up with a visit to try to explain it better, but he knew he couldn't give her what she was really looking for: closure. Only time would provide that.

———•———

By the next evening, Jonas was at peace with himself. He wasn't sure that what he was doing would produce the best outcome for Harrison, its patients, or Beacon Junction, but he was willing to trust that the FDA would act fairly, and he was willing to see how it played out.

He sat alone on the porch, *Anna Karenina* by his side. The September air was cool but welcome, and Jonas was enjoying a second pipe. Nobody needed to know. He used a new lighter that Mary Louise had given him as a present, a fancy-dancy thing that came in a leather case. Matches worked better, but he was trying not to be ungrateful.

When he finished the pipe, he took a short walk around the neighborhood, feeling generally pleased, at least until he came home and noticed the green Toyota SUV with the Massachusetts plates about a block from the Sunrise.

———•———

Mary Louise had been in a good mood since learning the news. She was frankly proud of herself for taking a stand and persuading Ed and Jonas that she was right. She was the only one in the group to have no misgivings.

It was about ten and she was sitting in her nightgown, brushing her hair and getting ready for bed and thinking about the menu for tomorrow's breakfast when she heard a knock on her inner door. She had given Ed a key to the outside door and assumed it was him, though it was unusual for him to come by so late or without calling.

But by the time that occurred to her, she had opened the door, and there was the client from Boston.

"You never returned my call," he said.

"How dare you!" She tried to slam the door, but his foot was already inside, and it sprang open.

"Now that's not very friendly of you."

"Get out before I scream," she cried, but he moved swiftly to grab her and cover her mouth, knocking a lamp over in the process. "Don't even try," he said. "You may have won the fight with Harrison, but I still know who half your clients are. How'd you like the whole world to know you're just a two-bit whore? And that includes your mother in the anything-but Paradise Nursing Home?"

She stopped fighting him as what he said registered, and he let her go.

"You work for them," was all she could say. The resignation in her voice told him he had won.

"Used to work for them. They seem to have lost interest in you. But I haven't."

She looked around the room, hoping for something she could use as a weapon.

"Don't worry, all I want is a freebie, and then I'll be on my way. What's one more or less to someone like you?" And with that he grabbed the front of her nightgown and tore it away in one motion.

"I don't mean to be dramatic, but if I were you I'd stop there."

They both turned to the door where Jonas stood. Mary Louise realized she was naked to the waist and pulled her nightgown together.

"Well, if it isn't the proprietor of this little whorehouse. The good lawyer turned madam in his old age. Do you expect me to shake in my boots at the sight of you?"

"No, but I've already called the police." He held up his hand to show the cell phone. "They should be here any minute."

"You sure you want that publicity?"

"Don't be a fool," Jonas said. "You think they don't know?"

Mary Louise actually managed a half smile. "You already know the mayor's a client," she said. "So is the chief of police.

How do you think he's going to react when he gets here?"

The man from Boston took a few seconds to consider that. He didn't seem to believe it, but apparently he wasn't willing to take the chance. He left.

Jonas locked the door after him and Mary Louise burst into tears. He went over to the bed to comfort her. She moved into his arms, still holding her nightgown closed.

"I better get a robe on before the police come."

"They're not coming," Jonas said. "Not unless a pipe lighter can send out an SOS." He held up the leather-cased lighter. "You know I don't have a cell phone."

She laughed. "That's okay. Sheriff Potter's not a client, in case you were wondering."

They heard a knock on the door and looked at each other as if to ask who that might be.

"Is everything all right in there?" Emma called through the door. "I thought I heard something break."

"Everything's fine," Jonas said and they both burst out laughing, knowing how it might sound to Emma to hear Jonas inside. They opened the door and explained, but only up to a point. "A little trouble, but it's all sorted out now."

Emma looked at Mary Louise's torn nightgown and then at Jonas. "Good thing you got pants on or you'd have some serious explaining to do." She winked at Mary Louise as they both said good night.

———•———

Anderson spent a week in Washington, accompanied by a team of experts on the CARC 2008 and Harrison's general counsel, who was still smarting because she'd been left in the dark on so much of what had happened. First, Anderson met with Catherine Delacourt and explained the problem and his plan to go to the FDA. He tried to fudge the timing, but when she asked him point blank when they first suspected a problem, he told her the truth.

The FDA gave him and his team a thorough grilling, promised to study the data and render a decision. In the meantime, they put a hold on sales of the CARC.

"You know, if you'd come to us right off, we might have been happy to let you handle this on your own," one official told him off the record. "We always triage these cases and Harrison's good record would have gone a long way to help you. But now that the press knows about it, we're going to have to take a very close look."

Before heading back to Beacon Junction, Anderson went back to Catherine and gave her an update. She listened impassively and then told Anderson she wanted his resignation and would put Parker in charge. When he told her he'd fired Parker and why, she asked Anderson to stay on just long enough for her to pick a successor. He agreed.

———•———

"You sure know how to keep a secret."

Nathan recognized Delacourt's voice right away. He'd been expecting the call. "Actually, I didn't know about it until last week," Nathan said. "It's my father who can keep a secret."

"Well, tell him we appreciate that he gave us a chance to go to the FDA on our own. If my mother had known about it, none of this would have happened."

Nathan wondered for a second whether that was true. He'd never know and it didn't really matter. "Maybe she should get more involved in the company," he said after a few seconds.

"We've been thinking about that. Can I tell you something off the record?"

Nathan hesitated but then agreed. He was sitting at his desk at the *Clarion*, poised over his keyboard to take any statement Delacourt wanted to make, but now he turned away from the computer and faced the window.

"Mom told Anderson he has to go. She asked me if I wanted the job."

Nathan took a breath. He'd been surprised and grateful that Delacourt had left town without talking to Emma. He didn't relish the prospect of his returning.

"Are you going to do it?" he asked cautiously.

"I don't think so, though I promised to think about it. I really don't have the qualifications to run a company like that. But I am going to take a seat on the board of directors, and I may even lead the search for Anderson's successor."

"The board's been pretty ineffective from what I can tell," Nathan said, recalling annual pro forma meetings to ratify decisions already made by the CEO.

"Well, we're going to change that. That's why I'm joining. And we'll put some better people on it."

Nathan stood up and walked toward the window. "I guess that means we'll be seeing you pretty regularly."

Delacourt seemed to understand the implication. "Yeah, but don't worry. I'm not going to put your mother on the spot. If she wants to tell me about my father, I'll gladly listen, but I decided to leave it up to her."

"That's quite a change from the last time we spoke."

Delacourt was silent for a moment. "I know. I took your advice and confronted my mother. It was pretty nasty for a couple of days, but eventually we had a long talk. About twenty years too late, but better than never."

"She still thinks he did it?"

"Oh yeah, that won't change. She still hates his guts, but she said some things that at least explain why she feels that way. I know it's only one side of the story, and I'll never be able to get my father's version. I'd still like to talk to your mother, but I'm beginning to realize there are some things I'll never know."

Nathan let out his breath in relief. "I'll tell her. I suspect she'll want to talk to you, at least try to answer any questions you have."

Delacourt thanked him and said he'd let him know when he planned to come back.

They were about to hang up when Delacourt reminded Nathan that the news about Anderson's dismissal was off the record.

"Yeah, but once you start a search, it'll leak out in no time. You ought to be prepared for that and keep me in mind."

"You mean let you break the news."

"Exactly."

———————•———————

Two days later, the *Clarion* came out with the stent story. Nathan's article explained that company officials thought they had solved the problem and didn't think anyone else was in danger. Nathan quoted several experts who said the law was vague and filled with gray areas, that Harrison had exploited them but so had a lot of other companies. One said it was no big deal. A watchdog group, on the other hand, accused the company of violating the law and threatened to sue.

With the stent on hold, so, too, were any plans to build a new production facility in Beacon Junction or anywhere else. The whole town was disappointed with that, even Nathan.

Mary Louise accepted the FDA's decision. She was certainly pleased that they had halted sales of the stent for the time being, but she was disappointed that they hadn't come down harder on Harrison and hoped that eventually they'd decide that

Anderson and others deserved to be punished. Jonas disagreed but didn't see the point in arguing. Ed agreed with Jonas, but he was still waiting for Mary Louise's decision and still too much in love to say or do anything that might upset her.

Anderson held a staff meeting at Harrison and told everyone that he thought the company could hold on for a while without laying anyone off, but that if stent sales didn't resume within a few months, that might be difficult. No one asked about it, but there were a few pointed questions about the *Clarion* story, and Sarah Egan, much to her colleagues' surprise, asked point blank if Anderson thought he had handled the controversy ethically.

He said he thought he had, that the stent was never a real problem and still represented a significant medical advance. Madeleine came to his support on that, and he was pleased to hear Craig speak up in his defense as well. Craig's role in making the problem public remained a closely held secret, and Anderson intended to honor his pledge to keep it that way.

Much to Anderson's surprise, he got a standing ovation when he adjourned the meeting.

———•———

One of the ironies of Mary Louise's living arrangements was that while she had full range of the kitchen, there was no private place besides her room to have a guest for dinner. She had tried cooking dinner for Ed at his place, but his kitchen was poorly stocked in appliances, utensils, and the many herbs and spices she liked to use, so on this particular September night she did most of the cooking at the Sunrise and brought it over to his apartment for the finishing touches.

Sensing that this was to be the big night, Ed asked his cleaning lady to make an extra visit, and he picked up some scented candles and flowers that he tried to arrange to create a romantic setting. But Ed still hadn't learned that scented candles upset Mary Louise's allergies, and the flowers—painted carnations—were a poor substitute for what Emma would have gladly donated from her garden. In the end, though, it didn't matter.

"Ed, this is the hardest decision I've ever faced, and I may be making a huge mistake, but I have to say no, at least for now."

She paused and watched him lower his head, but he didn't say anything. "Ed, I feel very strongly about you, and I really want to keep seeing you. Our relationship is special, and maybe someday it'll grow into something a lot more."

"But not now."

"Not now."

"You could move in here, and we could live together for a while. A trial."

"I need the room at the Sunrise. And think about what that would be like for you. You'd resent it every time I left. You'd end up hating me."

"You mean, no matter what, you won't quit seeing clients."

"I can't afford not to. Maybe someday."

"That makes it sound like I have to hope your mother dies."

She couldn't help but notice the change in tone and suddenly realized how easily things could get out of hand.

"Ed, please try to understand. And it's more than my mother."

"I can't stand sharing you with others."

"It's not like that. When I'm working, it's a whole different thing. It's just a job."

"A job you're not willing to give up."

"Of course I'd give it up if we were married. But I don't think we're ready for that. I've always been honest with you about working. I like certain parts of it. I like the independence it allows me. I like not having to work in some office."

"What's independent about sucking some guy's dick for money?"

"Ed, don't. Please. I'm sorry if this hurts you. I wish there were some way not to hurt you. And for the record, getting some boss coffee or typing his letters can be just as bad as sucking his dick. Only it pays less."

"You don't believe that."

"Yes, I do. I'm not saying it's the best job in the world, but I am my own boss. And that has become important to me."

"More important than being with the one you love?"

"I still want to be with you."

"Or maybe you don't really love me."

"I do love you, but I'm not sure what that means. The truth is, I'm not sure how much I'm willing to give up for it."

"Mary Louise, be honest. With yourself, as well as me. You don't love me. You might as well say it. It's obvious."

"Maybe you're the one who's not being honest. Have you really considered what it would be like for you? To have the whole town talking behind your back about how you married a hooker? Have you thought about what it would be like when you begin to question everything? When the first thing that runs through your mind every time you run into a guy in town is whether he was ever a client?"

The anger on his face morphed into a look of pain.

"Ed, why can't we go on as we have been? As friends and lovers, but with no exclusivity."

"Don't you understand? I love you. I don't want you to keep working."

She did understand it, and that's why she wasn't sure how much of his proposal was out of love and how much out of jealousy that she had other clients.

"I think you better leave," he said quietly.

She nodded and began gathering up the dishes she had carried over.

"Don't worry about that," he said. "I'll drop them off at the Sunrise in the morning."

"Ed, I don't want to lose you."

"I'm afraid you already have," he said as he closed the door behind her.

CHAPTER 27

October brought a chill but Jonas refused to let it keep him indoors. He was walking regularly now, and his favorite spot for reading and socializing was still the front porch. He sat in a different chair each time. No one took notice of it anymore, but for Jonas it was a reminder to himself of the way he had changed over the past few months. He was also working a couple of mornings a week at the senior center, volunteering help with legal issues or whatever else might come his way.

He had just settled onto the porch when Mary Louise glided onto the chair next to him.

"Don't mind if I do," she said.

"Don't mind what?"

"Joining you. I knew you were going to ask me. I was just saving you the trouble. Kinda chilly, though."

"You want my jacket?" He gestured toward the windbreaker that was draped over the railing, but she declined.

"Did you hear the news?" she asked.

"Yeah, Nathan called me. The stent is back on the market. Harrison got off with just a mild rebuke."

"Craig feels awful. He's happy with the decision, but thinks he made a big mess out of nothing. Told me he wished he'd never said anything to me. I think what he meant is he wishes he never met me."

"I doubt that."

"How do you feel? Did I drag you into this for nothing?"

"No, not at all. Telling the FDA was the right thing to do. The final verdict should be in their hands, not in Harrison's and not in ours."

"But in the end, I caused a lot of trouble for nothing."

"You did what you thought was right. Don't ever be sorry for that. And in the end, the company got a clean bill of health. Everyone can feel good about that."

She let out a sigh.

"Has Ed said anything?" he asked.

She laughed bitterly. "Ed doesn't talk to me anymore, and don't say you hadn't noticed. I just wish he'd be a little more grown up about it," she said.

"You mean the way he leaves the room when you come into it?"

"You'd think he'd stay away from the Sunrise if he was going to act that way," she said.

"Man needs to eat his breakfast."

"Man needs to use his brain, too."

"Could be he's so in love with you, he can't not come by. Can't not hope you'll change your mind."

"It's not a matter of that. You know it could never work."

Jonas tamped down his pipe and relit it. He was back to the Scottish mix of Black Cavendish and Latakia that he most preferred. He puffed for a while not saying anything.

"You do know it could never work, right?" she said.

"I trust your judgment. Seems a shame, though, if two people are in love."

"What's love got to do with it?" she joked. "Not much in my business."

"I think his point was to get you out of your business."

"Well, there you go. That's why it can't work. I don't need a savior. Not that kind, anyway."

"What kind do you need?"

She looked at him and laughed. Then a tear fell down her cheek. "Kinda wish you weren't taken."

"And that I were forty years younger?"

"I like you the way you are. Only you'd have to promise not to up and die on me just when it was getting interesting."

He reached over and took her hand. "Ed's a good man. In a lot of ways. You sure you want to send him packing?"

She hugged herself from the cold. "I better take that jacket of yours."

He handed her the jacket, and she wrapped it around herself. The tears were coming down her face in a steady stream, but she wasn't acknowledging them.

"You're not sure, are you?" he asked.

"Not sure of what?"

"That you want to lose Ed."

"I want to have my cake and eat it, too. That's the truth of it." She took out a Kleenex and wiped her face, blew her nose. "I like Ed and miss his company. But I'm not in love with him the way I'd need to be. And the fact is, he's not in love with me the way I need him to be. He's lonely and I'm his first good lay, but there's not much more to it than that."

"I don't believe that, and neither do you. I've talked to him enough to know that he really cares for you."

"Not enough." She let out a long sigh and then was quiet for a while. "I'm sure," she said finally. "It could never work."

Jonas put his pipe in his mouth. He was tempted to try to change her mind, but he knew he'd be doing it for himself more than for her. He couldn't argue with her feelings, but he hated what was coming next.

"Jonas, I have to go back to Boston. I can't stay here anymore."

He looked at her and nodded slightly. They sat for a minute. Neither made any attempt to hide the tears.

Finally, she got up, put her arms around him, and kissed his cheek. Then she went inside.

———•———

Jonas sat alone for the next hour, unable to return to his copy of *The Old Man and the Sea*. He had the windbreaker on now and the temperature was dropping. Emma appeared at the door and suggested it was time to come in, but he asked her if she'd sit with him.

"Only with some hot tea for fortification," she said. "You want some?"

He said he did, and a few moments later, she came out with a tray and two steaming cups. She was wearing a winter coat and gloves. The whole scene looked a little silly, and they both knew it.

"I thought you were having dinner with Sally tonight."

"I did. We walked over to Maria's, and when we got back, it looked like you and Mary Louise were having a serious conversation, so we went in the side way."

"Uh huh."

"That mean you accept my explanation or are you confirming it was a serious conversation?"

He smiled but didn't reply.

"It's nice that she confides in you," Emma said. "She's not as comfortable talking to Sally or me."

"I doubt that."

"No, it's true. I'm not sure why."

"Maybe it has something to do with what she does."

Emma seemed to think about that. "What do you mean?"

He shrugged. "I don't know. I'm no psychiatrist, but she

once told me that men can accept what she does a lot easier than women."

"Well, I'm sure that's true. Especially the men who are her clients."

"Careful or you'll prove the point."

She smiled. "I love Mary Louise. I think the world of her, and I'd be very concerned if she didn't know that."

"Have you told her?"

Emma looked at him and took a sip of her tea.

"Well, have you?"

"I'm thinking," she said. "Some things you don't have to say. They should be obvious."

"That sounds like my line. Are we switching roles in our old age?"

"I told you not to use that term with me." She took another sip. "But you're right. I'll tell her."

"She's going to leave us."

That surprised Emma. For a moment she was speechless. "Because of Ed?"

"Not just Ed. It's more complicated than that."

"I suppose she liked it better when she had a lower profile."

"Something like that."

"Is there any chance she and Ed can work it out?"

"No, and it would be a mistake if they even tried."

"You sound pretty sure."

"I am. More important, she's sure. I might even try to explain that to Ed when he calms down. If he calms down."

"You used to mind your own business a lot more."

"You saying I shouldn't talk to him?"

"No. I was just noting the change."

"Change has its time and place, like everything else."

"I didn't say it didn't. I wanted you to know that I noticed.

And that I'm glad."

He picked up his pipe, walked to the edge of the porch, and knocked the bowl against the railing to empty what was left of the tobacco.

"Shall we go in?" he asked, and picked up the tray with the empty teacups.

"Don't overdo it," she said, taking the tray from him. "I wouldn't want you changing so much I don't recognize you."

"How will I know when to stop?"

"Jonas, you're not really changing on the inside. You're just letting yourself out. You're going back to the man you used to be."

"Hmm."

He took the tray from her and put it back down on the table. Then he took her in his arms, and they kissed, softly and sweetly.

ACKNOWLEDGMENTS

I'd like to thank a number of people who helped me with the manuscript for *Hawke's Point*.

Margaret Meyers, my teacher and friend, provided invaluable advice and counsel after reading an early draft. Other faculty members at the Johns Hopkins University Writing Program, including Tim Wendel, Mark Farrington, and David Everett, were also very helpful, as were classmates who reviewed the opening chapters in workshops.

My sisters, Diane and Debra Willen, read later drafts and offered valuable input, as did Jim Roby, Richard and Debbie Gann, Kim Orr, Joan Berne, and Jerry Lenoir. My critique groups—The White Oak Writers and the Novel Experience—gave me the tools to improve my writing and continue to do so.

Thanks, too, to the many people in Vermont who welcomed me and talked eagerly about their wonderful state and helped refresh and update my memories of days spent there. Officials of the Food and Drug Administration were kind enough to brief me on regulatory and legal issues, although I should point out that I have taken minor liberties with normal FDA procedures for dramatic effect.

Valuable information on what it feels like to be a high-priced working girl came from the memoirs *Callgirl: Confessions of an Ivy League Lady of Pleasure* by Jeannette Angell and *Working: My Life as a Prostitute* by Dolores French.

My editors and designers at Pen-L Publishing also deserve my gratitude for their creativity, professionalism, and patience in shepherding this work from manuscript to a published novel.

Above all, thanks to my wife, Janet, for reading every draft, offering advice at each step, and providing unlimited support throughout the entire endeavor.

ABOUT THE AUTHOR

Mark Willen was born, raised, and educated in New England, where he developed a special appreciation for the values, humor, and strengths of its people, as well as the sense of community that characterizes so many of its small towns.

As a journalist, he has been a reporter, columnist, blogger, producer, and editor at The Voice of America, National Public Radio, Congressional Quarterly, Bloomberg News, and Kiplinger. Though based primarily in Washington, he has reported from datelines as varied as New York, Moscow, Cairo, Bei-jing, Buenos Aires, and Johannesburg. He has taught journalism ethics, and runs a website (TalkingEthics.com) that explores ethical dilemmas and the way people react to them.

Mark's short stories have been published in The Rusty Nail, Corner Club Press, and The Boiler Review. *Hawke's Point* is his first novel.

He lives in Silver Spring, Maryland, with his wife, Janet.

- ◆ -

If you liked *Hawke's Point*, please take the time to review it on Amazon, Pen-L.com, or your favorite site.

31871444R00181

Made in the USA
Charleston, SC
31 July 2014